Body Politic

Body Politic

Paul Johnston

St. Martin's Press
New York

Library of Congress Cataloging-in-Publication Data

Johnston, Paul, 1957–
    Body politic / Paul Johnston. — 1st U.S. ed.
        p. cm.
    ISBN 0-312-20279-2
    I. Title
PR6060.O417B6   1999
823'.914—dc21

                                                                99-29923
                                                                CIP

First published in Great Britain by Hodder and Stoughton, a division of Hodder Headline PLC

First U.S. Edition: August 1999

10 9 8 7 6 5 4 3 2 1

Body Politic

In the last decade of the twentieth century people bought crime fiction like there was no tomorrow – which soon turned out to be the case for many of them. It isn't hard to see why detective stories were addictive. The indomitable heroes and heroines with their reassuring solutions prolonged the illusion that a stable society existed outside the readers' security windows and armoured doors.

Since the Enlightenment won power in Edinburgh, the popularity of crime novels has gradually declined, though not as much as the guardians think. They would prefer citizens to read philosophical investigations rather than those of Holmes and Poirot, Morse and Dalgliesh, but even in the "perfect city" people hanker after the old certainties.

I often have trouble deciding what to believe. All the same, the message that the Council sent on my birthday gave me even more of a shock than the first time I heard James Marshall Hendrix playing the "Catfish Blues".

I shouldn't have been so surprised. Sceptics and detectives have the same general principle: the only thing you can be sure of is that you can't be sure of anything at all.

Chapter One

Ghost-grey day in the city and seagulls screaming through the fog that had been smothering us for a week. Tourists started to head up George IVth Bridge for the Friday execution. I was the only local paying attention. If you want to survive in Edinburgh, you've got to keep reminding yourself this place is weirder than sweet-smelling sewage.

My shift with the squad of Parks Department labourers was due to finish at four but I'd made up my mind long before that. I had an hour before my meeting with the woman who signed herself Katharine K. It was 20 March 2020, I was thirty-six years old and I was going to break the rules.

"Are you coming for a pint, Quint?" one of the boys asked.

It was tempting, but I managed to shake my head. There would have been no escape if they had known what day it was. The Council describes birthday celebrations as "excessively self-indulgent" in the City Regulations, but the tradition of getting paralytic remains. It's one of the few that does. Anyway, I had a sex session later on and if you're pissed at one of those, you're in deep shit.

"Course he isn't." Roddy the Ox wiped sweat and snot away with the back of his arm. "He'll be away to the library like a model arse-licking citizen." Every squad's got a self-appointed spokesman and I never get on with any of them. So I go to the library a lot. Not just to broaden my mind. I spend most of my time in the archives checking up on the people my clients report missing.

"Actually," I said, looking the big man in the eye, "I'm going to watch the execution." Jaws dropped so quickly that I checked my flies. "Anybody else coming?"

They stood motionless in their fatigues, turned to stone. Not even the Ox seemed to fancy gate-crashing a party that's strictly tourists only.

The way things are, I usually try to stick out from the crowd. Not this time. As I was the only ordinary citizen pushing a bicycle towards the Royal Mile, I tried to make myself inconspicuous. The buses carrying groups to the gallows gave me a bit of cover. So did the clouds of diesel fumes, at the same time as choking me. Fifteen years since private cars were banned and still the place reeks.

The mass of humanity slowed as it approached the checkpoint above the library's grimy façade. Rousing folksongs came from loudspeakers, the notes echoing through the mist like the cries of sinners in the pit. Some of the tourists were glancing at adverts for events in the year-round Festival which is the Council's main source of income. Among them were posters of the front page of *Time*'s New Year edition proclaiming Edinburgh "Worldwide City of the Year". The words "Garden of Edin" were printed in maroon under a photo of the floodlit castle. I've worked in most of the city's gardens but I've yet to see a naked woman – or a snake.

I kept my head down and tried not to bump into too many people with my front wheel. The guards had raised the barrier as the time of the execution drew near. Fortunately they weren't bothering to examine the herd of people. I felt a stickiness in my armpits that would stay with me till my session next week at the communal baths. Why was I taking the chance? The fire in my veins a few seconds later answered the question – I'd managed to get into a forbidden part of the city. I felt like a real anarchist. Till I started calculating my chances of getting out so easily.

I let myself be swallowed up by the crowd that had gathered round the gallows in the Lawnmarket. Guides were struggling to make themselves heard, speaking Arabic, Chinese, Greek, Korean. There was a small group of elderly Americans in transparent rain-capes. They were among the first from across the Atlantic; until recently the Council refused entry to nationals of what it called in its diplomatic way "culturally bankrupt states". A bearded courier in a kilt was giving them the sales pitch.

"The Royal Mile runs from the castle to what remains of Holyrood Palace," he bellowed, pointing towards the mist-covered lower reaches. "The palace was reduced to ruins in the rioting that followed the last coronation in 2002. The crown prince's divorce and remarriage to a Colombian drugs heiress signed the old order's death warrant." He paused to catch his breath and gave me a suspicious look. "The already fragile United Kingdom quickly broke up into dozens of warring city-states. Thanks to the Council of City Guardians, Edinburgh has been the only one to achieve stability . . ."

The propaganda washed over me. I knew most of it by heart. I wondered again about the note I'd found under my door yesterday. "Can't wait any longer," it read. "Meet me at 3 Lennox Street Lane five p.m. tomorrow if you want work. Katharine K." The handwriting was spidery, very different from the copperplate required in the city's schools and colleges. The writer must have been hanging about on the landing outside my flat for quite a time. Despite the fumes from the nearby brewery, the place was filled with her scent. I knew exactly what it was: Moonflower, classified Grade 3 by the Supply Directorate and issued to lower level hotel and restaurant workers. Beneath the perfume lay the even stronger smell of a client desperate for my services.

It was coming up to four thirty and the guides took a break from their shouting competition. Looking around the crowd, I was struck by how many of the tourists were disabled in one way or another: some were in wheelchairs, some were clutching their companions' arms, a few even looked to be blind. The Council had probably been working on a braille version of the hanging.

Then there was a hush as the condemned man was led up to the scaffold by guards in period costume. The prisoner's hands were bound and a black velvet bag placed over his head.

The guides started speaking again. The bearded man was explaining to the Americans that this was Deacon William Brodie, the city's most notorious villain.

"Here, in the heart of the city where crime no longer exists" – at least according to the Public Order Directorate – "Brodie committed his outrages. He was a cabinet-maker by trade, rising to become Deacon of Wrights and Masons. But by night he was a master-burglar, robbing dozens of wealthy house-holders."

Encouraged by their guides' gestures, the tourists began to boo. The English-speaking guide moved nearer the gallows. "Brodie was eventually caught, but not before his reputation had gained a permanent place in the minds of his fellow citizens. A century later the Edinburgh writer Robert Louis Stevenson used him as the model for his famous study of evil in *Dr Jekyll and Mr Hyde*. The man in the kilt gave a fawning grin. "Don't forget to pick up a souvenir edition of the book in your hotel giftshop."

Under the gibbet final preparations were being made. I followed them closely, trying to work out how they faked it. There was no sign of a protective collar. It even looked like the victim was trembling involuntarily. I remembered summary executions I had seen, members of the drugs gangs that terrorised the city in the years after independence being put up against a wall. They had shaken in the same way, sworn at the guardsmen to get it over with. To my disgust I found that my heart was racing as it had done then.

The presiding officer, dressed in black tunic and lace collar, shouted across the crowd from the scaffold. "On 1 October 1788 Brodie mounted the set of gallows which he himself had designed – to be hanged by the neck until he was dead."

There were a few seconds of silence to let everyone's flesh creep, then a loud wooden thump as the trap jerked open and the body dropped behind a screen, leaving the rope twisting one way then the other from the tarred beam. The spectators went wild.

I pushed my way to the side, wheeling my bicycle past the tartan and whisky shops towards Bank Street. I felt a bit shaky. It had struck me that maybe the execution wasn't just a piece of theatre for the tourists. I mean, staging mock hangings in a city where capital punishment has been abolished and violence of any kind supposedly eradicated is cynical enough. Actually getting rid of the small number of murderers serving life with hard labour in the city's one remaining prison would be seriously hypocritical. But with the Council you never know. It's always boasting about the unique benefits it's given us: stability, work and housing for everyone, as much self-improvement as you can stomach. But what about freedom? Even suicide has been outlawed.

I turned the corner. By the Finance Directorate, a great, dilapidated palace that had once housed the Bank of Scotland, the barrier was down and the city guardswoman standing in front of it was definitely not friendly. She stuck her hand out for my ID.

"What are you doing up here, citizen?" She was in her mid-twenties, tall and fit-looking. Her red hair was in a neat ponytail beneath her beret and the maroon heart – emblem of the city – was prominent on the left breast pocket of her grey tunic. On the right was her barracks name and number. The heavy belt around her waist provided straps for her sheath knife and truncheon; since the gangs were dealt with, the City Guard no longer carry firearms. "Well?" she demanded. "I'm waiting."

I tried to look innocent. "I was working at the museum, Wilkie 418 . . ."

She didn't buy it. "Your flat's in the opposite direction." She had the neutral voice that all auxiliaries acquire during training. The Council has been trying to get rid of class distinctions by banning local accents. It's a nice theory. "You've no business to come this way."

She ran her eyes over my labourers' fatigues and checked the data on my ID card – height five feet ten inches, weight eleven stone in the imperial system: bringing that back was one of the Council's stranger decisions. Hair black, a bit over the one-inch maximum stipulated for male citizens. Eyes brown. Nose aquiline. Teeth complete and in good condition. Then she glanced at my right hand to check the distinguishing mark, showing no sign of emotion. Finally she gave me a stare that would have brought a tear to the eye of the Sphinx. She had registered the letters "DM" that told her I'd been demoted from the rank of auxiliary.

"I hope you don't think I'm going to do you any favours." The sudden hard edge to her voice rasped like a meat-saw biting bone. "You've no business in a tourist area. Report to your local barracks tomorrow morning, citizen." She handed me an offence notification. "You'll be assigned two Sundays' community service and your record will be endorsed accordingly." She glanced at my face. "You could do with a shave as well."

I stood at the checkpoint with the neatly written sheet in my hand for a few moments. Cheering from the racetrack that had been laid over the disused railway lines in Princes Street Gardens came up through the fog. The seagulls had given up auditioning for the City Choir and now I could hear bagpipe music from the speakers beneath the streetlamps. It sounded more mournful than any blues song I ever played. My appetite for meeting the fragrant Katharine K. had gone completely.

"Oh, and citizen," the guardswoman called humourlessly from the sentry box. "Happy Birthday."

I was late of course. As I was cycling like a lunatic through the swirls of mist on the Dean Bridge, I almost went into the back of one of the city's battered delivery vans. Their drivers have a reputation for using the vehicles to shift contraband but this one was going so slowly he had to be on city business.

"At last." The woman came towards me from the door of the house in Lennox Street Lane, then stopped abruptly. She examined me as critically as the guardswoman had, staring at my mud-encrusted trousers like she'd never seen filth before. She had a face to write poems about: high cheekbones, lips as promising as a lovers' assignation and green eyes that flashed in the dim light and told me stories I hadn't heard for a long time. Then her nose twitched and the spell was broken. "You are citizen Dalrymple, aren't you?" she asked in a hoarse voice that I felt run up my spine like a caress.

She wasn't the first of my clients to be dubious about the way I look. I nodded and fumbled with the padlock on my bike; only an idiot relies on the City Guard to look after his property outside the tourist areas. At the same time I ran my eye over her. She was about my height, but her build had more going for it. The short brown hair that stood up on the top of her head would have made her look permanently surprised if she hadn't been as languid as a well-fed lioness. I wondered whom she'd eaten recently.

"Katharine Kirkwood," she said. "I wasn't expecting a labourer."

I took her hand and felt long, elegant fingers. Her scent washed over me like the tide of a lunar sea. "Quintilian Dalrymple," I said. "Investigator as well as labourer."

Her eyes blinked only once when she felt the stump of my right forefinger. "You give everyone that little test, don't you?" A smile nagged at the corners of her mouth. "How did I do?"

"Pretty well," I said generously.

"How did you lose it?"

"You don't want to know."

She looked at me curiously, then shrugged. "Come this way." She opened the street door and led me up dingy stairs to the first floor. That gave me an opportunity to examine her legs, black stockings beneath her issue coat. She passed that test too.

"You've got a key," I said. "Why were you waiting outside?" Katharine Kirkwood faced a door which needed several coats of paint. She turned slowly and handed me the keys, her face taut. "I'm . . . I'm frightened." I hadn't put her down as the type who scares easily. "This is my brother's place." All of a sudden her voice was soft. "It's ten days since I last saw him."

"That's not long. You know what it's like in this city. People are always being picked up for extra duties or . . ."

"No," she said with quiet insistence. "Adam and I, we're . . ." She left the sentence unfinished. "He'd have found a way to let me know."

I watched her as she leaned against the doorframe and tried to look optimistic. It wouldn't be the first time I found a body behind a locked door. If this one had been there for over a week, not even a jerrycan of her perfume would be much help.

"Haven't you been to the City Guard?"

"Those bastards?" Her tone was razor sharp. "I told them days ago but they still haven't found the time to take a look. Too busy licking the tourists' arses."

I nodded and knocked on the door less violently than the guard would have done. No answer. That would have been too easy. So I slipped the key into the lock and took a deep breath. Then pushed the door open and went inside.

Adam Kirkwood's flat conformed to the Housing Directorate's standard plan. In other words, it was a soulless dump. There was a square living room with the minuscule kitchen in a partitioned alcove, a bedroom off to the left and a toilet without shower or bath in the far corner. It contained the usual furniture; table, two stick-legged chairs, a sofa that looked like an elephant had been trampolining on it, a desk, uneven bookshelves and, to my relief, no body.

Katharine K. remained in the doorway till I beckoned, then came forward into the main room. "He's not here."

She breathed out slowly and turned to me. "Your turn for a test." She gave me a smile that was about as encouraging as the thumbs-down to a stricken gladiator. "I heard from one of the

9

girls at work that you find missing people. Convince me you've got what it takes, citizen."

"Call me Quint." I've had to get used to clients who think investigators are magicians. Sometimes I refuse to perform, but not when they're female and have her looks. "You want a demonstration?" I scrutinised her, taking my time. I enjoyed it more than she did. "So, you work as a chambermaid at the Independence Hotel, you live in William Street, you're left-handed, you burned yourself with an iron five, maybe six days ago and you spend a lot of your free time in the staff gym."

She wasn't impressed. "Come on, all that's obvious from my appearance. And everyone knows where Indie staff live."

I shrugged. "I haven't finished. You have an unusually close relationship with your brother, your parents are dead, you used to be an auxiliary and you have a dissidence conviction." I gave her my best smile. "Also, you like Chinese poetry."

She glanced at the tattered book that was protruding from her bag. "Very observant. But most of that is just guesswork." She didn't sound quite as sceptical.

"You reckon?" I don't usually reveal how my mind works and a lot of what I'd said was just supposition, but I wanted her to think I was as sharp as they come. Maybe I was trying to convince myself too. "I saw your handwriting, remember? Only someone who doesn't care what people think would write a note to a stranger without using copperplate. And you aren't in a hurry to get off to evening classes either. Demoted auxiliaries like us aren't allowed to attend classes in case we have a bad influence on the others."

Katharine K. nodded. "You were one too. I was beginning to wonder. Don't tell me – Public Order Directorate?"

I raised my hands in surrender. The way she had shifted the discussion from her past to mine was impressive.

"Guardsman?" she asked acidly.

"Not exactly." I went over to the kitchen. It was tidy, a cup and plate on the draining-board. "Do I get the job, then?"

"I suppose so." She was right behind me, looking at the crockery, then touching the cup carefully as if she were trying to re-establish contact with her brother. "How do I pay you?"

"No cure, no pay. If I find your brother, it's up to you what you give me. None of my clients has much to spare after buying the week's food and electricity vouchers. I often get whatever they can lay their hands on at work. I had half a pound of coffee last month."

"Riches indeed." She finally took her fingers away from the cup. "Why do you do it?"

I've never been too sure of the answer to that question myself. "It's a way of staying alive." I moved over to the sofa. "You'd better tell me something about your brother."

Katharine K. sat down beside me and took a piece of hotel notepaper from her book of poetry.

"Adam Peter Kirkwood," I read. "Status – citizen. Born 3.12.1995, height six feet two inches, weight thirteen stone twelve pounds, hair dark brown, nose snub, teeth complete, distinguishing mark none, employment Roads Department, Transport Directorate, address 3 Lennox Street Lane, next of kin Katharine Kirkwood (sister)." I nodded. "That'll do for a start. I don't suppose you've got a photo?" The Council has strictly controlled the taking of photographs, seeing them as a major element in the cult of the individual that had helped to destroy the United Kingdom.

She showed me a small, blurred copy of a handsome young man who was looking straight into the camera with the hint of a mocking smile on his lips. "Just this, I'm afraid." The only way people can get pictures of their loved ones is by sneaking photocopies of ID cards.

"I'll track down his file and see what it says. If it's been brought up to date."

"Can you do that?" She was staring at me. "I thought citizens' files were classified."

"Depends who you know." That line usually provokes admiration, but Katharine Kirkwood just looked puzzled. "He's twenty-four, so obviously he's done his year on the border."

"Finished it three years ago."

"And you last saw him when exactly?"

"Tuesday before last, 10 March. I came round here. I often do."

I looked around the small room, keeping to myself the fact that over the last three months I'd had half a dozen cases of missing young people. I hadn't found any of them. "Anything different? Anything been taken?"

She got up and walked about, picking up and laying down

objects that were clearly familiar to her. She went into the bed-room and re-emerged after a couple of minutes. "Everything's as it always is. Adam's very neat."

"Is there anything you haven't told me, Katharine?"

She looked like she was going to object to my use of her first name, but nothing came of it.

"I need to know. If it turns out he's part of some dissident cell, I'd prefer to be told before they start using me as a punchbag." She shook her head. "No, he's not a rebel. You can be sure of that." She raised her hand to her forehead. "What worries me most is how he was the last time I saw him. Kind of nervous – not frightened exactly, but excited, as if something important was about to happen. I've never seen him like that before. He wouldn't tell me about it. Said it was secret."

I didn't like the sound of that and went into the bedroom to conceal my expression. If Adam Kirkwood was into something classified, I'd be giving myself a headache for nothing. Still, maybe she was worth it.

Where he slept was unusually tidy, more like a barracks than a private room. The deal wardrobe contained labourer's fatigues like mine and the few casual shirts and trousers that the average citizen possesses. A pair of size twelve running shoes took up one corner. When you look round a place you normally form an impression of the person who lives there. Not in Adam Kirkwood's case. I felt like an archaeologist breathlessly opening a golden sarcophagus to find nothing but dust and moth-eaten shrouds.

Back in the main room I continued snooping around, aware of Katharine's eyes on me.

"How are you going to track him down?" she asked.

I sat down on the sofa beside her. "I'll check the archives first. I know my way around there. I've got contacts in other places too – the Misdemeanours Department, the Labour Directorate – to see if he's been drafted into the mines or on to one of the city farms" – I skipped the hospitals, where unidentified bodies turn up more often than you might expect in a city whose population is carefully monitored – "the Deserters' Register. Did your brother ever talk about crossing the border illegally?"

Her eyes narrowed. "That's what the guard asked too. Adam isn't a deserter any more than I am. I don't like the Council but Edinburgh's safer than all the other cities. Neither of us wants to leave." She moved her hand to her eyes quickly. "It's my fault. I influenced him. He could easily have become an auxiliary. It was because of me that he didn't. He let his work at college go, failed all his exams and ended up as a labourer." She looked over at me. "Sorry . . ."

"Don't worry, I'm not proud. You haven't told me why you were demoted."

Her eyes opened wide and glinted shafts of ice. "That's got nothing to do with this. What about you? Why did they kick you out?" She looked down.

"Why do I have the feeling that I've suddenly grown jackass's ears?" I waited for her to raise her eyes again but she didn't oblige. "Forget it. I'll have to trust you."

"How kind." She smiled bitterly then stood up. "I've got the night shift. When will you know something?"

I moved over to the bookshelves. "In a couple of days. I live in Gilmore Place, number 13. Come round about eight in the evening." I pulled out the book that had attracted my attention. It was the same edition of Chinese poetry translations Katharine had in her bag. Between pages twenty and twenty-one I came across a single foreign banknote. I kept my back to her. "Any idea why your brother would have secreted fifty thousand drachmae in his copy of this?"

She was at my side instantly, staring at the garish pink bill. "I haven't the faintest idea," she said, her voice fainter than it was hoarse. "What's it worth?"

"More than you or I will earn this month. But where did he get it? You know it's illegal for Edinburgh citizens to have foreign currency."

Katharine shook her head in what looked like bewilderment. I was almost sure she knew nothing about this part of her brother's life but you never know – she could have been the most accomplished actress in the city. Glancing at her profile, I made another discovery. The line of her nose was exactly the same as Caro's. I thought I'd got over seeing aspects of her in other women. This case was already full of surprises.

I wheeled my bicycle back to Gilmore Place. It was dark now and the fog was even thicker than before, but City Guard vehicles were still careering about like decrepit maroon dodgems. My watch had finally succumbed to the soakings it got every day in the city's parks so I didn't have much idea of the time. Fortunately curfew wasn't imminent. Then I remembered the sex session. All citizens have to attend a weekly session with a partner allocated to them by the Recreation Directorate. The Council claims we get a more stimulating sex life, but everyone knows it's just another way of keeping an eye on us. At least it was a home fixture this time. A month ago I ended up stranded for the night at a crazy woman's flat in Morningside. She got her money's worth. Thank Christ the regulations forbid further encounters between partners of my status.

Back in my place I sank into the sofa, which was even more hamstrung than the one at Adam Kirkwood's. My room, a testament to Housing Directorate grot, was so similar I almost thought I was back at his. The only difference was that I had a lot more books. One of the few Council decisions I completely go along with is the banning of television. As a result Edinburgh citizens are seriously well read and cheap copies of most kinds of books are available. Nothing too subversive, of course, and writing in any Scots dialect is right out. I've forgotten all the dirty bits from Irvine Welsh books I memorised when I was a kid. But the worst thing the idiots in power have done is to ban the blues, though they had their reasons. My collection of recordings is hidden under a tartan rug with my guitar case on top. I listen to them with my head against my moth-eaten speaker, straining to hear and hoping the neighbours won't report me. What a thrill.

The street door three floors below banged open and heavy, ringing steps sounded on the stairs. Only the City Guard and citizens working in the mines are issued with nailed boots. Either I was about to have sex with a large female miner or someone in number 13 was in trouble.

I should have known that someone was me. My door took a pounding before I could get to it.

"Citizen Dalrymple?" The auxiliary was tall and barrel-chested, the kind of guy who gets picked first in playground team games. His black hair was longer than mine and the regulation beard thick on his face. "I'm Hume 253." He handed me an envelope bearing the seal of the Council. "This is for you."

I opened it, expecting one of the public order guardian's regular warnings to keep my nose out of his directorate's business. Instead I read: "CONFIDENTIAL: Murderer codenamed Ear,

Nose and Throat Man appears to have resumed his activities. Accompany Hume 253 to Council meeting."

I was having trouble standing up, let alone concealing my shock from the guardsman.

"Are you coming, citizen?" the guardsman asked with an unusually patient smile.

I followed him out. Halfway down the stairs we passed a middle-aged female citizen with tired eyes and a soft, sad face. I wished I could have spent some time with her, but she was better off without me.

"I hear there's been a murder," Hume 253 said in a low voice. He must have been in his late twenties and on the surface he looked like a typical muscle-bound guardsman, but his enthusiasm was surprising. The average auxiliary these days displays about as much emotion as the tarts who service the tourists in the city's hotels. "What do you know, citizen?" he asked.

"Nothing," I lied as I climbed into the battered Land-Rover.

"The first killing in the city for five years," the guardsman said. It sounded like he approved. He let in the clutch and set off round the corner even faster than his kind normally drive.

I hung on to the worn edges of the seat and wondered exactly what kind of birthday present I was about to be given.

Chapter Two

"I don't want to die."

The fog had now reduced visibility to a couple of vehicle lengths. Only the knowledge that the disciplined citizens of Edinburgh wouldn't be jaywalking enabled Hume 253 to head towards the Royal Mile at high speed. Fortunately there weren't any tourists around Tollcross.

"Don't worry," the guardsman said cheerfully. "I passed out top of my driving course."

"Great." I blinked in the chill air that was whistling in through numerous holes in the bodywork. The best of the Land-Rovers were reserved for border patrols and farm protection. "What time is it?"

"Coming up to seven," Hume 253 said without taking his eyes off the road for more than a second. "The Council's daily meeting has been brought forward an hour because of the killing. That shows you how seriously they're taking it, doesn't it, citizen?"

"Call me Quint, will you?"

He knew I was trying him out. "Use of first names is prohibited between auxiliaries and ordinary citizens. So is inducing a guardsman to break regulations." He glanced at me, then laughed. "I seem to remember that my name's Davie, Quint."

So I'd found a guardsman who wasn't completely robotic. The more dedicated of them even address their barracks colleagues by number. "How long have you been in the Public Order Directorate, Davie?"

"Seven years, ever since I finished auxiliary training. I like it.

I'm going to stay in the guard. Not even six consecutive tours on the border put me off."

That sounded more like your typical guardsman. I was interested in his background, though. "Did you have anything to do with the last operations against the drug gangs?"

He looked at me suspiciously. "How do you know about those?" Five years ago the Council sealed the border around what used to be Midlothian and laid into the remaining heavily armed criminals who had plagued the city since independence. Those guys were led by a ruthless bastard who called himself Howlin' Wolf, after the blues singer. There was some evidence that the Ear, Nose and Throat Man was one of the gang. The high casualty rate among guard personnel had led the Information Directorate to suppress all the facts, despite the success of the mission.

"You were involved, weren't you?" I said, waiting for him to nod. "How do I know about the operations?" I wondered if I would manage to shock an auxiliary. "I ran them."

"Shit!" he gasped, taking his eyes off the road long enough to make me nervous. "You're Bell 03."

The sound of my old barracks number was definitely not sweet music to my ears. "Used to be Bell 03," I corrected.

"They still talk about you in the directorate," Davie said. He was more excited than any auxiliary I'd ever seen. "If it hadn't been for you . . ."

"Fewer people would have died," I said, looking away. "That's all in the past. I don't want to talk about it." I wished I hadn't encouraged him. The stump of my forefinger was tingling and my gut felt like something with a sharp beak had just hatched in it.

The Land-Rover turned sharply into Mound Place and I caught a glimpse of the city from the high point; the blaze of illumination through the fog in the tourist area at the centre was like a weird version of the northern lights, but the suburbs where the ordinary people live had been cast into the outer darkness.

Davie pulled up outside the mock-Gothic façade of the Assembly Hall. The Church of Scotland used to hold its annual gathering here. It was typical of the Council's desire to replace religion with its own philosophy that it chose this location rather than the former City Chambers or Parliament House. They probably had too many associations with democracy. Banners were draped around the blackened walls proclaiming the Council's ideals; "Education, Employment and Health", "Edinburgh – Independent and Proud" and "The City Provides". Deep down I still felt some admiration for them. Then, beyond the flagpoles, I saw the memorial stones inscribed with the barracks numbers of auxiliaries who had died for the cause. Caro's name survived only in my mind.

"You all right?" The guardsman sounded strangely concerned. "Know your way?"

"I've been before the Council often enough, my friend. Thanks for the lift."

"Don't mention it. I'll be waiting to take you back." A grin split his face. "If they leave you in one piece."

I nodded wearily, remembering that Council meetings were more rigorous than City Guard physical training sessions, though at least they didn't take place at half past five in the morning. Then I felt the envelope in my pocket. What the hell was it all about? I raced up the steps three at a time.

Council members sat round a great horseshoe table in the main hall. I always used to find the setting a bit theatrical, but I could just remember the building's use as a venue in the Festival before independence. I sat down between the ends of the horseshoe, suddenly very aware of my dirty fatigues in the bright lights that were directed at me. I screwed up my eyes and saw the guardians. Behind them was the large bust of Plato that was the only concession to art in the austere chamber.

"Citizen Dalrymple." The deputy senior guardian's voice hadn't changed in the five years since I last heard it. She must have been over seventy by now. When I was a kid, she was a frequent visitor to my parents' house. She was the only university professor I ever met who found children more interesting than her subject – well, she was a sociologist. She also had a liking for vintage champagne. I wondered when she'd last sampled that. "It is some time since we last had the pleasure of seeing you," she said drily.

"I haven't been counting the days, guardian." Like all those who pass through the rank of auxiliary, the city guardians don't use names. The roof would have come down if I'd addressed her as Edith.

"I'm sure you haven't. I think you know most of the Council members. Only my colleagues in the Medical and the Information Directorates are relatively new appointees."

I looked at the red-haired woman to her left, then at the improbably handsome man with the mane of silver-blond hair. His thin fingers formed an arch beneath his nose, giving him the appearance of a monk at prayer. The speaker was wrong. I knew Robert Yellowlees well enough. Before the Enlightenment he had played rugby for Scotland. After the party won the last election and took the city into independence, he worked as a surgeon. Later his research into neurology and endocrinology became known around the world, as journals I saw in the library confirmed. He could have jumped ship and worked anywhere, but he preferred to stay and move slowly up his directorate. He'd been in the pathology department when I was in the Public Order Directorate.

I couldn't avoid the unwavering glare of the figure sitting next to Yellowlees. While the other Council members had studied expressions of gravity on their faces, the public order guardian at least showed what he really felt – which was hatred of my guts.

The deputy senior guardian glanced at the unoccupied chair in the centre of the horseshoe. "I'm afraid the senior guardian is again unable to attend the meeting due to illness."

First I felt relieved, then uneasy. I made myself ignore both emotions.

"To the business in hand. Today's meeting has been brought forward because of the murder that has been reported." The speaker took a deep breath. "The murder of a female auxiliary right in the heart of the city." She was unable to restrain a shiver. "This was an act of unspeakable barbarity."

"Can it really be the otolaryngologist after all this time?" Yellowlees, the medical guardian, looked at me quizzically. I remembered he used to refer to the Ear, Nose and Throat Man by the technical term.

"It's incredible. After all the work that's been done to divert the urge to criminality . . ." The high-pitched voice trailed away. I looked at the bald head of the finance guardian which was glinting under the lights as he moved back and forwards animatedly. You'd have thought he'd be more concerned about the city's tourist income, but deviant behaviour had always been one of his specialities. Though he'd been a well-known economics professor before the Enlightenment, in certain Edinburgh bars he was more famous for his pursuit of male undergraduates. Under the strict celibacy rules that guardians submit themselves to, the only person he'd have laid hands on recently would have been himself.

"Quite so," the deputy senior guardian acknowledged, sympathetic but eager to continue. "I will not go into the details of this atrocity as I do not wish to prejudice the opinion of citizen Dalrymple. He is to investigate and find the murderer."

So that was it. For a nasty moment I thought the Council was finally on to me, even though I'd disposed of the ENT Man's body in a site I knew had never been disturbed. No matter how many times I told myself it was an accident, that he'd skewered himself on his own knife, I was responsible. I tried to strangle him like he strangled Caro. I wanted to kill the animal and that's what counts.

Hamilton, the public order guardian, shot to his feet, the iron line of his jaw visible even under his beard's thick grey curls. "I object."

I can't say I was surprised.

"This matter comes under the jurisdiction of my directorate. Citizen Dalrymple . . ." He paused, then repeated my name like it tasted putrid. "Citizen Dalrymple chose to withdraw his services from the Council at a critical time – while, I might add, the Ear, Nose and Throat Man was still at large. If it is indeed the case that the killer has struck again, this citizen can be seen as responsible. He never completed his investigation." The city's chief policeman looked round his colleagues. "Besides, he has been working as a labourer in the city's parks since then. What possible use can he—"

"One moment, guardian." The speaker interrupted him without raising her eyes from her papers. "There is to be no discussion about this. The senior guardian has sent a written directive." She turned to him. "You will provide citizen Dalrymple with everything he needs to track down the murderer." She looked around. "That applies to all directorates." Her eyes rested on me. "I'm afraid you may find the city's resources in the fields of forensics and criminology rather meagre. There has been little call for such expertise recently."

The public order guardian sat down noisily.

"We are dealing," continued the speaker, "with the killing of a city auxiliary. This raises several concerns. The most significant of these would appear to be public awareness and the potential effect on the tourist industry. Your thoughts, please."

The information guardian got up, her flaming hair standing out above the sombre grey of her tweed jacket. She proposed keeping all news of the murder out of the *Edinburgh Guardian* and of Radio Free City. She was worried that such a major crime could lead to a loss of confidence in the Council. The public order guardian nodded vigorously in agreement. I might have been more convinced by the argument if the information guardian hadn't once been an award-winning investigative journalist on the *Scotsman*. People who change that much always make me suspicious. Anyway, I'd heard all this in the past. One of the most disturbing things about the Council is its obsession with secrecy. If the aim is to educate citizens to think for themselves, it seems to me that they should be trusted not to revolt as soon as things go wrong. Then again, who am I to talk? I've kept my mouth shut about what happened to the ENT Man and that makes me as egocentric as a pre-Enlightenment politician. Christ, how low have I sunk?

Whenever I give myself a bad time, it isn't long before I start looking for an alternative target. There was a whole shooting gallery of them in front of me.

"Excuse me," I said politely. Hamilton was the only one who smelled a rat; his glare was steelier than the toecaps of a guardsman's boots. "I suppose it's theoretically possible that my fellow citizens won't find out about the murder, but in my experience word always gets out, especially when measures are taken to keep things secret." I gave the public order guardian a cheerful smile, which deflected his hard man's stare for a second. "I mean, I heard about this supposedly confidential crime not long after I got your message."

That provoked more gasps than I'd expected, but Hamilton's reaction was about what I guessed it would be.

"I want the name of the citizen who informed you immediately," he demanded, his fists clenched.

I shook my head slowly. "No chance." I might have known my former chief would assume it was an ordinary citizen who had told me rather than one of his own auxiliaries.

"That will do," said the speaker sternly. "There is no need for names. Citizen Dalrymple's point is taken."

I sat back as the discussion turned to the danger of tourist volumes being affected if the murder was publicised. I couldn't see the Chinese being too bothered. Beijing became a Dantean pit of underworld activity in the years following the country's economic expansion. The Greeks weren't likely to object either. Since the discovery of oil in the Aegean twenty years ago, they've acquired a crime rate worse than those of Chicago and New York put together.

I found myself remembering the metaphor of the body politic, which had been a favourite propaganda device in the early years of the Council. It was probably one of my father's ideas. The ordinary citizens were the body of the city-state, while the guardians were its heart and brain and the auxiliaries its eyes and ears. But what if the heart was growing weary and the mind was no longer reliable? What if the eyes no longer provided 20-20 vision and the ears heard only what they wanted to hear?

The debate finally drew to a close and the deputy senior guardian looked at me. "So, citizen, we will expect a report from you every evening in person."

I didn't want them to think I was too much of a pushover. "And if I choose to remain with the Parks Department? No doubt the public order guardian would prefer that."

The speaker's expression froze. "I would remind you that this is a matter of the utmost importance, not just for the Council but for the whole city. You are not being given a choice, citizen. Failure to obey this instruction would have a very detrimental effect on the private investigation activities you pursue in your free time." The threatening tone was at odds with the guardian's white hair and wrinkled face, but I knew it was real enough. They let me trace missing people because auxiliaries have plenty of other work to do. I've even done the guard a good turn occasionally by letting them know about minor illegalities I turned up. But if I got on the wrong side of the Council, that would count for about as much as kids in one of the city's schools saying they hadn't done their homework because they reckoned Plato was irrelevant to the modern world.

So I shrugged and accepted the job without showing how interested I was. Rule one: never show your clients that you're fascinated by their case.

"Very well. The public order guardian will take you to the scene of the crime."

"One small point," I said. "I've got an offence notification for tomorrow morning." I heard Hamilton snort derisively and wished I'd picked up a few more public order violations. He might have ruptured himself.

"That is waived," the speaker said, without hesitation. "Citizen, I notice your watch has stopped. Never mind that you're breaking regulations, how do you expect to conduct a murder enquiry without a serviceable time-piece?"

I liked her turn of phrase. If I'd closed my eyes, I could almost have believed I was in a Sherlock Holmes story. "I'll get one, guardian," I said and turned to leave. "Without a moment's delay."

The public order guardian overtook me on the stairs and went over to a pair of auxiliaries in civilian clothes. He looked almost as imposing as he imagined he did in the tweed jacket and corduroy trousers worn exclusively by members of his rank, the brogues on his feet shining like a schoolboy's prize chestnuts.

"Hurry up, Dalrymple," he said over his shoulder. "This isn't a Sunday outing."

"Where's the body?" I asked in an even voice.

"The body?" he repeated, his eyes fixed on a point several inches to the right of my face. "We aren't going to see the body. Weren't you listening to the speaker? I'm taking you to the scene of the crime." He glanced at his watch. "There isn't much time."

I turned to the keen-looking young men who were standing behind their chief like a pair of little girls holding a bride's train. "Run away and play. This is grown-ups' business."

The guardian hesitated, then waved them back. "You can't talk to auxiliaries like that, Dalrymple," he hissed.

It was about time I got my relationship with my former boss sorted out. "Hamilton, you're still as much of a jackass as you used to be." I wasn't sure whether my use of his name had shocked him more than the animal imagery. "We both heard exactly what was said in there. I'm reporting to the Council, not to you. You're supposed to give me whatever I want." So far the show was going well. He looked like he'd swallowed a six-inch fishing hook. Time to reel it in. "So where's the fucking body?"

Hamilton went on the retreat. "It was a collective decision of the Council."

I looked at him in disbelief. "Don't tell me. You've moved the body, haven't you? I bet that's not all. I bet you've cleaned up after it too."

"Calm down, man," said Hamilton, signs of guilt I'd normally have enjoyed disturbing his features. "We couldn't wait any longer."

Outside I could see Davie standing by the Land-Rover. "Where's the scene of the crime?" I asked as I moved off.

"Stevenson Hall, the men's toilets on the ground floor." The guardian tried to keep up. "Aren't you coming in my vehicle?"

I didn't bother answering.

Davie looked impressed as he started the Land-Rover. "You've got guts, having a go at the chief."

"Maybe." I looked across at him. "But there's something I haven't got and you can supply it."

He turned on to Castlehill and headed for the corner at what used to be the Tolbooth church. It's the most soot-blackened building in central Edinburgh. Maybe that's why they've turned it into a strip joint. A group of enthusiastic Thai tourists had gathered outside.

"What do you need?" asked Davie.

"Your watch," I replied, putting out my hand like the beggars used to on Princes Street before the Council turned them into more productive citizens.

Through the fog the bagpipes were still wailing. I could just make them out above the roar from the Land-Rover's defective silencer.

"It's all yours." Davie handed a watch over that was a lot better quality than mine. "Anything else I can do? I'd give a lot to be in on this." His willingness to help was like a small child's and about as suspicious. What was he after?

I thought about it. I'd be needing an assistant, I was sure of that. On the other hand, he was a sworn servant of the Council.

Beware guardsmen bearing gifts.

Chapter Three

A large crowd was milling around outside Stevenson Hall; it used to be the Usher Hall, but the Council preferred the name of one of the city's most illustrious writers to that of the brewer who paid for the building. Its great dome was lost in the mist.

I had half an hour before the musical version of *Kidnapped* was due to begin. Shoving through the mass of people, I could see what had inspired the guardians' decision to remove the body. Cancelling the event would have caused a riot.

"Citizen, where do you think you're going?" A pale guardswoman stepped forward from one of the entrances, a hand on the grip of her truncheon. Ordinary citizens aren't allowed near Festival performances without special permission.

"It's all right, guardswoman," the public order guardian called from behind. "He's with me." It sounded like the admission caused him more angst than your average existentialist could handle.

"Sorry, guardian. He didn't look . . ."

"Never mind how I look," I said, suddenly feeling sensitive about my appearance. "Open the door, will you?"

Hamilton nodded and the guardswoman obliged. I found the men's toilet and was confronted by a sentry who looked like he wrestled elephants in his spare time and wasn't in the habit of losing.

"Let him pass," the guardian shouted from down the hall.

Before I went in, I rested my hands on the door for a few seconds and breathed in deeply. First impressions are important, especially when, thanks to the Council, there wouldn't be much to go on. Then I pushed the swing door open and ran my eyes around glistening marble and porcelain, seeing myself reflected in the row of mirrors. The smell of disinfectant was overpowering.

I almost hit the ceiling when one of the cubicle doors banged open. An arse in yellow overalls backed out.

"Right then, that's them all done." The old man straightened up slowly and gave me a leer. "Come to see the mess? Well, you're too late, son."

"Out, auxiliary," Hamilton ordered. "Now!"

The cleaner grabbed the bucket he'd put down at my feet and scuttled out past the guardian with his eyes lowered.

"Too late all right," I said, dropping to the floor. "Where was the body?"

"She was lying on her left side, head in that corner and back facing outwards." Hamilton pointed to the far right. "The bin for paper towels, which was empty, had been moved down this end."

I crawled forward with my magnifying glass. The tiles were almost dry. Pretty soon I gave up the search.

"Not a trace. You'll have to give that cleaner a commendation."

"Calm down, Dalrymple. I issued a permit and plenty of photographs were taken." Even in a major crime enquiry, the use of cameras has to be authorised. "They're being developed now."

"Wonderful. And what about all the other scene of crime activities? Sketches, collection of physical evidence, pathologist's report?"

"We followed procedure by the letter," Hamilton replied testily. "You're not the only investigator in the city. We also dusted for fingerprints all over the room and in the hallways – my people are checking records now. And don't forget, we've still got the post-mortem to come. We're sure to find traces of the killer on the body."

"Are we?" I found it hard to share his optimism. "Who's the pathologist?"

"The medical guardian."

I didn't make it obvious to Hamilton, but I found that interesting. You'd think Yellowlees would have more pressing duties. Still, he did carry out the post-mortems on the ENT Man's victims, so it made some sense.

"Who found the body and when?"

"A guardswoman: the one who tried to stop you outside. She came to relieve the victim at 0600."

"Jesus. She came on duty fourteen hours ago, found a colleague murdered and is now on crowd control? You're still treating your people like shit, Hamilton."

"Spare me the lecture," he said, avoiding my eyes. "For your information, she was taken back to barracks in the morning and allowed to rest after she'd given her statement. I told her commander to send her back after you were assigned the case. I presumed you'd want to talk to her."

"That's about the first thing you've got right so far." I'd forgotten how easy it was to bait my former boss. This time I got a reaction that was almost human.

"Look, you insubordinate little turd," he said, the veins around his eyes swelling like a nest of purple snakes, "you may think you're something now you've been let back into the fold, but to me you'll always be a prima donna who ran away when things got tough. If you don't want me to stamp all over you when this investigation's finished, you'd better observe the rules. For a start, don't call me by my name."

"Yes, guardian." Being told what to do always brings out the worst in me. "Sorry, guardian. Can I go now, sir?"

Hamilton kicked the door open, his face red.

"Where's the guardswoman now?" I asked over my shoulder.

"In the manager's office."

"I'm going to talk to her. Alone."

The guardian's reply was lost as the doors were opened and a horde of tourists stampeded in.

Napier 498 was standing by the barred window with her hands behind her back. She looked exhausted, her shoulders drooping and her forehead resting on the glass. I saw she was very young.

"I'm Dalrymple." I put my hand on her shoulder and felt the muscles tense. She turned, eyelashes quivering, then pulled herself together in proper auxiliary fashion and moved away from my touch. "You can call me Quint. What shall I call you?"

She pointed to the barracks number on her tunic, but let her hand drop almost immediately. Then, in little more than a whisper, she said, "Linda."

I led her to the swivel chair and sat on the desk next to it.

"I know exactly how you feel, Linda, believe me. But I have to hear what you saw."

She kept her eyes down. "I made a statement. There's nothing more."

I've never read a statement that tells the whole story, no matter how careful people think they're being. I leaned closer. "You know who I am, don't you?"

"The guardian told me you have Council authority."

"That's not what I mean."

She looked up at me, her eyes less like an exhausted doe's. As I expected, the jungle drums hadn't taken long to beat.

"You were Bell 03. You wrote the *Public Order in Practice* manual we studied during the auxiliary training programme."

I nodded. "Some of your teachers probably told you that a lot of the material is irrelevant now that crime in the city has been controlled. But you saw what was done to one of your colleagues. Do you think any of your teachers can catch the killer?"

Napier 498 shook her head. "Catching the bus back to barracks is about the best they can do."

I smiled at her, overjoyed that cynicism was alive in the City Guard. "On the other hand, my record is a bit better."

"Legendary, more like," she said, colouring slightly.

"Thank you." Looking at the young woman, I suddenly felt a stab of guilt. I had turned tail and left the next generation in the shit. Then I thought of Caro and managed to justify what I'd done. "So trust me, Linda. Tell me what you found." I waited, but the gentle approach wasn't enough – I could tell by the way she was leaning away from me. I would have to shock her out of the reluctance to talk that's drummed into auxiliaries. "Your written statement is only a skeleton." Feeling like a worm, I hit her with my carefully chosen metaphor. "Flesh it out."

It never fails. The guardswoman's eyes narrowed and she sat up straight. "All right, citizen Dalrymple," she said, avoiding my first name like it might put running sores on her tongue. "I've been on the morning shift at Stevenson Hall all week. The guard vehicle dropped me off just after 0600 this morning – we were late because of the fog. We could hardly see a thing on the way down from the castle."

I was feeling bad about what I said to her and had an uncontrollable urge to make friends. "You're in the barracks up there?"

She nodded, giving me a suspicious glance.

"How much more of your tour of duty have you got left?"

"Four months." There was a slight loosening in the muscles round her mouth.

"Going to apply for another one?" I could see she was puzzled by these personal questions. They might have been a waste of time, but I reckoned I'd get more out of her if she didn't think I was a plague-carrier.

"I'm not sure." She gave a tremor. "I doubt it, after today."

I nodded. "Go on."

"The fog was even thicker around the hall. Because I was late, I ran to the door . . ."

"Did you see or hear anything unusual?"

"No. As I said, the fog was really dense. I could hardly even see the lights in the building." She paused. "And there was no sound. I didn't hear the Land-Rover driving off. It was like I had cotton wool in my ears."

"So you wouldn't have heard anyone walking or running away?"

She shrugged. "I don't think so."

I kept on at her. "Are you positive you were alone in the street? You didn't have any intuition that someone else was there?"

"Yes. No." She looked at me helplessly. "You're deliberately confusing me."

"No, I'm not. It's important."

"Yes, I did feel alone. I told you. I . . . I remember I shivered. I suddenly felt afraid. I ran to the door to find Sarah." The name made her choke and she bent forward, her hands over her eyes.

I let her have a few moments, then asked, "Her name was Sarah?"

Linda wiped her face quickly. "Sarah Spence. Knox 96. I knew her from the first day of my auxiliary training. She's . . . she was older than me – in her mid-thirties. She ran physical training classes on top of her normal guard duties."

"Describe her to me."

"Short and stocky, brown hair and eyes, a lot of freckles. The kind who would have turned to fat if she hadn't done so much exercise." A strangled sob escaped before she could get in its way. "Oh God, she was always so full of energy, laughing . . ."

"Obviously she could defend herself."

"Of course. She trained me in unarmed combat. That made

it even more of a shock." She straightened herself up again. "Of a shock," she repeated, her voice falling away.

I gave her time to compose herself.

"So I knocked at the door and waited to be let in. She didn't come. I knocked again, then pushed the door. It was unlocked – against regulations. I was surprised, but I was still keen to see her before she was picked up. Her Land-Rover had been delayed too. So I walked in and called her name a few times. No reply."

"Did you notice anything in the hallway? Anything strange?"

"No, they didn't find anything."

"I'm not asking about what anybody else found, Linda. I'm asking if you saw anything."

She frowned then shook her head. "No, there was nothing."

"All right. Go on."

"She wasn't there – at the guardpost by the ticket office, I mean. The mobile phone was there, on standby, but there was no sign of Sarah. I walked down the corridor calling her name. Then I got to the men's toilets and, I don't know why, I pushed open the door. I hardly broke my stride, so I only caught a glimpse of it out of the corner of my eye . . ."

"It?"

She looked at me like I was a schoolboy who had just wandered into a research seminar on advanced cybernetics. "The blood, of course." She began to shake. "It was, oh God, it was as if someone had thrown a bucketful over her."

I slipped off the desk and held her jerking shoulders. This time she didn't shy away. "Was there any on the floor near the door: footprints, stains, anything?"

"No!" she screamed. "No!" Then her struggling subsided. "No, there wasn't." Suddenly her voice was normal again. She stared at me in bewilderment. "But how could that be? She'd been . . . torn apart, but the blood was only in the corner where she was lying."

"Yes, how could that be?" I tightened my grip on her bony shoulders. "Tell me exactly what you saw as you approached her."

"The gaping hole," Linda replied without hesitation, her voice as bereft of emotion as a hanging judge's. "The great hole in her abdomen. Like an animal had taken a bite out of her." This time she didn't sob, but she seemed unaware that the door had opened quietly. The public order guardian came in.

"What about her face?" I asked quickly. "Did you see it?"

"No, thank God. Her tunic was wrapped around her head. It was soaked in blood." She was looking at the floor. "Is it true what I heard, that her liver was cut out?"

"You shouldn't pay attention to gossip, guardswoman," said Hamilton firmly. "Have you finished, Dalrymple?"

"Scarcely even begun, guardian," I replied. "Scarcely even begun."

"Where to now?" Davie asked. "The infirmary?"

I was looking at the mobile phone that was fitted beneath the Land-Rover's rusty vent. "Yes, the infirmary. Remind me about reporting procedures in guarded premises, will you?"

"Every hour, on the hour. New code word each time."

Which is a pretty good example of the Council's mania for security. No wonder they need so many auxiliaries. I didn't share my thoughts with Davie, though I had a feeling he might have agreed.

"So what happened at Stevenson Hall last night? Did the killer time his arrival and departure to avoid the calls, or was he just lucky? Or . . . I wonder." I glanced at the bearded figure beside me in the dim light from the dashboard. This was a chance to find out how enthusiastic he really was. "Davie, while I'm at the post-mortem can you talk to the guard commander who was on duty this morning? Tell him you're working with me; he'll know that I have Council authority by now. Find out whether Sarah – I mean the dead guardswoman Knox 96 – gave all the correct responses."

"No problem."

Most auxiliaries would have had a hard time taking orders from an ordinary citizen, but Davie didn't seem to care. Maybe I would be able to make use of him. If he managed to squeeze an answer out of the commander.

The Land-Rover swung into Lauriston Place, just missing a horse-drawn carriage containing four tourists. We came to the gateway of the city's largest hospital. It bore the ubiquitous maroon heart emblem and the legend "The City Provides". Is that right? I thought. Provides what? Mutilation for female auxiliaries?

Before I was five yards away from the vehicle, I heard Davie speaking on the mobile.

*   *   *

I walked into the mortuary and my nostrils were instantly flushed out by the sweet and sour reek of formaldehyde.

"Ah, there you are, citizen," said Yellowlees, the medical guardian, with a warm smile. He looked so welcoming that I clenched my buttocks. Then I remembered the reputation he had for womanising years ago. "We're ready to begin." He was standing next to the slab where the cadaver had been laid out.

Hamilton came in, his face turning greyer than his beard when he saw the dead guardswoman. He'd always been squeamish at post-mortems. I'm not particularly proud that I can turn my feelings off temporarily. A nursing auxiliary with a bust like the figurehead on a tea clipper handed us masks and gowns.

Yellowlees nodded to her. "Very well, Simpson 134, start taking notes on –" he glanced at the tag on the subject's ankle – "Knox 96."

"She had a name, you know."

They all stared at me.

"Sarah Spence. In case you're interested."

Simpson 134 was the first to look away.

"Really?" Yellowlees turned briefly to the nurse, his eyes meeting hers above their masks, then stepped closer to the body. "It hardly matters now, does it?" He started the preliminary examination.

I soon realised that the medical guardian hadn't forgotten any of his pathologist's skills. The mortuary assistant scarcely got a look in as Yellowlees involved himself in everything, removing the plastic bags from head and hands, taking samples of dried blood from around the wound in the abdomen, scraping underneath the fingernails, telling the photographer exactly what angles he wanted. Then he lifted the tunic from around the head. I leaned forward. This was the interesting bit. As Sarah Spence had been lying on her left side, that part of her face and limbs was dark blue in post-mortem lividity. I saw immediately that her ears were intact and her nose unblocked. The guardians and I exchanged glances.

Yellowlees bent over her neck, then motioned to his assistant to turn the body over. "No doubt about the cause of death. Strangulation by ligature."

"The Ear, Nose and Throat Man's modus operandi," said Hamilton, nudging me.

"What?" I had suddenly been back in Princes Street Gardens, pulling a ligature of my own round a much thicker neck.

"All twelve of his victims were despatched that way."

Caro's face flashed before me, then was gone.

"Quite so," said Yellowlees. He pointed to the deeply scored line in the victim's flesh. "You can see the contusion where the ligature was twisted with considerable force. Unfortunately the killer took it away with him. We'll check for fibres, but it's possible he used strong wire."

Like I did.

"Turn her to the front," Yellowlees ordered, bending to lift the eyelids. "Note the haemorrhaging to the conjuctivae." He took a syringe and plunged the needle into the right eye. Hamilton stepped back quickly. "The vitreous humour. I should be able to give you a fairly accurate time of death after I've tested for potassium."

"What's your estimate from the body temperature?" I asked.

"I don't much like estimates," the guardian said, his eyes narrowing. "Still, you need all the help you can get. I'd say between four and six a.m.; as the body was found just after six, we're already in the frame."

I nodded and watched as he started examining further down the cadaver, cutting and plucking hairs then applying swabs to the vagina and rectum.

"There's extensive damage to the anus consistent with violent buggery."

"As with almost all the ENT Man's victims, male and female," said Hamilton.

"Correct." Yellowlees lifted his mask and lowered his face to the dead woman's buttocks, then sniffed.

"Jesus Christ." The public order guardian gagged and turned away.

"Curious." Yellowlees stood up straight and glanced at me. "A hint of spermicide. Tests will confirm that."

"A condom?" I said. "The Ear, Nose and Throat Man never used them."

"And we still never managed to track him down from his DNA profile." The medical guardian shook his head impatiently.

"He managed to keep himself out of all the Council's numerous files," I said, looking at the pair of guardians. "Pretty good going." He was a cunning bastard. Even though I buried him,

I never knew his name. Members of the drug gangs always used aliases. I don't think the other Howlin' Wolf headcases knew his identity either. After I got rid of him, I didn't try to find it out. Maybe I should have.

Yellowlees had replaced his mask and was peering at the arms and chest. "No evidence of a struggle. She must have blacked out immediately. It happens." Now he was over by the abdomen, reading off measurements. "Wound made by three incisions, forming a flap of skin six and a quarter inches by eleven inches by five and a half inches; said flap was pulled down to allow access to the liver, which was then removed."

"What kind of blade?" I asked.

"Non-serrated, single-edged, extremely sharp." The medical guardian shrugged. "As to length and thickness, I can't be sure."

I looked into the blood-encrusted hole. "Any evidence of medical knowledge?"

"Not a great deal. The killer knew where to locate the liver, but he could have found that out in any encyclopaedia."

"What about bloodstains? Surely he would have been soaked."

Yellowlees nodded. "I would have thought so, though bear in mind that the victim was already dead when mutilation took place. There wouldn't have been any spurting."

Hamilton came closer. It looked like he was only just winning the battle against vomiting. "We found all her clothing apart from the tunic in a neat pile under the washbasin nearest the door. Her equipment was laid on top. There were no stains on any of it."

I looked at him. "And there were no traces of blood anywhere except in the immediate vicinity of the body."

"That's right," said Yellowlees. "What are you getting at?"

"I'll tell you what I'm getting at. I think the killer took off his own clothes as well as the victim's. I think he cut her open when he was stark naked, then washed the blood off in one of the basins. He's some sort of cleanliness freak."

Simpson 134, the nurse, was staring at me, her eyelids so wide apart that I felt my own straining in sympathy. After a few seconds the medical guardian moved to her and put his hand on her arm briefly.

"I'd expect there to be traces of blood on the basin he used," he said.

"Not after the Council's decision to send in the city's number one cleaner."

Yellowlees ignored the sarcasm. "As I remember, the ,oto-laryngologist didn't use to mind if he left bloodstains." That was a typical guardian understatement. The ENT Man treated his victims' blood like it was paint and he was Jackson Pollock.

"What are you saying?" demanded Hamilton. "That this isn't the same killer? The victim was strangled by ligature, sodomised and had an organ removed. That was the pattern in the past. What more do you want?"

I wanted an explanation of a lot more: like why the ears weren't cut off, why the nose wasn't blocked with earth, why the face hadn't been beaten till it was more black than blue, why a condom had been used and why the scene of the crime hadn't been left like a room in some late twentieth-century slasher film. And that was just for starters.

Yellowlees looked like he was thinking along the same lines. He glanced at Hamilton doubtfully, then turned back to the body. His assistant had finished shaving the head and groin.

"Let's get on," said the medical guardian. He picked up a dissecting knife and made a large Y-shaped incision from neck to pubis, leaving the larynx intact for further examination. The sternum was then split and the dead woman's chest prised apart. That was when the public order guardian left.

"There's more to this than meets the eye," Yellowlees said. Even guardians sometimes speak in clichés.

"I'd go along with that," I said, suddenly noticing that the statuesque nurse was following the surgeon's every movement like she had been hypnotised. Not even auxiliaries are that brainwashed usually.

I left them to it. I'd attended too many post-mortems in the past. Perhaps a five-year lay-off had turned me into a sensitive soul; perhaps there's just a limit to how much of the human body's interior you can take. Unless you're a medic. Or a serial killer. I had a nasty feeling that was what I was up against, even though there was only one body in the morgue. At least I knew it wasn't the ENT Man. I'd have gone through the whole of his autopsy, but I couldn't allow there to be one. What happened was between me and him alone. I owed Caro that much.

Hamilton ambushed me in the foyer. Even though it was late in the evening, there were still patients waiting to be seen. Some of them were speaking a language I didn't recognise.

"Here. I've got these for you." The public order guardian looked like he desperately needed a cigarette, but the Council banned them years ago. He handed me a mobile phone and an embossed card bearing the Council seal. It authorised me to demand full co-operation from any guardian, auxiliary or citizen. "Anything else you need?" he asked mordantly. "Apart from a shave and a change of clothes." I could see he hadn't forgotten my jibe about the cleaner. It was hard to resist another one.

"I saw the hanging today. Do you ever use it to get rid of undesirables?"

Hamilton's eyes sprang open like a pair of Venus flytraps that hadn't seen a bluebottle for weeks. He stepped towards me as I jumped into the Land-Rover.

"Looks like you did it again," Davie said as he accelerated away. "What is it between you and the guardian?"

"You're better off not knowing. Take me back to my place, will you?"

"Right. I spoke to the guard commander who was on duty last night. Every call to Stevenson Hall got the correct response except the one at 0600. Napier 498, the guardswoman who was relieving the victim, made an emergency call at 0609. By that time a vehicle was already on its way to check out the place."

"Thanks, Davie." I made the decision. "What do you say to a temporary transfer? I need someone to work with me on this case."

"Bloody brilliant." He gave a great laugh that echoed round the Land-Rover's rattling shell like a crazed rodent trying to get out of a bass drum. "I wouldn't miss this for anything."

Either he was one of Hamilton's best undercover men selling me a double dummy or he really was excited. I was too tired to work out which. The streetlights flashed three times in quick succession, making me blink.

"Curfew coming up. You better get a move on or you'll have to arrest me for being out after my bedtime."

"Don't worry, I'll vouch for you," he said with a grin. "Even if the chief won't."

The fog closed in around us as the lights were extinguished outside the tourist area to conserve electricity. In the early days, when the Council still called itself the Enlightenment and the nuclear power station at Torness was operational, citizens had to be off the streets by midnight. More recently, curfew time has been brought forward to ten o'clock. Whatever that points to doesn't come under the definition of enlightenment in any dictionary that I know.

Chapter Four

I was playing rhythm guitar in the band, cutting some riffs Muddy Waters could have related to, when the ENT Man appeared. Then I was on him, my blood on his filthy jacket. His head turned towards me as I garotted him. In the light above the path I saw his teeth. They were as blue as a cheese that had been forgotten for decades in the deepest recesses of an underground storeroom in Copenhagen. The bastard was grinning, taunting me because he knew he could break my grip. When he got bored, that's what he did. Threw me sprawling to the ground, then came for me. I didn't think I had a chance of tripping him, but he went down like a hamstrung bull. On to his own knife. The beat drove on. Eventually I realised someone was hammering on my door. I staggered towards it.

"Morning." Davie examined me. "I won't ask if you slept well. You look like . . ."

"What's in the bag?"

"Barracks bread." He thrust it into my hands. "A sight better than anything you'll get in your local bakery."

"The coffee's over there." I went to dress.

"Coffee?" he called after me. "Where did you get that, citizen?"

I was groggier than a sailor's oesophagus, but it almost sounded like he was doing an imitation of your average hyper-inquisitive auxiliary. That wasn't enough to get him out of jail. As far as I'm concerned, people who thrive on getting up early belong to an alien race which has managed to infiltrate us without anyone noticing. Not a bad description of the Enlightenment.

Daylight was no more than a faint grey line under my tattered curtains. "What the hell's the time?" I shouted.

"You tell me. You've got my watch."

I found it in the carpet of dust under my bedside table. Ten past six. "Jesus, Davie, when I asked you to call me, I didn't mean at the start of your shift." The guard start two hours earlier than everyone else to police the rush hour.

He came in with a mug for me. "What shift? I thought murder investigations went on twenty-four hours a day."

"Up yours, guardsman."

He smiled and went back into the living room. While I was tying the laces of my boots, I heard him strum my guitar and have a go at "Such a Parcel of Rogues in a Nation". It was an Enlightenment favourite before independence but he couldn't do it much justice because of the state of my strings.

When I came out he greeted the clean black sweatshirt and trousers I'd found at the back of the wardrobe with a whistle.

"Citizen Dalrymple, you look almost respectable."

"Call me Quint if you want to stay on the case."

"You'll do anything to be different, won't you? A spell down the mines is what you need."

"They tried that once." I gulped coffee. "They didn't invite me back. Apparently I was a disruptive element."

Davie nodded slowly. "I can see that." He put my guitar back in its case. "You any good with this?"

"I haven't played for a long time."

"I noticed. What happened to your E-string?"

I had a flash of the ENT Man falling into the pit with my guitar string still round his neck. Then I thought of the dead guardswoman. Maybe she'd been strangled with a guitar string too. The idea disturbed me – too close for comfort.

I frowned at him when I realised he was still waiting for an answer. "I lost it, years ago. You know how difficult it is to get things like that replaced in Edinburgh."

He looked at me dubiously then followed me to the door.

The victim had been stationed at Knox Barracks on the west side of Charlotte Square. The building was formerly one of the city's record offices. After independence its façade had been ruined by the addition of rows of dormitory windows. The Council chose it as a guard depot because it's close to the tourist hotels and shops at the West End of Princes Street, and because it's within sprinting distance of the guardians' quarters in Moray Place. The dark, mist-sodden stonework looked like the hull of a long-lost battleship sunk beyond the range of the most sophisticated depthfinder.

Davie stopped the Land-Rover outside. I was remembering when there were parking meters on both sides of the road. I gazed into the fog that was still a thick carpet over the city. In the grass-covered centre of the square there used to be bookstalls and tents where writers made speeches at the time when the Festival only lasted three weeks every summer. Now there are booths containing slot machines and roulette wheels – for tourists only. Guard personnel stood at the gates even at this early hour.

"Try not to draw attention to me, Davie," I said before I got out.

"And how am I supposed to do that?" he said with a laugh. "Unless you grow a beard in the next two minutes, every auxiliary in the barracks is going to notice you."

"Well, anyway, let me go ahead, then see if you can find anyone in the recreation area. Tell them you were a friend of Knox 96 and see what kind of reaction you get." I shoved the rusty door open. "You can draw a replacement watch from the stores as well."

"You think of everything, bossman."

Which unfortunately was not the case. At that moment I had no idea how I was going to get anything but the most grudging of answers from the occupants of Knox.

At the entrance my way was barred by a grey-bearded guardsman. Most auxiliaries these days look like they're just out of primary school, but a few have survived from the early days. My ID and authorisation were scrutinised and the details entered in a logbook.

"I thought it was you, sir." The guardsman's eyes were suddenly more welcoming, though he didn't risk a smile.

Not that I had a clue who he was. His use of a proscribed form of address and the low number on his chest – Knox 31 – showed the length of his service. The twenty city barracks were originally set up in 2005 with fifty members each. Now they all have five hundred serving auxiliaries.

The guardsman waited while a group of his colleagues in running kit passed on their way to the all-weather track in Queen Street Gardens. I tried to place him but failed.

"Taggart, sir. I was with you in the Tactical Operations Squad."

Now I remembered. Even when I was in the directorate, I used names rather than barrack numbers – Hamilton used to love me for that. "God, Jimmy Taggart." I sneaked a quick handshake. "I didn't recognise you. All that grey hair."

This time he smiled. "Pressure of being an auxiliary, you know." The smile faded. "I'm not joking. You're well out of it." He looked away from my face. "I was in the back-up group the night we took out the Howlin' Wolf gang up on Soutra. If only those fuckin' phones hadn't gone down . . ."

It was impossible to shut out the flashing lights from the flares, the brittle sound of gunfire, then the screams of a woman I only identified when it was too late. I clenched my fists hard and managed to bring myself back to the present.

"Sorry, sir, shouldn't have mentioned it." Taggart stepped back as more auxiliaries came by. They glanced at me curiously. "Well, you'd better get up to the commander's office. You're here about the killing, aren't you?" He came closer again. "I knew Sarah Spence."

I looked around the hallway. "Can we talk later?"

He nodded. "I've got a break in a couple of hours. The refectory's usually quiet then." He acknowledged another colleague. "Don't believe everything they tell you."

"I'm not expecting them to tell me anything at all." I walked down the corridor and breathed in the familiar barracks smell: bleach mixed with sweat and the reek of overcooked vegetables. The only light came from the high, dirty windows.

The commander was waiting for me outside her office. She was younger than me, her dark hair in the regulation ponytail and her mouth set in a straight horizontal line beneath pale cheeks and cautious eyes. There's nothing like a senior auxiliary's welcome to make you feel optimistic about the future of the human race.

"Citizen Dalrymple," she said. "Your reputation precedes you."

"Meaning that the public order guardian told you to expect me."

Straight-mouth nodded and led me into her office. It was

furnished in the usual austere fashion; it wouldn't do for ordinary citizens to think that auxiliaries lived comfortable lives. Not that any ordinary citizens would have got as far as her office recently. The large windows looking out over the square were all the room had in its favour. The carpets and curtains were worn and the antique desk could have done with the services of a restorer. Over the fireplace was the city's maroon heart flanked by the words of the slogan. "The City Provides". It was faced on the opposite wall by the motto of the rank of auxiliaries: "To Serve the City". This is one of the Council's better jokes – well, one of its only jokes, and unintentional at that. The fact is, the Council deliberately inspires competition between the barracks, which means that they serve themselves first. "Loyalty to your barracks" is the auxiliaries' real watchword. This leads to a pathological reluctance to disclose anything to outsiders, and you don't get much more of an outsider than me.

I decided to go in feet first. "So, what can you tell me about Sarah Spence?" I smiled as Knox 01's eyebrows shot up. "I mean, Knox 96."

"Knox 96," she repeated emphatically, opening a file. "Born 7.10.1986, height five feet two inches, weight nine stone two pounds, hair brown, eyes brown, distinguishing marks heavily freckled face and arms, completed studies at City College of Physical Education July 2007, started auxiliary training programme 1.9.2007, entered Knox Barracks on completion, 31.8.2009, served as physical education instructor—"

"I'm a big boy, commander," I interrupted. "I can read files for myself. Tell me things that aren't in there. Like did she have a lot of friends in the barracks? Did she have any contacts outside Knox? Did she prefer men or women at sex sessions?"

Her mouth looked even straighter than it had been. "Most of that is in the file, citizen," she said coolly. "For your information, she took male and female sexual partners."

"You're not answering my question. Which did she prefer?"

"What bearing can that possibly have on her murder?" The commander actually looked irritated. That was a good sign. Maybe I would find something out. "Oh, very well. Judging from personal experience I would say she preferred women."

She seemed to be expecting me to comment, so I didn't.

"As regards friends, yes, she was popular. She was the kind of person who organises, who's at the centre of things. She had no enemies I ever heard of." The commander was avoiding my eyes. "I don't think she had many contacts outside either. She was very much a Knox person." She stood up and handed me a list of barracks numbers. "These are the people she's . . . she was closest to." Suddenly her mouth wasn't straight any more. "Find him, citizen," she said, her voice taut. "Find the animal who did that to her." Then she twitched her head and became the senior auxiliary again.

"I'm working on it, commander," I said and left her to her files.

On my way to the refectory I passed the barracks gym. There were several pairs practising unarmed combat. I watched the auxiliaries in maroon judo suits going after each other with carefully controlled violence. The fact that the city was served by ten thousand trained killers didn't make me feel that great.

I saw Davie in the far corner of the eating room and ignored him. Taggart got up and led me to the self-service counter. I took a pint of milk and a plate of haggis and mixed vegetables. They serve that kind of food on a twenty-four-hour basis in barracks because of the shifts auxiliaries work. The food's better than what ordinary citizens can find in the subsidised supermarkets too. Since I'd missed dinner the previous evening, I decided against making a complaint at the next Council meeting.

"How did you get on, sir?"

"Stop calling me that, Taggart. I'm just an ordinary citizen now. Call me Quint."

"Sorry." He scratched his beard. "I was a constable before the Enlightenment. Things like that stick in the mind." He sat watching me eat and I knew he was wondering whether he could get away with bringing up the past again. I didn't give him any encouragement. "Did you find out anything useful?" he asked eventually.

"Not much. You know what it's like in barracks. They'd rather have their fingernails pulled out than talk about a colleague."

Taggart nodded. "I'm usually like that myself, but this is different. A murder, for fuck's sake. After all this time."

I studied the burly face opposite me. He had a two-inch scar above his right eye that had been sewn up by someone a lot less proficient than Yellowlees. "What do you think about it then?" I had a feeling he wanted to tell me something.

He leaned closer. "I'm a bit bothered by a couple of things. I'm sure you'll have heard that Sarah was all sweetness and light, a cheery soul and all that. It's true enough – as far as it goes. She wasn't always like that. There was a hard side to her as well. She was really sharp with people who went against her. I heard stories about her taking it out on girls who . . . you know . . . said no to her."

A pair of eager-looking guardswomen approached, making Taggart sit back rapidly.

I waited till they had gone. Even if he was right, I'd have a job getting any of his female colleagues to admit it. "What was the other thing?"

He leaned forward again. "I often do the night shift on Saturdays. I saw Sarah go out after midnight more than once. She always had an authorisation."

I lost interest in my food faster than a croupier in one of the city's casinos sizes up a tourist's wallet. "When was the last time?"

"Two weeks ago."

"But I checked the duty rosters." I looked through my notes. "Two weeks ago she had morning fitness classes and the afternoon shift at Stevenson Hall."

Taggart bit his lower lip and nodded slowly. "Like I say, it's a bit strange, isn't it?"

"Auxiliaries' movements in the central area aren't logged, of course."

"No, but since she had an authorisation, there should be a reference in the rosters."

"I don't suppose you can remember which directorate stamped her authorisation?" I knew before I'd finished the question that a positive answer was about as likely as the Supply Directorate doubling the sugar ration.

"I'm back on watch in a few minutes," Taggart said, collecting the crockery like a good auxiliary.

I needed to squeeze him a bit more. Whatever the Council thought about the ENT Man, I knew for a fact he wasn't at work again. But there were similarities in the modus operandi, Hamilton was right about that. I was going to have to carry out my own private investigation into the bastard's background. That meant doing what Taggart wanted and talking about the old days. I felt sick.

"What were you saying before about the Howlin' Wolf gang?" I asked as nonchalantly as I could. "Did you ever hear what happened to the survivors?"

Taggart didn't show any surprise at the question. I saw he was the kind of veteran auxiliary who spent most of his free time boring the arses off his younger colleagues with tales of his heroic past. "I saw one of them the other day," he said, screwing his eyes up as if the coincidence stung him like an onion. I knew the feeling. "A pal of mine was in charge of a squad of prisoners clearing rubble at Fettes. I recognised him from the tattoo on his arm. They all had them, remember? This one's said 'Leadbelly'. Christ knows why."

Christ and me. They were all blues freaks. The Ear, Nose and Throat Man had "Little Walter" on his arm. I suppose they thought that was really funny.

Taggart would have gone on for hours, but he had his shift and I had my lead.

It was obvious from Davie's face when I got back to the Land-Rover that he hadn't got much out of his fellow auxiliaries. At least he was wearing a new watch.

The sheer walls of the Assembly Hall loomed out of the mist like a smoke-blackened Aztec sacrifice pyramid. I jumped out as soon as Davie stopped and sprinted into the building. Arriving late for a Council meeting was a good way to commit suicide. I'd been working in the archives and had lost track of time.

The medical guardian was on his feet when I got into the chamber.

"Never mind explaining, citizen," said the deputy senior guardian, raising her hand. "Our colleague has been giving us the results of the tests he ran on the victim. Unfortunately, they don't seem to be much help."

That didn't come as much of a surprise. I was too busy being relieved that the senior guardian was absent again.

Yellowlees looked at me without blinking, then acknowledged the speaker's remarks. "I'm afraid that's the substance of it. From the tests I can at least say that Knox 96 was in good physical condition and was not under the influence of drugs or alcohol of any kind. Nor did I find any trace whatsoever of the murderer – no hairs, blood, skin, semen. And no traces from the ligature. I can place the time of death between five and six a.m. from the potassium level in the vitreous humour." He looked around at Hamilton. "I can also confirm that there were traces of spermicide from a standard-issue condom in the guardswoman's rectum."

Hamilton was gazing unperturbed into the middle distance. Behind him was a board with photographs of the ENT Man's victims. That didn't exactly raise my spirits.

The speaker was trying to attract my attention. "Have you made any progress, citizen Dalrymple?"

"Not much. The medical guardian was lucky. At least he had a body to work on." I looked round the horseshoe table. The guardians suddenly found their papers more interesting than me. Which wound me up even more. "All I got was the best-cleaned shithouse in the city."

That got their attention. They probably hadn't heard one of those words for a long time. "I'll tell you this. I reckon there are going to be more killings. The bodies must be left where they're found. I haven't got a chance otherwise."

Some of them looked like they weren't too surprised to hear that.

"All right, citizen, you've made your point," said the deputy senior guardian drily. "Your report, please."

"I've been working on the victim's background." I saw Hamilton move his eyes upward dismissively. That was all the confirmation I needed to keep some of what I'd discovered to myself. "There's nothing irregular. I also spent some time with the auxiliaries from the public order directorate who handled the case before I was brought in. Again, there's nothing significant to report. Fingerprints found in the lavatory and corridor are either those of cleaners, who all have sound alibis, or are not registered in the archives, indicating they belong to tourists. There's no shortage of those in Stevenson Hall every night. The hotels have been checked and they all report that their residents were in by the tourist curfew of 0300."

"What's the point of all this?" Hamilton demanded, jerking his thumb at the board behind him. "We know who the killer is."

"Hardly," said Yellowlees. "Even if the ENT Man has started killing again, we don't have any idea of his identity."

The speaker raised her hand. "One moment. Are we to understand there is some doubt that the Ear, Nose and Throat Man is involved?"

"Absolutely none," said Hamilton, as firmly as a member of

the Inquisition who'd just been asked if there was any possibility Galileo could be right about the solar system.

The deputy senior guardian didn't buy it. She turned to me. "Citizen?"

It was a tricky one. Life would have been a sight easier if I'd told them what happened to the ENT Man. They probably wouldn't even have thrown me into the cells for keeping quiet about it for five years. At least until I caught this killer. But it wasn't just my secret. It was all I still shared with Caro, lost beautiful Caro, whose photo, thank Christ, was obscured by Hamilton's head.

"We're waiting," prompted the speaker, her voice sharper.

I let Caro fade away. And decided to keep our secret. "Well, there are a lot of inconsistencies in the modus operandi. The ENT Man removed organs from his victims, but he also took their ears and blocked their noses, sometimes with earth, other times with pieces of cloth."

"He may have run out of time in Stevenson Hall," said Hamilton.

"You think so? This murder looks to me like a carefully calculated killing. The person who did this knew how to avoid the patrols and gain entry to a protected building."

"Whereas the otolaryngologist," said the medical guardian, his fingers forming a pyramid under his chin as he repeated the term, "the otolaryngologist tended to keep out of the way of guard personnel."

Except in two cases, I thought.

"As I remember," the shrivelled finance guardian said, "he didn't clean up after himself either." The old man glanced at the photos and twitched his lips.

Hamilton was shaking his head. "The woman was strangled, mutilated and sodomised. What more evidence is necessary?"

"Evidence that will enable citizen Dalrymple to catch him," said the deputy senior guardian. "There seems to be precious little of that." She looked at me again. "If you are dubious that it is the same killer, what grounds do you have for expecting more murders?"

It was a good question. They might give the impression of inhabiting a world light years away from the rest of us, but there's nothing wrong with the guardians' intellects. Except perhaps the public order guardian's.

"There was an outburst of serial killing in the years before the UK broke up. I read all the reports. The likelihood of a murderer who gets away with a killing of this kind doing it again is overwhelming." I was trusting a hunch as well, but I didn't think that would impress them.

"You'd better make sure you catch him then," said Hamilton grimly. "I propose that we increase the number of patrols in the tourist area at night. And that we continue to suppress all news of the guardswoman's death."

"You realise that every auxiliary in the city knows about it by now," I observed, giving him a grim look of my own.

"Auxiliaries are sworn servants of the city," said the speaker loftily. "They will not divulge the news to ordinary citizens."

And a formation of pigs had just been spotted over Arthur's Seat. "Even if they don't," I said, "it's possible that the killer needs publicity. By denying him that we may increase the chances of him doing it again." They all looked at me sternly. "Let's face it, censoring the news of the ENT Man's activities didn't exactly help us catch him."

I caught a glimpse of the bust of Plato at the rear of the chamber. The Enlightenment used his ideas as the basis of the new constitution and they're still debated every week in all the barracks. "You're the students of human nature," I said, trying to provoke a response. None of them reacted. It looked like I had them where I wanted. "By the way, I've taken on a guardsman as my assistant."

Hamilton was as reliable as one of Pavlov's dogs. His eyes sprang wide open and his fists clenched.

"Hume 253 is his barracks number," I continued. "He'll report to me alone during the investigation. No objections, I hope."

If the deputy senior guardian disapproved of my tone, she concealed it. Which is more than can be said for the public order guardian. Now he looked like a dog that had just been fed something worse than standard-issue haggis.

I hadn't finished with them. "It seems to me that we're failing to address the most important question raised by this case."

"No doubt you're about to tell us what that is," said Hamilton in a strangulated whisper.

I closed my notebook and stood up. "You're right, guardian – I am. What's behind the timing? It's five years since the ENT Man last killed. Suddenly his modus operandi is repeated in part and a guardswoman is murdered in Stevenson Hall in the early morning of 20 March 2020. Why?"

Back at my flat I cleared everything off the table and sat down to turn dross into gold. As I told the Council, the archives had yielded nothing worth reporting. I'd a faint hope that I would find some detail that had been omitted from the barracks documentation concerning the dead woman. Even a juicy big Public Order Directorate stamp showing that something had been censored would have done – then I could have squeezed Hamilton about it. But there was nothing. It didn't take me long to come to the conclusion that I was as much at sea as the owl and the pussycat. At least they had a pea green boat.

The knock on the door came as a relief. I assumed it would be Davie, then with a shock I remembered Katharine Kirkwood. Maybe she couldn't wait until tomorrow. Her brother had been missing from my thoughts as well as from his flat. Still, the idea of laying eyes on her again was not unpleasant. I was disappointed.

"Billy?" I tried and failed to sound unsurprised.

"Quint, how the hell are you?" The short figure in a beautifully cut grey suit and pink silk shirt pushed past me. On his way he rammed a brand of malt whisky I hadn't seen for a decade into my hands.

"Christ, Billy, how did you find me?" I closed the door. "More to the point, after all this time, why did you find me?"

"I'm pleased to see you too. What kind of a welcome is that, for fuck's sake? I'm your oldest friend." William Ewart Geddes, Heriot 07, one hundred and ten pounds of financial genius and calculating bastard, walked into the centre of the room and looked around under the naked light bulb. "Nice place you've got here, Quint," he said with a sardonic grin. "I see you've still got your guitar. Not being a naughty boy and playing the blues, I hope."

There was a time when Billy was as fanatical about B.B. King and Elmore James as I am, but that was before the Council banned the blues on the grounds that music has to be uplifting or some such bollocks. The fact that most of the drugs gangs idolised bluesmen had nothing to do with the decision, of course.

"No, I haven't played for years," I said. "Not since I was demoted." I opened the whisky and inhaled its peaty breath.

"That's the last time I saw you as well. Why the sudden interest?"

Billy accepted a chipped glass reluctantly and sipped the spirit neat, his small grey eyes blinking. The sparse beard that covered his thin face showed definite signs of officially disapproved clipping.

"You know how it is," he said. "No fraternisation between auxiliaries and ordinary citizens." He grinned again, showing suspiciously even teeth. "Still, you've had time to cool off. And now I hear you're back in favour—" He broke off to examine the small, blurred photo of Caro on the wall, the sharpness in his expression dissipating. The three of us had been at the university together. He looked like he was going to say something about her, but the glare I gave him made him change his mind.

"As for finding you, that was easy. I'm deputy finance guardian, remember. All I had to do was pull your rates sheet." He sat down gingerly on the sofa after inspecting it for anything that might damage his suit. Personally I'd have stayed upright if I'd been him.

"Deputy finance guardian? You look more like a stockbroker. Remember them?"

Billy laughed. "The clothes are nothing. You should see my flat."

"No, thanks. I'm only a citizen. Luxury's bad for my character." So's jealousy. I couldn't resist having a go at him. "Or so they used to say in the Enlightenment, didn't they?"

"Something like that," Billy mumbled, his cheeks reddening. The party had alway taken second place to his personal ambitions. Obviously they were now in the process of being achieved. "Listen, Quint, how about a night on the town? I've got a car."

"You're full of surprises."

"There's a new nightclub in Rose Street."

"Nightclub? You mean a place where semi-naked women prance around and tourists pay inflated prices for shitty whisky?"

"So you're interested." Billy raised an eyebrow. "You'll need a change of clothes."

I drained my glass. "I'll wear a tutu if I have to."

As I dragged my only suit out of the wardrobe, I almost managed to convince myself that I was only going because I wanted to find out why Billy had turned up after five years. But as I always turned the light out during sex sessions, it was also a long time since I'd seen a woman in anything less than a layer of off-white Supply Directorate underwear. Men are animals.

The Toyota that Billy drove might well have been the newest vehicle in the city. I decided against asking him where he found the petrol to run it. He'd either have ignored the question or revealed some deal I didn't want to know about. The Council banned the private ownership of cars because it was unable to negotiate a favourable price with the oil companies for anything except poor quality diesel. I wondered what its members thought about the deputy finance guardian's wheels. I had a flash of the clapped-out 2CV he used to have when we were students. The problem then wasn't obtaining fuel, it was finding somewhere to park. Now Lothian Road stretched ahead of us like a long deserted runway whose controller had turned the landing lights on in the forlorn hope of attracting some passing trade. Looking around, I realised that the fog was less thick.

Billy accelerated hard down the hill past Stevenson Hall and jerked a thumb. "It happened in there, didn't it?"

I might have known. He wanted me to fill him in about the murder. I fed him some scraps which he accepted impassively but which, I was sure, he was storing away in his memory. At school Billy was famous for his ability to memorise pages of material in seconds. Coupled with his business acumen, that had sent him straight into the Finance Directorate in the early years of the Council.

"Your parents all right?" he asked as he swung the car into the pedestrian precinct of Rose Street and acknowledged the guardsman who waved him through. When we were boys, Billy was a constant presence in our house in Newington. His own parents were divorced.

"Growing old with about as much grace as those archbishops the mob walled up in St Paul's years ago – the old man especially." Then I remembered that the next day was Sunday. Despite the investigation, I'd have to find time for the weekly visit.

"Don't suppose you see much of your mother," Billy said as he pulled up. "Right, let's get in amongst them."

The Bearskin was brightly lit. A pair of hypothermic girls wearing tartan shorts and crowned by headgear consistent with the club's name flanked the entrance. Placards in a variety of languages laid out the treats in store for prospective customers: live music ("the hottest in the city"), top quality food and the widest selection of beer and whisky in Edinburgh, as well as a floorshow Bangkok would supposedly have envied in the years before its decline.

Billy pushed through the mass of Chinese and Middle Eastern men – I couldn't see any female customers – and led me in without any money or ID appearing. The manager, despite his dinner jacket, smoothly shaved face and slicked-back hair, was an auxiliary, like most of the staff in clubs and casinos.

"Come on, Quint, I've got a table at the front." Billy went down a short flight of steps towards a thick curtain. It was opened by a beaming girl with dead eyes. Her skirt would only cover her knickers if she stood very still. A wave of sound broke over us.

The activities on stage were hard to avoid. Billy was already at a table, eagerly following the spectacle. I tried to play it cool, but my eyes were drawn all the same. The place was packed, the audience making almost as much noise as the band, whose members all wore kilts. A banner above proclaimed they were the only jazz band in the world with a bagpiper. Fortunately he seemed to have the night off.

We were very close to the tangle of limbs on the stage. The costumes suggested that the scene was set in the sixteenth century. Most of them were strewn across the floor. Mary, Queen of Scots, her petticoats lifted over her back, was being penetrated from the rear by a wiry young man presumably meant to be her secretary Rizzio. As the music rose to a crescendo, he withdrew, flipped his royal partner on to her back and started to tear off her remaining clothes to the raucous accompaniment of the crowd.

Billy turned to me with a desperate smile on his face, then glanced over my shoulder and nodded. I followed the direction of his eyes and saw an old friend, though she didn't seem to be very happy to see me. Patsy Cameron must have been in her fifties but she still looked the part, dressed up in a black velvet evening gown that showed the amount of bosom you'd expect from the madam of a cathouse in a Western. Which is more or less what she'd been before the Council decided to make use of her in the Prostitution Services Department. Patsy and I had got on pretty well when I was still in the directorate. Now she was avoiding my eyes like they'd give her an X-ray from twenty feet away.

Looking back at the stage, I saw that the queen was now completely naked. She sat up and gazed out at the audience. My heart missed so many beats that it hurt. She was without doubt the most stunningly beautiful woman I'd ever seen in my life. Although the tresses of her red wig partially obscured her face, the perfectly proportioned features were still visible. As were her full, hard-tipped breasts and limbs that looked like the pure white marble of an ancient statue. She moved her eyes slowly around the room, giving certain individuals the benefit of her erotically charged but totally inscrutable stare. The girl at the curtain's eyes had been dead, but this one's were on a different plane altogether – both superior and all-knowing, detached but at the same time infinitely provocative. I felt seriously out of my depth.

Then Rizzio, another member of the zombie eyes club, pushed her down, squatted on her chest and offered her his long, thin penis. She took it in her mouth and clutched his bony buttocks with her hands. The music started to build to a climax again as Mary, Queen of Scots inflated her cheeks in exaggerated movements. Eventually Rizzio pulled out and fountained over her breasts.

That was when I had another shock. Rubbing my eyes in the smoke from the tourists' cigarettes, I looked again. There was no doubt about it. The queen's left hand was normal, but the right one was a textbook example of polydactyly. Like everyone else, she had one thumb – but she also had no fewer than five fingers.

Chapter Five

Davie arrived at eight o'clock on the dot and almost fell over laughing when he saw the state I was in. I turned my nose up at his offering of barracks bread.

I only managed to formulate a coherent sentence after dosing myself with black coffee. "What do you know about Heriot 07, Davie?"

"The flash bastard in the Finance Directorate? He's got a reputation for looking after himself."

"How come he hasn't been nailed then?" I wasn't too happy about the way Billy had thrown his weight around at the night-club. After the show had finished he got a hold of Rizzio and one of the waitresses and tried to interest me in a foursome. I prefer sex with women whose eyes have a bit more life in them. Besides, I was too pissed to do anything.

"Things have changed since you were an auxiliary," Davie said, shaking his head. "I'm beginning to see why you got out. You were one of those who thought the city should stay like it was in the early days, weren't you?"

"I was an idealist. Most people were then."

"Not any more, pal." His voice was harder. "While you've been doing your Philip Marlowe impersonation, a fair number of senior auxiliaries have been acting less altruistically. There's no shortage of smart operators like Heriot 07 who get what they can from the city. They cover their arses. If they're spotted, they pay people off. Or arrange a good kicking."

"Sounds like Chicago under Al Capone."

"Or London before the UK fell apart."

"Don't the guardians have any idea of what's going on?"

"That's the big question, isn't it?" Davie was looking twitchy. "Don't ask me, I'm only a guardsman." He turned away. "What are we doing today?"

I gulped down the last of my coffee. "It's Sunday. I have to call in on my father." Even when I was in the directorate, the visit had been a fixture. Hamilton, always the understanding boss, used to complain about me taking a couple of hours off on the city's single weekly rest-day. "But before that, we're going to look for a convict."

The fog had lifted completely and we drove along Comely Bank in bright sunshine. After the checkpoint between the tourist area and the suburbs, the surroundings took a rapid change for the worse. Although the streets were cleaned and rubbish collected regularly everywhere, the road surface, pavements and buildings were crumbling. In the centre, squads of cleaners, painters, masons and gardeners worked round the clock. Not in the parts where tourists never set foot. A flash in the sky caught my eye. A large silver and blue plane droned overhead on its descent to the airport – probably the daily flight from Athens with another load of tourists for the city's museums and fleshpots.

I looked at a small group of citizens gathered outside a church. Although the city is officially a secular republic, religion is tolerated as long as it conforms to the Council's standards of loyalty and civic responsibility. The thin but enthusiastic figures in their Sunday-best suits and dresses – smart enough despite the limitations of clothing vouchers – showed no dissatisfaction with the regime. People generally don't. In the sixteen years since the Enlightenment came to power, the Council has managed to retain the trust of the overwhelming majority of citizens. Probably because most of them haven't forgotten the economic chaos and the violence on the streets in the years before the last democratic election.

"You stay in the Land-Rover," I said as Davie pulled up at the East Gate of what had once been the most striking building in north Edinburgh. Fettes College, once one of Scotland's foremost public schools, production line for generations of the politicians who had eventually brought the UK to ruin, was blown to pieces in 2009. I remembered playing rugby under the great grey-blue fairy castle walls when I was a kid. After independence and the abolition of private education, the school's proximity to the gangland area of Pilton had made it an attractive base for the drug traders. The Council concentrated on establishing order in the city centre first, then moved to retake Fettes. Bad idea. The gangs were better armed than the Parachute Regiment. Although the Council eventually drove them out, the buildings were blown up to show the guardians what the gangs thought of them. The top of the college's spire now lay hundreds of feet from its foundations. A small group of shaven-headed prisoners were loading stones on to a decrepit lorry.

"What do you think you're . . ." The guardsman shut up when he saw my authorisation.

I studied the labourers. They were sweating in the sunlight and had their shirt sleeves rolled up. That made it easy to spot Leadbelly.

"Bring that one to the Land-Rover," I said to the auxiliary. "Gently."

"Number thirty-five," he barked. "Get your arse over here."

I followed, shaking my head. You can always trust the guard to put people in the mood to co-operate.

"Wait outside, will you, Davie?" At least he did what I asked. I got into the driver's seat and beckoned to the prisoner to get in the other side. He was tall and I could see he had once been a hard man. Five years of the Cramond Island diet had turned him into a passable replica of a mummified corpse. He kept his eyes off me.

"So, Leadbelly, been digging any potatoes recently?" The reference to one of his namesake's best-known songs made him look at me quickly enough. A grin spread across his cracked lips and I saw that he had a serious shortage of teeth.

"'Digging My Potatoes' – shit, it's fucking years since I heard that. You know the blues?"

I nodded.

He gazed at me incredulously. "You know Huddie Ledbetter?"

"'Lining the Track', 'Matchbox Blues' – I've got some recordings from 1942."

He smacked his bony thigh. "You have? Christ, I'd bend over in front of a guardsman to have a listen to them."

"You may not have to go that far." I gave him my most encouraging smile.

His grin faded. "What do you want from me, man?" He peered at my clothes, noticing the lack of barracks number. "Who the fuck are you anyway?"

"Call me Quint."

"Quint? What kind of name is that?"

"There was a time when I was known as Bell 03."

"Is that right?" He leaned towards me. "You and me have had dealings."

You never know when it's going to happen, but sometimes you get lucky. I had been trying not to get excited by the slight chance that Leadbelly would turn out to be the gang member who put me on to the ENT Man. And it turned out he was. If I believed in a god, I'd have said thank you.

"You wrote me the note saying that the killer we were looking for would be in Princes Street Gardens the next Saturday night. You said he was going to get himself a tourist and really put the shits up us."

Leadbelly held his bloodshot eyes on me like he still needed final confirmation.

"At the end you wrote 'Axe the fucking . . .'"

"Psycho," he completed. "Okay, man, you're the genuine item." He grabbed my knee with a clawlike hand and brought his mouth close to my ear. "So did you?"

I didn't answer. He got the message though.

"What do you want now then?" he asked eventually.

"Tell me everything you know about him."

"After all this time?" He ran fingers with black nails over his scalp. "What's the point?"

"I've got Robert Johnson on tape too," I said.

"Never." He watched me nod in confirmation. "You're really something, man, you know that? Better get your notebook out then." He blinked and held his eyes shut for a long time, as if he were steeling himself to dive off a cliff. "Right, here it is. We called him Little Walter. Fuck, that was a good one. He must have been six foot two and sixteen stone."

At least. I felt his weight on me again, falling back as I tightened the ligature.

"And he was a shite. Fuck knows where the Wolf found him. He wasn't one of us, he didn't come from Pilton. He was good in a fight, mind, a handy man to have around. But he was weird, man. Christ, he was fucking insane. He had scars all over him; I'm sure he'd done most of them himself. And his breath reeked too. His teeth were even more rotten than mine."

I remembered. The bastard cocked his head, seemed to listen out. Then came the blue flash of his teeth in the light and the pitted skin of his face as he turned.

"And he was so fucking out of control. He once told me that he used to come when he throttled people. After I saw how he left that auxiliary woman in the farmhouse up on Soutra, I thought enough is a fucking nough."

I saw Caro lying on the stone floor, her left foot jerking like she was stretching it to get rid of cramp.

"I mean, he lived in a world of his own, man. He never paid any attention to our music, I don't think he even liked the blues. I'm sure he only let us tattoo him because he got a thrill from the needle." Leadbelly stopped and licked his lips as if he'd bitten into a putrid tomato. "Why are you making me talk about the sick fuck, for Christ's sake?"

"You ever hear his real name?"

"What do you think? We only used our gang names." He laughed harshly. "Like you assholes only use your barracks numbers."

"Not me, pal. How about family? Ever hear him talk about anyone he was close to?"

He choked on another laugh. "Close to? That shite only ever got close to the people he butchered. How come you never caught him? He left enough evidence, didn't he?"

"I nearly caught him once in Leith. He went back to the same place . . ."

"Yeah, he told us all about that. He reckoned he was something really special after he got away." He raised a finger. "Wait a minute, I do remember something about a relative. A brother. Walter said he was a right wee wanker and he'd shown him a thing or two when they were boys." He shook his head. "Didn't mention a name, though."

"Or anything about where he'd grown up, where he went to school, anything like that?"

"He was as silent as the grave I hope you put him in about all that."

I bet he was, the cunning bastard. "Anything else that could help me identify him?" I asked in desperation.

Leadbelly shrugged. "Here, can I get back now? The others'll be thinking you're getting me to rat on them."

"Wouldn't be the first time."

"Not fair, man. I did you a good turn. Walter was an animal."

I closed my notebook. End of the road. What the hell had I been doing? I knew where the butcher was; why was I raking around in dead man's dust? The chances of someone copying his modus operandi imperfectly were about as small as my chances of finding out the ENT Man's identity. I had to forget the old obsession once and for all.

The prisoner climbed out. Before closing the door, he leaned back in. "What about those recordings of Huddie?"

"Don't worry, I'll get them to you."

It was obvious he didn't believe me.

"Give me half an hour." I left my mobile phone with Davie and ran into the house in Trinity.

As a former guardian, my father had been given the large room that took up the whole third floor of the Victorian merchant's house. When he resigned in 2013, the Council's plans for the provision of homes for all the city's old people were well advanced, driven by the need for every able-bodied citizen to be available for full-time work. The old man was in his late sixties then and had no problem with the fifty-five steps to his room. He liked being alone, away from the resident nurse's prying eyes. But recently he'd begun to wheeze and he lived in fear of being moved downstairs. I knew that was about as likely as the roulette tables being opened to ordinary citizens – he had a tendency to wander off and the nurse wanted him as far from the front door as possible.

I opened his door without knocking. "Hello, old man."

"Hello, failure." My father didn't look up from his desk in the window but continued to run his finger along the page of the book he was studying. Finally he stopped and marked his place carefully.

"At least the fog's lifted." I was looking out over the Firth of Forth from the high window. I could make out the island of Inchkeith, which the Council once used as a penal colony. Further west I could just see the top of what remained of the Forth railway bridge – both it and the road bridge had been severed during the fighting that followed the city's declaration of independence. It suited the Council's policy of isolation from the rest of the country to leave the bridges unusable.

My father rose to his full height of six feet four inches and looked down at me, his breath catching in his throat. He never opened his eyes fully, which gave the impression of someone who was only half awake – that's my earliest memory of him. Like most things to do with him, it was deceptive. He was one of the quickest-thinking people I've ever met.

"What's happened to you, lad? You look almost respectable."

"I know. It's something I need to talk to you about."

The old man's eyes flashed and a sardonic smile grew across his mouth. "You surprise me. Don't tell me you want advice from a senile has-been, Quintilian."

He was the only person who liked calling me by my full name. He did choose it, much to his wife's disgust. Classical names were a tradition in the Dalrymple family and since the old man's academic field of expertise was rhetoric, the Roman orator Quintilian's name had been doubly appropriate. I'm not complaining. At least he didn't call me Demosthenes.

"This is serious, Hector." Even when I was at primary school, he'd insisted I address him that way. I don't know whether he subscribed to some late-eighties belief in equality between parents and children or whether he just liked the sound of his own name.

He sat down on the sofa beside me and stretched out his legs. Even indoors he always wore the guardians' tweed jacket and heavy brogues though he was no longer entitled to them. The polish from the old brown shoes made my nostrils twitch.

"Fire away, then," he said encouragingly. He was more sympathetic to his fellow men's weaknesses than some of his activities as one of the original guardians suggested.

"I've been taken on by the Council. To investigate a murder."

His eyebrows rose and he began to question me in detail. I didn't mention the ENT Man. He'd never heard about him.

"So what do you think?" I asked when he'd finished interrogating me. "You were information guardian. Should the Council be suppressing all news of the killing?"

He got up slowly then glared down at me. "Certainly not. You're as much to blame as they are. You should have seen where this would lead."

I didn't have a clue what he meant, but it was usually worth giving him some slack. "Which is where?"

"It's obvious, isn't it?" he shouted. "Why did I resign from the Council?"

I'd had enough of riddles. "What's that got to with it?" I shouted back.

"Answer the question, boy!"

The only way was to humour him. I bit my tongue. "All right. You left because you thought the guardians were going beyond the principles of the Enlightenment and taking too much power for themselves."

"Exactly." He was nodding his head like a teacher whose thickest pupil had just grasped that two and two don't make five. "Which, for all the high-mindedness of the first Council members, would inevitably lead to corruption."

"And murder?"

"Why not? I'd say that this killing is a direct result of the Council's concentration of power in directorates personally controlled by its members."

Now he'd lost me. "Hang on a second. Lewis Hamilton's got about as much idea of how to handle a murder case as I have of respecting my elders and betters, but you can't deny his directorate's cut down crime in general. What's corrupt about that?"

Hector shook his head. "You're taking what I said too narrowly. I'm talking about the regime as a whole. If there's no debate, no opposition, as has happened now that absolute power rests with the Council, there's bound to be a lowering of standards, just like there was in the House of Commons before it self-destructed."

He may not have been a guardian any more but he still spoke in the long sentences favoured by that rank. Still, what he'd said about corruption had made me prick up my ears. "How come you've never spoken about this before?" I asked. "Have you given up on the Enlightenment completely now?"

"Of course not." The old man went over to his desk. "When we founded the Edinburgh Enlightenment at the turn of the century, we were convinced that the only way out of the political and economic nightmare in the United Kingdom was by decentralising power. Not the feeble assemblies that some of the old parties had set up, but the real thing – regional government by bodies of experts, some of them even philosophers like Plato's guardians. Here, I want to show you something." He started rummaging around in his papers.

I thought about the early years. I was still at school when the party was formed – sixteen, and almost as fascinated by Edinburgh's new politics as I was by the blues. The world was changing day by day. Oil in the Aegean had lead to the end of American investment in the North Sea and a slump in the UK's already weakened economy. At the same time China, bolstered by the return of Hong Kong, had become the dominant economic power and the USA had reverted to the self-obsession that's a hallmark of their history.

It wasn't long before crime reduced the majority of British cities to battlefields. Drugs were the country's only significant industry. The government reintroduced the death penalty in 1999 and became increasingly assertive in its handling of foreign policy, egged on by the tabloid press. Following a European Union directive to withdraw British forces from Gibraltar, Downing Street threatened the use of nuclear warheads against Spanish ships. This resulted in international sanctions and the sealing of the Channel Tunnel. The catastrophic accident at the Thorp installation at Sellafield in 2003 was the final straw. The country fell into total disorder and the Enlightenment got the opportunity it needed. Edinburgh citizens voted the party in with a huge majority after a London mob barricaded MPs in the chamber during their last emergency debate and burned the place to the ground. I can't say I was too upset.

"Got it." Hector held up a piece of paper triumphantly. "Read that."

I looked at the typed sheet. It was a page from the minutes of a Council meeting six months after the election victory. I studied it with mounting amazement. "'As a result of negative votes by the education and public order guardians, we do not approve the information guardian's proposal that the Council commit itself to resign en masse if evidence of corruption in any directorate is brought to light.'" I glanced at my father and whistled. "Jesus. You tried to get them to agree to that and they refused?"

His eyes were unusually wide open. "You see what I mean? That proposal was an integral part of the Enlightenment's planning from the beginning – it was the ultimate safeguard. But once we were in power, people's priorities changed."

"I'm not surprised Hamilton voted against it, but the education guardian . . ."

"Who is now the senior guardian." The old man sat down, his limbs suddenly loose and his jaw slack. "From that day on I never felt the same about the Council. I stuck it out for another nine years, but organising propaganda is hard when your heart isn't in it."

It was one of the few times I'd seen my father looking like he needed support. I wish I'd shown him that I felt for him, but neither of us was ever much good at displays of emotion. The Enlightenment deadened us completely.

Pretty soon afterwards Hector sat up straight. His periods of introspection were always short. "Look on the bright side, Quintilian," he said. "People are better off than they were and they know it. Electricity and water may be in short supply, but there's enough. There are no cars or private telephones or personal computers. There's no television, though only a cretin would choose to sit in front of what used to be served up every evening. But think of all the benefits: jobs, a reliable health and welfare system, safety in the streets, education throughout their lives for all." He glanced at me and smiled ironically. "Except for people who've been demoted, of course." He looked away, shaking his head. "Those were our ideals and they've actually been achieved. Sometimes I still find it hard to believe."

I admired his ability to criticise the regime and then salute its achievements, but I wondered how close he was to the reality of life in the city now. "I saw Billy Geddes last night," I said, then told him about the Bearskin.

"Sounds like he's turned out to be one of the backsliders I was talking about," Hector said scathingly. He was never keen on what he referred to as "affairs of the cock".

"Maybe he isn't that bad," I said, scrabbling around for something to put up in mitigation. "Maybe he's just keen on cars and flash clothes."

"I'd have him down the mines before he could zip himself up."

He had a point. I was having a hard time with Billy myself.

"I never agreed with all that entertainment for the tourists," the old man added. "At least the gambling and whoring. I'm no Calvinist, but to me that's just dirty money."

I had a sudden vision of the perfect woman on the stage and

wondered how she'd got involved in that kind of work. "The Medical Directorate checks all the women regularly," I said. "There hasn't been a case of AIDS for years."

"Not that we've been told about," Hector said. "There hadn't been a murder . . ."

Boots were pounding up the stairs. The noise grew louder, then Davie burst in, my mobile phone in his hand.

"Quint, you're wanted. Come on."

"What is it?"

Davie struggled to catch his breath. "They've found another body . . . in Dean Gardens." He looked at my father, then back to me. "Male this time . . . same modus operandi, it seems."

Hector was looking worried. I didn't feel too good myself.

"Sounds like you've got a psychopath on your hands, Quintilian. Be careful."

Davie set off out the door and I followed. "I'll try to come again next Sunday. Keep well, old man."

Halfway down the stairs I heard him calling out. Something about me not telling him if I'd seen my mother. At that moment, she was the last thing on my mind.

Chapter Six

"Shit, Davie." I clutched the seat. "I told you, I don't want to die."

"Don't worry. There hasn't been a fatality on the roads for years." He kept his foot on the floor and called ahead to the next checkpoint. We raced through and were soon crossing the Dean Bridge. The parkland dropping steeply down to the Water of Leith was bright green in the sunlight, the only trace of the days of fog a silver sheen on the leaves and grass that had almost evaporated. Along with the last slim chance of this being a one-off killing.

Then the Land-Rover swung round hard into Academy Place and I remembered two things. The first was irrelevant, a desperate attempt by my mind to distract itself from what lay in the park; it had come to me that the street used to be called Eton Terrace before the Council took steps to change all names with suspect cultural connotations. The second thing gave me a jolt of electric-chair proportions. Adam Kirkwood's flat, where I'd been with Katharine two days earlier, was a couple of hundred yards further on. I hoped to hell he wasn't the latest corpse.

I counted six guard vehicles, including the public order guardian's with its maroon pennant. The windows of the houses lining the street were filled with spectators. No chance of the Council keeping this killing quiet.

Lewis Hamilton emerged from the gap in the railings where the gate to these formerly private gardens had been. "Dalrymple, it's about time you turned up." His cheeks had an unhealthy tinge and I reckoned he'd been closer to the dead man than he would have liked.

"Who found the body?" I headed down the slope to the bushes where a group of guardsmen and women stood.

"We did," said the guardian. "A woman who refused to identify herself telephoned from the callbox at the end of the bridge. Probably one of the local residents who didn't want to get involved."

"Very public-spirited of her."

"There are rotten apples in every barrel, citizen."

That was too inviting to ignore. "I thought your directorate had got rid of all of them."

He gave me a glare that made me feel a lot better. "Clear the way," he ordered curtly. It wasn't the first time I'd seen him taking things out on his auxiliaries.

I pulled on rubber gloves and dropped to my knees. There were a lot of footprints on the grass at the edge of the bushes but it was clear they were all recent – from the guard and the woman who'd raised the alarm. It was also obvious what had drawn her to the spot. The stench of decomposing flesh was like a curtain I'd just poked my head through. Beyond the branches a discoloured mass was visible. Even at ten yards' range I could see that the body was completely naked.

There was a small clearing beyond the outer foliage. I approached from an oblique angle to avoid touching any footprints. As I got nearer the corpse their number increased and I marked the deepest indentations so that casts could be taken. I already knew what kind of footwear had made them – non-nailed citizen-issue boots, size twelve. That was all I needed. The Ear, Nose and Throat Man took size twelves. That's how I was sure the man in Princes Street Gardens that night was him, even before I got close. He was wearing a pair of ancient cowboy boots with square toes – I'd found prints from them at several of the murder sites. Jesus. He couldn't still be alive. I clung to that certainty. After he skewered himself, I pushed him into the foundations of the stand they were building beside the new racetrack. Then I heaped a great load of earth over him till I passed out because of the loss of blood from my finger. But I came to before the workmen arrived the next morning and I saw them pour the concrete over him. It was a coincidence, the shoe size, but it shook me for longer than it should have.

I crawled around with my magnifying glass but found nothing else in the way of traces. No fibres from clothing, no buttons torn off in the struggle, no strands of hair.

Davie came in on his hands and knees, carefully avoiding the marks I'd drawn around the footprints. He looked across at the body and grimaced. "How long do you think he's been here?"

I couldn't put it off any longer. "I was just getting round to having a look."

Davie was holding a handkerchief to his face. "After you."

"Thanks a lot." I moved forward. The man was lying on his left side, his limbs swollen under greenish purple skin. The abdomen was grotesquely distended. A couple of yards behind his head was a neat pile of clothes, boots placed on top. He was short, no more than five feet five inches, and heavily built. At least I could be sure he wasn't Adam Kirkwood. I could also be sure that something violent had been done to the lower part of his back.

Taking a deep breath, I bent over the blackened hole. And almost threw up. It was seething. I had an idea there would be insect infestation, but not this much. The temperature under the fog carpet hadn't been too low so the maggots were fat, clustered over what was left of the flesh around the ribs. I reckoned they were in the third instar of growth. The flies had laid their eggs in the cavity which had once been occupied by the dead man's right kidney. I turned towards the upper part of the body and froze solider than the permafrost on a Siberian steppe. Something had moved.

"What is it?" Davie asked immediately.

I shook my head to shut him up. Again there was a quick, confined flurry. It came from the right armpit. I leaned forward slowly, drawn on despite the urge to escape my stomach manifested by the mug of coffee I'd drunk earlier. Then I saw it.

The rat was so bloated that it could hardly pull itself out of the corpse. It looked at me with glassy eyes then opened its mouth to pant. Its head twitched from side to side as it calculated angles and distances for its escape. I wasn't planning on getting in its way.

It made its move with surprising speed. The long hairless tail was past me even before I could sit back. But it hadn't taken account of Davie. He grabbed the tail and held the animal at arm's length. I hadn't put him down as a pet lover. The rat wriggled frantically and tried without success to bite him. It was too fat to double up.

"Don't we want to examine it?" Davie asked. "The stomach contents might . . ."

"Jesus Christ, let the bloody thing go. We've got a whole, well, almost a whole body to dissect. Not to mention about a million bluebottles."

There was a rustling noise behind me.

"What have you got there, guardsman?" asked Robert Yellowlees. "We can always use those in the labs. Give it to my assistant."

Davie grinned at me and departed.

The medical guardian inspected the body, running his rubber-sheathed hands over the limbs and sniffing like a discerning wine drinker.

"You were right, citizen," he said. "We're dealing with a multiple murderer. Whether it's the otolaryngologist or not." He pointed to the victim's neck. "Strangled by ligature like the guardswoman. And an organ removed. There isn't much doubt that it's the same killer."

I looked at the dead man's swollen face. He had a misshapen nose that had been broken at some stage. There was no evidence of it having been blocked. The ears were intact too. His close-cropped hair was grey and I put his age at around forty-five. The mouth, caught open in a rictus that looked like he was trying to call for help and yawn at the same time, revealed discoloured teeth and gaps where several had fallen out. Another one who hadn't taken advantage of the city's dental services.

Yellowlees was writing notes. I went over to the pile of clothes. In the breast pocket of a donkey jacket I found a wallet containing only an ID card. There were none of the booklets of food, clothing and electricity vouchers that citizens usually have on them. Still, it seemed hard to believe robbery was the motive. Any self-respecting thief would have taken the ID to sell to the dissidents. No self-respecting thief would have had a man's kidney out.

I read that the victim's name was Rory Talbot Baillie, aged forty-eight, driver in the central vehicle pool.

"Around ten days since he was killed," Yellowlees said, a thin smile flashing on his lips. "Before you ask. The entomologists will be able to confirm that from the maggots. I'll run my own tests as well, of course. I'd say that the kidney was removed with a blade very similar to the one used in the other murder." He turned to go then stopped. "Oh, and the anus was penetrated. Will that do you for the time being?"

I spent three hours supervising the scene-of-crime auxiliaries. They seemed to have a reasonable idea of what they were doing. Perhaps they'd read my manual. Davie certainly had. He took charge of the photographer and made sure all the angles were covered. We had some trouble taking plastercasts of the footprints as the ground was still soft, but eventually we got some good ones. An auxiliary got on to the Supply Directorate and was told that two thousand three hundred and six pairs of size twelve citizens' boots had been issued in the previous year. That was a great help.

Hamilton came over when things were winding down and the body was long gone. "What do you make of it, Dalrymple? It's our man, isn't it?" His cheeks were glowing like those of a believer who's just had his faith confirmed by a thumbs-up from an effigy of his god.

"Bit early to say," I said, keeping encouragement to a minimum.

"Come on, man. Size twelve footprints. What more do you want?"

"There's no shortage of large men in Edinburgh," I observed. "Thanks to the Medical Directorate's dietary guidelines."

The guardian was impervious to irony. I've often noticed that with members of his rank.

"Damn the fog." That made me bite my lip. Now he sounded like an eminent Victorian. "The body would have been found much more quickly under normal weather conditions."

"I checked with the meteorology centre. The fog came down on the afternoon of Friday the 13th. We're waiting for an accurate time of death, but it looks like the murder happened when the atmosphere was still clear." A thought struck me. "Of course. It must have been at night. And this area's outside the central lighting zone."

The guardian looked at me dubiously. "So?"

"So no witnesses. Your people are taking statements from residents but I'm not holding my breath."

"No. There would have been a call by now."

"But if it was night, how did the killer see what he was doing?"

Hamilton stared at me. "What are you getting at?"

I stared back. "He must have had a torch. Tell me, guardian, who are the only people in Edinburgh issued with torches and the batteries for them?"

"Auxiliaries," he mumbled.

"Sorry? I didn't catch that."

"Auxiliaries," he repeated, his eyes steely. "Guardsmen and women, as you full bloody well know." He turned away, wiping his mouth. This time he resembled one of the faithful who's just been tempted into heresy by a hirsute gentleman with a full set of horns and hooves.

"Who won that round?" asked Davie. "Don't tell me. The chief looks like he's going to throttle someone."

"Very apt. Let's leave him to it."

"Where to? The infirmary?"

"Yellowlees will be desperate to start the post-mortem, but there's somewhere else I need to go first." I gave him directions to Adam Kirkwood's flat.

The lane was quiet. I got Davie to park round the corner so we'd be less conspicuous. That was a waste of time. The sound of his boots on the pavement told the locals that the guard was on its way.

The street door was open. I led him up the stairs to the flat. The door was closed. I got out the strip of plastic I always carry.

"How about knocking?" Davie suggested.

"I thought your lot preferred to break doors down."

The lock clicked and I pushed the door open slowly. A familiar scent filled my nostrils.

"What the fuck are you doing?" Katharine Kirkwood appeared from behind the kitchen curtain with a carving knife in her hand. "Quint. God, you nearly gave me a heart attack."

"Put the knife down, citizen." Davie had his hand on the butt of his truncheon. "Slowly."

"It's all right," I said. "This is one of my clients. Katharine Kirkwood, Hume 253. Also known as Davie."

They looked at each other suspiciously.

"Quint, what's going on?" Katharine asked after she'd put the knife back in the drawer. "You break in here with a guardsman in tow. I thought you were an independent investigator." She gave me a questioning look. "At least that's what you led me to believe."

"I am." I opened my arms in a feeble display of innocence that I could see she didn't buy. "I've been taken on by the Council for one particular job."

She walked over to the sofa and picked up her bag. Despite the limited choice of clothing in the city, she had managed to dress in an idiosyncratic way. The tight black trousers made her legs look even longer than they were and the long chiffon scarves, magenta and brown, gave her an exotic air.

"And this job includes sniffing around my brother's flat, does it?"

"Not exactly. Look, I can't tell you what's going on . . ."

"Of course you can't." Katharine gave Davie a glare that Lewis Hamilton would have been proud of. He put back a book he'd taken from the shelves. "It's classified, like everything else official in this place."

"Right. I needed to check if your brother was here, that's all."

"Well, as you can see, he's not." She moved towards the door.

"And you haven't seen him since we last spoke?"

"No, I haven't." Her voice had softened. "Have you found anything out?"

I didn't fancy telling her I'd done nothing about her brother at that point. "Look, come round to my flat tonight as we arranged. I can't talk now."

She nodded without looking at me and headed out. "Since you managed to get in on your own, I suppose you can close up again when you've finished."

I checked the place out. Everything was the same. There were no more foreign banknotes in the book of Chinese poetry and the size twelve running shoes didn't look like they'd been moved. Davie watched me with undisguised curiosity.

"Who was that female?"

"I'll tell you later. We'd better get up to the infirmary."

"You're forgetting this." He held up a clear plastic bag in which he'd put the long-bladed knife Katharine had brandished.

"Well done, guardsman. You beat me to it."

The post-mortem went on for hours. A team from the university zoology department spent an hour removing the insect life from Rory Talbot Baillie. Then Yellowlees confirmed what we already knew concerning the cause of death and the wound in the back. I could have spent the afternoon in the archives looking into the dead man's background, but that could wait till the morning. One reason for staying in the mortuary was to watch Hamilton's face change colour more often than a chameleon in a disco. As long as I was there, he felt he had to be too. Simpson 134, the nurse with the prominent chest, took notes – when she wasn't following the medical guardian's every move.

As I was leaving, Hamilton came up. "You know, Dalrymple," he said in a low voice, "your idea about the torch and batteries doesn't mean a thing. The Ear, Nose and Throat Man could easily have got hold of them on the black market. And remember, the boots were citizen issue, not auxiliaries'." He stepped back, looking pleased with himself.

There was something in what he said, but I didn't feel like letting him off the hook. "I'm glad you admit that there is a black market in the perfect city, guardian." His scowl encouraged me to go on. "And as for the boots, correct me if I'm wrong, but aren't auxiliaries issued with standard boots for fatigues?"

He didn't correct me. There was something else I was tempted to bring up but I decided to keep it for the Council meeting. The guardian looked like he had enough to wrestle with for the time being.

Before the meeting I stood by the railings and looked down over Princes Street Gardens. The last race had just finished and the tourists were going back to their hotels to get ready for a night on the town. There was no way the butcher could have been alive when I buried him, no way he crawled out before the concrete was poured – I would have seen a trail. I remembered the sick grin on his face as he slashed my finger off with one of his knives and felt myself shiver. No, he was dead all right. The alternative was too horrific to consider.

I passed by the Land-Rover on my way into the Assembly Hall. If Davie was surprised by the request I made, he didn't show it. I pocketed what he gave me and went inside.

The guardians were less disturbed than they'd been after the first murder. You can get used to anything. A cynic would say that the death of an ordinary citizen was less important to them than an auxiliary's, but even I wouldn't go along with that. They were concerned enough, but they showed their usual tendency to get bogged down in philosophical debate. This time the subject was cannibalism. We never determined what the ENT Man did with the organs he removed. The possibility that he ate them had been difficult to overlook. The same applied now.

The deputy senior guardian caught me looking at my watch. "You don't seem to have much to contribute on the subject, citizen."

"It's all a question of evidence, guardian. We don't know why the killer's removing the organs. Since there's nothing to back up any conjecture, why waste time talking about cannibalism?"

"Very practical," she said drily. "How do you think we should be proceeding?"

"First, we should publish full details of this murder in the *Guardian* tomorrow. You'll find that half the city knows already, so you may as well give the killer some publicity. That may prompt him to do something careless."

The red-headed information guardian nodded in agreement. Even ex-journalists love a murder.

"Very well," said the speaker. "Subject to the senior guardian's approval. What else?"

"I have a question," I said, feeling around carefully in my pocket. "For the medical guardian."

Robert Yellowlees was watching me, his fingers in the usual pyramid under his nose. "Go ahead, citizen," he said.

I took Davie's auxiliary knife out. The naked blade flashed in the light from the spots above the horseshoe table. "Could the weapon used to remove the organs have looked anything like this?"

The guardians looked like a flock of pigeons that had been infiltrated by a ravenous cat.

Except Yellowlees. He smiled broadly. "Long, well-honed blade, single edge, non-serrated, sharp point – yes, it fits the bill. Not exclusively, of course."

From then on the atmosphere was distinctly frosty. If there was one thing that had never been obtainable on the black market, it was auxiliary knives. I think they got my drift. The trouble was, I was no nearer to catching the lunatic who'd done the cutting.

*   *   *

"You look pissed off," Davie said as I climbed into the Land-Rover.

"Pissed on, more like. I'm having difficulty convincing our beloved guardians about something."

"Want to talk about it?"

I thought about that. Over the past five years I'd got used to working things out on my own, with a bit of help from the old man occasionally. But the fact that Davie didn't know about the ENT Man might be an advantage. "All right. Drive up to the Lawnmarket. We don't want Hamilton to see us having a heart-to-heart, do we?"

On the Royal Mile the souvenir shops were still open, tourists wandering around with their purchases in lurid tartan plastic bags that invariably clashed with their clothes.

"Pull up over there." I pointed to the gallows where I'd seen the hanging two days before. "Have you ever heard any rumours about the mock executions they stage here?"

"Rumours?" He looked puzzled. "The only story I heard was the executions were the chief's very own idea. He persuaded the tourism guardian to go ahead with them."

"Is that right?" I wondered if Hamilton was clutching at any way, even as theatre, to keep the ultimate deterrent alive. Or had he taken it upon himself to dispense summary justice? "Forget it," I said to Davie. It seemed to have nothing to do with the case and I didn't want to test his loyalty too hard.

I needn't have worried. He'd already forgotten the subject and was busy exchanging smiles with a guardswoman who'd walked up.

"Friend of yours?" I asked as she moved away.

"Auxiliaries don't have friends, citizen. You know that." Then he grinned. "I have spent the occasional sex session with her though."

"Oh aye. Don't you think those sessions are a bit soulless?"

"Why? There's nothing wrong with safe sex." He was avoiding my eyes.

"What about emotional involvement?"

He shrugged. "What about it? It just gets in the way."

"Come on, Davie. Haven't you ever fallen for a woman?"

"I thought we were going to talk about the investigation."

"We are. Just answer that simple question first."

He let out a long breath. "All right. Yes, I've been in love, whatever that means. Satisfied?"

I gave him a smile. "For the time being. Right, let's look at the second murder. Yellowlees and the forensics people will confirm the time of death tomorrow. I'm not expecting any surprises, so what are we going to do?"

"Check family, friends, workplace of the victim."

"Yes, there's going to be plenty of legwork over the next few days. But there are other angles too. Put yourself in the murderer's shoes. Or boots."

"Killing someone in a public park isn't a job you'd do in daylight."

"Good one, Davie. That's just what I said to your boss."

He scratched his beard. "So the murder happened at night . . . Christ, he must have had a torch." He turned to me. "Now I understand why the guardians were down on you. You think it was an auxiliary. Bloody hell, Quint."

"Hang on a minute. There isn't much to go on. The boots weren't auxiliary issue. All I'm saying is that we should open our minds to the possibility."

He didn't go for it. "There's no way one of us would go around throttling people and removing their organs, no way."

I hadn't expected him to be convinced easily. In fact I'd have been suspicious if he hadn't objected. The auxiliary training programme is so intense that self-doubt is an early casualty. I put my hand in my pocket. "Here's your knife, by the way."

He looked at it for a moment. "You told them one of these could have been used on the victims, didn't you?"

"Actually, it was the medical guardian who said so."

"But you asked the question."

"I asked the question."

He shook his head slowly. "Have you got a burning desire to spend the rest of your life down the mines?"

I laughed. "I told you. They won't have me back there. Any other thoughts?"

"The killer's clothes. They must have been heavily blood-stained. It's too bloody cold at this time of year to go prancing around in the nude like he did in Stevenson Hall."

"I agree. I got Hamilton to organise search parties in a mile radius from Dean Gardens. There's a good chance he'll have dumped his clothes."

"Meaning he had others with him to change into."

"Meaning, as if we didn't know it, that the murder was carefully planned."

Twilight was well advanced though the bright lights on the Royal Mile made it hard to tell.

"Come on," I said. "We'd better get going. I've got a meeting with Katharine Kirkwood."

Davie started the engine. "You haven't told me who she is."

I looked down the street to the ruined palace. "I haven't found that out myself yet, my friend."

Chapter Seven

Davie parked outside my flat and joined me on the pavement.

"What are you doing?" I asked.

"I'm coming with you."

"No, you're not. This has nothing to do with the murders."

He looked dubious. "Why did we give that knife to forensics then?"

"Just covering every angle. See you in the morning."

He laughed. "If you're sure you can manage on your own."

"Goodnight, guardsman." I pushed open the street door. Traces of her perfume confirmed that she was in the vicinity. I ran up the stairs.

Katharine Kirkwood was sitting against my door, knees apart. "Here you are at last." She examined her watch in the dim light of the stairwell. "I've got to get home by curfew time."

I led her into my rooms. "You don't have to worry about that." I showed her my Council authorisation.

She glanced at it. "I suppose this means you're going to stop looking for Adam." She fixed me with an acid look. "If you ever started."

I went over to the table and picked up the whisky bottle. "Drink?"

She shook her head dismissively.

I didn't fancy drinking on my own. "Sit down. I need to ask you some questions."

"About Adam?"

I nodded slowly. "What were you doing in his flat this morning, Katharine?"

"What do you think? I'm worried about him." She looked away. "I miss him."

"Look, I'll be straight with you. I was called to a Council meeting straight after I met you on Friday evening. I haven't had time to check anything about your brother."

"Great." She stood up and walked to the door.

"I haven't finished."

Katharine opened the door. "But I have," she said over her shoulder.

I had to tell her. "There's been a murder."

She stopped dead in the doorway.

"Don't worry," I added quickly. "Adam wasn't the victim."

She came back in. "So that's what all those guard vehicles were doing at Dean Gardens." She sat down opposite me. "You're investigating that?"

"Among other things."

Katharine took her bag from her knees and loosened her coat. "You must be a real detective."

"I have some relevant experience."

"What's this murder got to do with me? Or with Adam?"

I decided to try the victim's name out on her. "Do you know a citizen called Rory Baillie?"

She shook her head after a few moments' thought.

"Did you ever hear your brother mention that name?"

The same reponse. It seemed genuine. "Rory Baillie was killed by someone wearing size twelve citizen-issue boots."

Katharine was looking straight at me, her elbows resting on her knees. She wasn't going to give me any help.

I shrugged. "Your brother takes that shoe size, he lives down the road from the murder site and he hasn't been seen for over ten days."

Her eyes opened wide. "You think Adam killed someone?"

"No. But I need to find him so I can rule him out as a potential suspect."

She stood up and stared down at me. "You've got it all wrong. Adam couldn't kill anyone. He may be tall and strong but he's never been aggressive."

"I need to know more, Katharine."

She raised her left hand to her forehead and drew long fingers across it. "All right." She sat down again, her hotel-issue skirt riding up over black-stockinged thighs. She didn't pull the skirt back down. "It was true what you said, even if you were only guessing. I'm very close to Adam. Our parents were doctors, Enlightenment supporters. Not that they had time to get very involved with the party, they were so busy. Adam and I were often on our own at home. He's so much younger than I am. I was always looking after him." She gave a curious, winsome smile that changed the appearance of her face completely. "I still think of him as a little boy." Then her expression hardened again. "Our parents died in the flu epidemic of 2010. Adam was fifteen. I was in the City Guard at the time. They gave me the afternoon off to get him settled into the orphans' barracks."

"They're a caring crowd in the Public Order Directorate."

She nodded without smiling. "That was when I first had doubts about the system."

"And doubts are something auxiliaries aren't allowed to entertain."

"You've been through the same process, haven't you, Quint?" She was doing it again – turning the discussion away from her to me.

This time I wasn't going to let her get away with it. "So why exactly were you demoted?"

Katharine finally became aware of the state of her thighs and covered them in a rapid movement. She held her lower lip between her teeth for a few moments. "A couple of months later I finished my tour of duty in the guard. I was transferred to the Prostitution Services Department."

I had a flash of Patsy Cameron, that department's head, in the Bearskin and wondered if Katharine knew her. "In what capacity?"

She laughed harshly. "It said 'General Duties' on my transfer papers. You can imagine what that meant."

I looked at her and tried to work out how much of what she'd said was true. Then I heard the sound of a Land-Rover pulling up in the street below and thought of Davie. I was guilty about excluding him, but I reckoned Katharine wouldn't have said anything with a guardsman present.

There were footsteps on the staircase. I opened the door just before the knocking started.

A slim female form in a guard uniform fell against me. "Sorry, citizen," she said with unusual civility. She handed me an envelope.

I recognised the seal immediately. "That's all I need." It was a summons to the senior guardian. "We haven't finished," I said to Katharine. "Can you wait here? I'll be back as soon as I can."

She looked at me then nodded. "Why not? My place isn't any better."

I expected to find her there when I returned about as much as I expected the murderer to give himself up without a fight.

The guardians pride themselves on their rejection of private property and the trappings traditionally enjoyed by those in power. Their ascetic lifestyle and separation from members of their families are an example to auxiliaries, as well as a guarantee of their probity to ordinary citizens. But like all fanatics, they ruin their case by overstatement. The senior guardian's Land-Rover must have been the oldest in the fleet, the maroon pennant fluttering over bodywork that wouldn't even have had scrap value in the days when there was such a thing as a used car market.

The guardswoman was used to the ancient vehicle's ways, dextrously slipping from gear to gear without too much stirring of the slack lever. If she had any idea of who I was, she wasn't showing it. She stopped at the Great Stuart Street barrier and pointed the direction.

"It's number . . ."

"Don't worry, I know which one it is. Thanks for the ride."

The auxiliary's face remained impassive. "I'll be waiting for you here."

I couldn't resist the temptation to slam the door. The guardsman who checked my ID wasn't impressed.

"You are aware of the regulation about silence in the proximity of Moray Place, aren't you, citizen?"

"Must have slipped my mind."

He let me into the circular street which contains the guardians' residences. Their demand for silence was a typical example of their tendency to overlegislate. It's one thing to exclude all vehicles from the street, but telling citizens to keep quiet as they pass is comical. Not that any action is taken over the racket from the gambling tents in Charlotte Square; tourists can make as much noise as they like as long as they keep spending money.

The senior guardian had retained control of the Education Directorate and lived where the Educational Institute of Scotland had been located before independence. The black door opened a second after I put my finger to the bell and a female auxiliary in a grey suit admitted me.

"Go up to the second floor, citizen."

I climbed the elegant staircase slowly, trying to put off what was about to happen. It was over a year since I'd been in the building and then I'd been torn to shreds. I ran through the report I was going to make and tried unsuccessfully to decide which of my ideas I should come clean about.

Another administrative auxiliary opened the high door to the guardian's study. I walked in reluctantly, rubbing at a dusty mark I'd just noticed on my trousers. The room was lit by a single lamp which cast a glow around the desk and left the walls and peripheral furniture in gloom. The city's senior executive was standing, back to me, beside the thick curtains.

"Good evening, citizen." The voice was lower than it had been, but its edge was still perceptible.

I walked up to the desk. "Hello, Mother." I waited for her to turn, knowing that my use of that form of address would have annoyed her. "You sound tired."

The laugh that prompted was humourless, almost bitter. I was surprised. Whatever else I could accuse my mother of, she'd never let self-pity get the better of her.

"If only being tired was all I had to put up with." Then her voice softened. "Do not look away, Quintilian, I beg you."

This was very strange. Not only had she used my full name, which she'd always disliked, but she almost sounded like she was getting emotional. Then I got a real shock. As she'd guessed, my first reaction was to take my eyes off her. After a struggle, I managed to hold my gaze steady.

"My God, Mother, what's happened to you?"

She was still unbent despite her seventy-four years, but there the resemblance to the woman I'd known ended. She had put on a lot of weight. What remained of her hair, which had once been a mass of thick curls, was sparse, giving the impression that handfuls of it had been pulled out. There were purple lesions on her arthritic hands and a pinkish rash on her face. But it was the shape of her face that had changed most. Even the year before it had still been finely drawn, the cheekbones prominent and the skin delicate. Now it was round and swollen, the eyes sunken. Moon face, I thought. She looked like the man in the moon.

She sat down slowly, laying her arms out on the surface of the desk. "It's the lupus."

"But it was never like this before." I wanted to sit down badly but I wasn't going to without an invitation. "You just had occasional fevers and pain in your joints, didn't you?"

"Sit down, for goodness sake," my mother said irritably. Hector and I had always been wary of rousing her temper. "Don't worry, I still have fevers and joint pain. Apparently I've been lucky to escape these recent symptoms for so long."

The Georgian chair I was sitting on was seriously uncomfortable. "And there's still no cure?" I asked, moving my legs.

"Sit still!" She shook her head. "Not yet. The medical guardian's treating me with something he's optimistic about. Up until last month all he could prescribe were painkillers and drugs for the lesions. The problem is to stop the disease advancing. It seems systemic lupus erythematosus can attack any organ – kidneys, heart, even the brain." She smiled for the first time since I'd arrived. "Maybe your old mother's finally going to be certifiable."

I looked away, catching a glimpse through the gloom of the single work of art the guardians allow themselves to choose from the city's collections. For some reason my mother had taken a Renoir of a buxom woman suckling a child.

"I have approved the Council's recommendation to publicise the second murder," she said, opening the thick file in front of her. Clearly she was still able to work even though she wasn't showing up to meetings. "I gather you are doubtful that these latest killings are the work of the Ear, Nose and Throat Man."

"Because of the differences in the modus operandi."

She looked at me sternly. "Is that the only reason?" She waited to see if I had the nerve to answer. I didn't. "I'm not going to press you about what happened five years ago. I wasn't senior guardian at the time, so it doesn't directly concern me."

She was my mother at the time, but given the guardians' renunciation of family life, I suppose that didn't concern her either.

"I know that you were under a lot of pressure, running the operations against the drugs gangs as well as the investigation into the murders."

This was her attempt at compassion. No mention of Caro, of

course. She knew about our ties, but it suited her to see us as nothing more than a pair of auxiliaries who spent time together only on duty and at sex sessions.

"I also know that you were never one to shirk your duty, Quintilian. For all your childish egocentricity. Do we understand each other?"

I don't know how much she understood me, but I knew what she meant all right. She was twisting my arm. Any displays of petulance during this investigation and she'd start asking awkward questions about that night in the gardens.

She turned a page. "I also gather you think an auxiliary might be involved."

"There's a chance of that."

"A lot of circumstantial evidence, if you ask me. Anyway, you're forgetting one essential point."

"What?" I demanded. I was pretty sure I hadn't overlooked anything significant.

"The inherent illogicality."

I nodded slowly and tried to restrain myself. I might have known she would bring philosophy into it. She was a professor in that department at the university before the Enlightenment came to power. "You mean auxiliaries are trained to serve the Council so blindly that they can never break the law?"

She refused to be drawn. "Auxiliaries, like all citizens, are encouraged to think for themselves. There's no question of them following instructions blindly. The whole thrust of our educational system is towards the fostering of independent but discriminating thought."

"Spare me the lecture, Mother."

"It is not a lecture. There are certain basic precepts that the people accept, one of which is the inviolability of the body." She smiled briefly. "Despite what's happened to my own body, even I can uphold that. We abolished capital punishment for that reason, we eradicated physical violence in all its forms from the streets."

"Someone slipped through the net. In fact, a lot of people did. There's no shortage of rejects. Look at me. The system didn't want me."

She raised a finger. "You, Quintilian, were always wilful. But even you would accept that the city is a better place now."

"Maybe," I conceded. "But at what cost?"

"Cost? There is always some cost. In the past the poor and the unemployed bore it. Now everyone makes sacrifices. Surely you don't disagree with that principle?"

"Not as far as it goes. But what about the effect on people's hearts and minds?"

"Since when have you been an expert in those fields?" she asked caustically.

I stood up and leaned over her desk. "I don't have to be an expert to see that someone out there has been so messed up by your system that he's going around cutting people up."

She nodded reluctantly. "I'll grant you there's at least one madman in the city. Who knows? Maybe there's a cell of dissidents at work. The point is, how do we put a stop to the killings?" Apparently it was a rhetorical question, as she raised her hand shakily to shut me up. "Listen carefully. No doubt you think we guardians are out of touch with the realities of life in Edinburgh. All right. I'm prepared to concede that some of my colleagues would be better off in retirement homes like your father."

I'd have been surprised if there was any display of emotion to go with this mention of Hector.

"But I'll say this too," my mother continued. "If – and I see it as only the remotest possibility – if an auxiliary is involved, there will be some entirely logical reason. So concentrate on the question of motive. An auxiliary is incapable of acting irrationally, I assure you."

I was an auxiliary when I went after the ENT Man, but she didn't know that, of course. Maybe that was a rational act. I looked at the moon-shaped face and devastated hair. I couldn't help myself admiring her. But I knew without recourse to philosophical definitions that admiration is not the same as love.

"I'll bear that in mind, Mother," I said as I turned towards the door. "Unfortunately I've got even less of an idea about the killer's motive than I have of his identity."

In the Land-Rover on the way home I looked out at the city. The streets shone in bright moonlight and the floodlit mass of the castle rock reared up to my left – the illuminated heart of the Council's regime. At least that's how it's presented to the tourists. Citizens are more inclined to remember it's the headquarters of the City Guard.

I made myself go over the points I'd chickened out of bringing up with my mother. She always did have an imperious air that made contradicting her difficult, but this time I'd done even worse than usual. I wanted to ask her why she'd voted against the anti-corruption safeguard my father showed me. She'd probably just have wheeled out the standard line about how the citizen body now trusted the Council implicitly, while in the past they'd justifiably no faith in either their elected or hereditary rulers. Given the chaos inspired by the last UK government and the discredited monarchy, I couldn't have argued with that. But were the Council and its servants still worthy of that trust?

I also wished I'd had the nerve to ask her how much she knew about the activities of senior auxiliaries like Billy Geddes. I'd have liked to know what she thought she was doing drafting me on to the investigation without so much as a personal note too. She wouldn't even have bothered replying to that question.

It was only when I found myself on the pavement in Gilmore Place breathing in lungfuls of exhaust fumes that I remembered Katharine. No doubt the guardswoman would have reported the presence of a female citizen in my flat to my mother's office. Much joy might she have of that piece of information. The smile froze on my lips when it occurred to me that Katharine had probably been back in her own flat for a long time.

I opened the door and fumbled for the box of matches by the candle.

"Is that you, Quint?"

I jumped like a ewe surprised by a sex-starved shepherd. As the flame flared, I saw that she was sitting in the same place on the sofa. "Shit! Why didn't you light the candle?"

"Candle?" She shrugged. "I'm not afraid of the dark."

"Well I am," I shouted. "I assumed you'd gone."

"Why?" She sounded puzzled. "I said I'd wait for you."

I nodded. "Sorry. I just had a testing time with the senior guardian."

"Yes, you look like you've been in a fight. Have a drink." She pushed the bottle towards me. "Do you often visit the senior guardian?"

I shook my head and poured some whisky. I had a feeling she was about to start picking my brains.

"Want to talk about it?"

I did, but how could I trust her? Anyway, I was suddenly

feeling completely exhausted. "It's classified," I said, resorting to the coward's defence. "Look, I'm going to have to crash. We can talk in the morning. You take the bed. It won't be the first time I've passed out on the sofa."

"Quint?" Katharine said quietly, lifting the candle and pointing to Caro's photograph. "Who is she?"

My stomach knotted. I took a couple of deep breaths. "Someone I lost," I said in an even quieter voice than hers.

She looked at me but didn't say anything else.

"Goodnight," I said abruptly. I wanted to be alone.

She got up. "I want to help, Quint. To find Adam, I mean. And . . ." She didn't finish the sentence.

"There are some clean sheets in the bottom drawer."

"I'm the last person who needs clean sheets," she said over her shoulder. "Goodnight, sweet prince."

I was ready to drop but sleep didn't come immediately. I was thinking about what had led to Katharine's demotion. I'd sometimes heard rumours that the Prostitution Services Department used auxiliaries as undercover tarts to gather information on tourists in the city's hotels. Like most men who never go with whores, I always found them desperately alluring. A vision of Mary, Queen of Scots in the nightclub came to me; the way she'd gazed out over the crowd made it seem like every man there was naked and under her power. Then I thought of Katharine in my bed next door. Caro was absent from my dreams that night.

I often hear music in my sleep. This time it was Bessie Smith. She was singing "Mama's Got the Blues".

Chapter Eight

I was following Caro up a hillside. No matter how hard I tried, I couldn't get any closer to her. The Ear, Nose and Throat Man was coming up on me though. I could smell the stink from his rotting teeth. Eventually Davie's pounding woke me.

"You should give me a key, Quint," he said. "Then I could bring you breakfast in bed." He took in the clothes scattered around the sofa. "Or not, as the case may be." He went over to the electric ring. "Did you forget where the bedroom is?"

"Shut it, guardsman." I struggled into my trousers. Then I noticed that the bedroom door was open. On the neatly made bed I found a note. "Morning shift. Thanks for the bed. *I want to help*. K." I still wasn't sure how to take the offer.

The mobile phone rang as I was finishing the coffee Davie'd made. He answered it, his back straightening, then handed it to me. "The chief."

"Dalrymple? Get yourself down to Dean Terrace." Hamilton sounded like a teenage boy who's stumbled on his father's store of dirty magazines. "We've found a plastic bag full of clothing."

"I'm on my way. For Christ's sake, don't touch anything."

By the time I'd got my jacket on, Davie was already halfway down the stairs.

"That's it down there." Hamilton pointed at a shiny maroon object that was lodged between two rocks under the bridge.

I put on a pair of rubber gloves and clambered down. The Water of Leith sucked and pulled at the piles as it flowed past.

It was only a couple of feet deep and choked with vegetation. Looking back to the slopes of the park four hundred yards upstream where the body had been found, I wondered if the river could have carried the bag this far. I leaned forward and lifted it up. I had to pull hard to dislodge it. A sodden sleeve flapped about like the neck of a dead swan.

One of the forensics team stood waiting with a photographer. I handed him the bundle and watched as he removed a labourer's tunic and trousers, both size extra-large, then a pair of thick socks. There were bloodstains on everything.

"Apart from the sleeve, everything is dry," the scientist said.

"Meaning the bag was carefully placed there, not swept down by the water," I added.

Hamilton looked at me uncomprehendingly. "Have your report ready as soon as possible," he said to the forensics man, who was packing the clothes carefully in separate bags. Then he led me away. "What do you mean the bag was placed there?"

"If the bag had just been dumped in the water, how likely is it that the contents would have been dry?"

He nodded slowly. "But couldn't the murderer just have dropped the bag off the bridge as he was sneaking off? Maybe a guard vehicle made him panic."

"I don't think so. It was wedged solid between the rocks."

Hamilton gave me a confused look. "Explain."

"It's simple enough. The killer wanted us to find his clothes."

The guardian laughed. "Don't be ridiculous, man. How often do murderers deliberately plant evidence?"

I could think of several cases but there was no point in quoting them to him. I knew what he was going to say next as well.

"Anyway, however the clothes got here, they rather put paid to your theory about the killer being an auxiliary, don't they?" He smiled with more satisfaction than guardians usually allow themselves. That was a mistake.

"I had the impression that all barracks keep a stock of labourers' clothes for auxiliaries engaged in maintenance work."

The smile disappeared quicker than the sun on an August morning in the city. "You don't give up, do you, Dalrymple? Until the going gets tough." He turned on his heel and headed for his Land-Rover.

"Not again," groaned Davie as he came up. "The guardian's going to have your head if you're not careful."

"I'm sure he'd love to have it over his fireplace in the castle. Find anything out from forensics while I was distracting your boss?"

He grinned. "Is that what you were doing? As a matter of fact, I did. That carving knife we gave them. No traces of anything human."

I walked away from the river.

"Let's go and see the widow."

Davie drove down the broad avenue where the regional police headquarters used to be located. The buildings, surrounded by a high barbed-wire fence, are now Raeburn Barracks, responsible for Pilton to the north where the drugs gangs used to hang out. Ahead of us lay the ruins of Fettes where I met Leadbelly. I remembered that I hadn't sent him the recordings I'd promised. He wouldn't be surprised.

I slumped down in the seat. "Christ, Davie, if evidence was oxygen, we'd have suffocated days ago."

"Aye, there are a good few dead ends. The guard didn't turn up any witnesses at Dean Gardens, I heard. Surprise, surprise." He glanced at me. "Still, maybe we'll find out something from Baillie's wife."

I wasn't sure whether that qualified optimism was his own or a result of auxiliary-style positive thinking. Looking at the forbidding estate ahead – growths of grey concrete against the steely estuary – I wished I could share it.

Before the Council took charge I'd never been to Pilton. Although the area isn't much more than a mile from the northern extent of the city centre, it belongs to a different world. The drug traders recruited their hard men from the gangs that had always operated there. It was the city's open sore until the Public Order Directorate went in and the real fighting started. Since then the Housing Directorate has done what it can to rebuild and the streets are patrolled by the City Guard, but the place still looks like a war zone. Every window is fitted with solid shutters that are closed as soon as night approaches. I wondered when Hamilton had last been down here. Let alone the senior guardian.

A group of adolescents of both sexes was gathered round a lamppost that stood at a crazy angle. They watched us pass sullenly.

"Shouldn't they be at school?" My mother's educational planning set great store on the removal of truancy from the list of the city's social problems. There were squads of auxiliaries who went around counselling parents and pupils about the value of attending school.

Davie laughed grimly. "You want to make them go?"

"No." I didn't fancy the tough faces and empty eyes much. "What is the city coming to?"

"Don't ask me. I haven't finished the political philosophy course yet." He pointed ahead. "It's that block there."

We had reached the centre of a web of streets uncluttered by any vehicles. There were no people around here; all were busy at whatever work the Labour Directorate had assigned them. The dead driver's wife was to have been picked up by a guardswoman from the bakery where she worked as a counter assistant and brought home.

Inside the street door the sharp smell of disinfectant didn't disguise the inadequate sewerage. Working for the Parks Department meant that I was allowed to live just outside the tourist area. If I'd lived in Pilton, I wouldn't have been a drop-out from the system for long.

The information board in the lobby told us that Baillie R. and J. were in flat C on the third floor. I ran up concrete stairs that had been chipped away by the residents' heavy boots. The door of the flat had once been dark blue. I paused to draw breath then knocked softly. A heavily built guardswoman opened up immediately.

"Where is she?" I asked, looking round the room. Its standard-issue sofa and armchair, dining table and chairs all showed signs of wear, but the place was spotlessly clean.

"She went to the toilet," said the guardswoman, Raeburn 244.

I went over to the table where a large Bible lay open. It was over a hundred years old, the heavy type as stern as the Church which had authorised it.

"How long has she been in there?"

Raeburn 244 looked at her watch then met my stare with wide eyes.

"Shit!" I ran down the narrow hallway that led to the other rooms. "Mrs Baillie? Are you in there?" I shoved hard with my shoulder without waiting for an answer. The poor quality wood and hinges gave way as fast as an old-style princess before an offer from a tabloid newspaper.

A thin woman was crouching over the toilet bowl. At first I though she was throwing up. Her head, brown hair flecked with flour from the bakery, was moving backwards and forwards. Then her hand shot up and pulled the chain with surprising speed. I saw a mass of colour in the foaming water which didn't look like vomit. Pushing her out of the way, I rammed my hand down as the last of it was disappearing. A soggy lump caught in my extended fingers. I heard the woman sobbing.

"I hope you haven't been eating this, Mrs Baillie," I said, shaking my head. "It isn't good for you."

The pinkish mess had unravelled into what was clearly a banknote. Although the writing was in a foreign alphabet I had no trouble identifying it. I'd seen one in pristine condition a few days earlier. It was a fifty thousand drachmae note, all the way from Greece's sun-kissed shores and oil-rich waters.

"How many of these did you manage to flush away, Jean?"

The woman's eyes followed Davie and the guardswoman, who were taking the flat apart. "I'm no' sure. Maybe ten."

Half a million drachmae. In a city where foreign currency is restricted to tourists and the needs of citizens are covered by vouchers, that's big money, especially for a driver to have.

"Where did your husband – I presume it was your husband, not you?" I watched her carefully as she nodded. "Where did he get this money?"

"Ah dinnae ken, citizen, honest ah dinnae."

"Watch your language," said the guardswoman.

I raised my hand to silence her. The last thing I needed now was for Jean Baillie to be reminded of Council language policy. I didn't give a bugger if she said "ah dinnae ken".

The woman had lowered her head after the rebuke and her veined hands shook against the maroon of her overall. She eventually looked up when I didn't speak, eyes pleading for another question to make things easier. I kept quiet.

"He . . . Rory . . . he worked extra shifts. At night, a lot of the time. I only found that money this morning . . . I was tidying up his clothes in the wardrobe." Her voice almost broke, but she held on.

I believed her. "You don't have any children, Jean?"

She shook her head slowly. "I couldn't. Or he couldn't." She dropped her head again. "He tried hard enough."

That sounded promising. I changed the subject temporarily. "You read the Bible a lot?"

"Aye." She was suddenly more in control of herself. "I go to St Margaret's every Sunday." Like most of the believers who remain in the secular city, she was ardent about her faith.

"And your husband? Did he go with you to church?"

Jean Baillie laughed, a harsh scrape from a throat dried in the bakery for years. "Rory? He wouldnae go near a church. He spent all his time chasing fancy women and . . ." Her voice tailed off.

"And what, Jean?" I asked softly.

She stared up at me fiercely. "And nothing. I don't know what else he was doing."

"Why did you try to get rid of the money?"

She shook her head but didn't answer. The guardswoman came over but I waved her away. I was sure Jean Baillie hadn't done anything criminal. The same couldn't be said for her husband.

The widow wasn't able to answer my other questions either. She didn't know any of her husband's workmates; she didn't know where he'd been on the night of his death. I tried a long shot.

"Did Rory ever mention an Adam Kirkwood?"

I saw Davie look over and stare at me. We waited for the woman to reply. In vain. Eventually she shook her head slowly, hopelessly.

Down in the street the same group of teenagers had gathered near the Land-Rover. They hadn't touched it yet, but I reckoned it wouldn't be long before they had a go. When we came out of the block, they shambled away with calculated nonchalance.

"Get on the mobile and tell the directorate to send a squad down to search the sewers," I said to Davie as we climbed in. I caught a glimpse of Mrs Baillie at her window. She was gazing out to the north where the hills of Fife were visible beyond the Firth of Forth. I was pretty sure that for all its marauding gangs and violence, she was praying to her god to pluck her up in a pillar of fire and lift her over there.

Another one whom the system failed.

As we were passing Raeburn Barracks, Davie turned to me. "Why did you ask her about that Adam Kirkwood guy?"

I came clean and told him about Katharine and her brother. He didn't seem too pissed off at being excluded.

"You think he and Baillie might have met in the vicinity of Dean Gardens on the night of the murder?"

"It's possible." I took the banknote I'd found in Adam Kirkwood's flat from my wallet. "There's also the small matter of this."

Davie whistled. "Christ, the same currency and denomination. I told you we'd get lucky."

"Yes, but keep it to yourself for the time being." I gave him a Hamiltonesque glare. "And wipe that bloody grin off your face, guardsman. All this does is make things even more complicated."

He nodded, the smile still on his lips. "I'm assuming we're heading for the drivers' mess in Melville Street."

"You know, you're too bright to be in the guard, Davie. Ever thought of a transfer to the Parks Department?"

He shook his head violently. "No way. I couldn't face clearing up all that horse shit after the races."

"We're going to be clearing up a lot worse than that in the near future, my friend."

Yellowlees came on the mobile as we were driving over the Dean Bridge. "I've just finished comparing notes with the entomologists, Dalrymple. We've concluded that the time of death was between four and six a.m. on Friday 13 March."

"It certainly wasn't a lucky day for Rory Baillie."

"What? Oh, I see what you mean. You might like to know that the killer used a condom in this case too." The guardian paused as if he were waiting for me to volunteer information. "Making any progress?" he asked when I didn't.

"Slowly but surely," I lied, then signed off.

We left the guard vehicle on Queensferry Street and walked round the corner to Melville Street. Davie stopped at a kiosk and took a copy of the *Edinburgh Guardian*.

"Look, Quint, you've made the front page."

"That's all I need." They'd dug out a photograph of me so that the killer would know who he was up against. Above it was the headline "Dalrymple Investigates". I read the beginning of the lead article out. "'Quintilian Dalrymple, former senior detective at the Public Order Directorate, has been appointed to head the investigation into the murder of a citizen in Dean Gardens.'" I looked further down. "Jesus, listen to this. 'Citizen Dalrymple, who was forced to retire from active service because of ill health, has the full confidence of the public order guardian.' Two heaps of your favourite substance in one sentence, Davie. They've printed the number of my mobile, too. Wonderful."

Davie didn't seem too keen to hear any more of that in public. He grabbed my arm and led me down the street, taking back his paper. "Come on, citizen. Time to play detective. Here's the drivers' mess."

An open door led into a broad hallway. The building had once been a school, then offices, before it became the centre for all drivers of city vehicles apart from the guard's. The Transportation Directorate has overall control of the facility, but the drivers have always had a reputation for being individualists – as far as such creatures survive in Edinburgh.

The auxiliary in charge was middle-aged and overweight. I decided to play things low-key and kept my authorisation in my pocket. He didn't show any interest in my request for information about Rory Baillie. The magazine he was looking at did pertain to vehicles, but only in as much as they offered partially clothed women the means of sexual gratification.

"I hardly knew the man," he said. "Go and see Anderson, the drivers' co-ordinator."

Davie leaned across the desk, grabbed the magazine and jammed it up against the auxiliary's neck. "I don't like what I'm seeing here, Ferguson 73." He glanced at me. "Show him your authorisation. Obviously he's been too busy to read the *Guardian* today."

The auxiliary slumped forward as Davie pulled the magazine away. He rubbed his throat and gulped, his jowls vibrating like a petrified chipmunk's. Within seconds he'd called Anderson on the internal phone and told him to bring the relevant files.

I smiled at him while we were waiting. The fat man's skin had acquired a sheen of sweat. Auxiliaries have been demoted for obstructing the bearer of a Council authorisation, but I had a feeling he was more worried about his magazine. He would have paid a Scandinavian tourist plenty for it.

The co-ordinator bustled in with an armful of folders. He was balding, with the professional driver's paunch and fondness for black leather. If leather trousers had been available from the city's clothing stores, Anderson would have had a wardrobe full of them. As it was, his jacket was scuffed and his belt looked like it was about to give way. He must have had both items since before the time of the Enlightenment. Only his standard-issue boots looked new. The shine on them suggested he'd once been in the army.

"Hello there, gents," he said cheerily. "Here's all the stuff I've got on Rory: personal file, time sheets, medical record, the lot." He dumped the papers on his boss's desk and shook his head. "Poor sod. We thought he'd been drafted to the farms or down the mines." He turned to me. "Is it true what they're saying, that one of his kidneys was cut out?"

"It is." I motioned to him to sit down. "We'll go through the records later. In the meantime, I'd like you to fill me in about Baillie. How well did you know him?"

"Hardly at all," he said with a shrug. "Even though we were in the army together." He ran his hands down his jacket. "Rory was a secretive bugger."

"Tell me everything you can about him," I said.

The sun appeared suddenly above the buildings and light flooded into the room, making everyone screw their eyes up. The fat auxiliary mopped his face with a filthy handkerchief.

"Good driver," the co-ordinator said. "Plenty of experience in all kinds of vehicles – cars, Land-Rovers, trucks, ambulances, oil tankers." He looked at Davie and me. "There hasn't been much call for armoured cars since you lot dealt with the gangs," he added ironically.

"Watch it," growled Davie.

"Did he have any particular speciality?"

"Not really. As Ferguson 73 will confirm, we run a fair system here." His emphasis on the word "we" made it clear who was really in charge. "Everyone changes round regularly to maintain efficiency."

"Very commendable," I said, not buying that explanation for a second. "Why do I get the impression you're stonewalling, citizen? Would you like Hume 253 here to take you up to the castle and interrogate you with his friends?"

Anderson's shoulders dropped and his cocksure attitude vanished in the sunlight. Ferguson 73 started waving his hands about in a belated and wholly unnecessary attempt to make his subordinate see reason.

"Look, citizen," the driver said desperately, "I don't know anything about what Rory was up to."

"But you suspected something."

Anderson nodded. "Aye. I mean, we've always had a reputation for being on the make, we drivers, especially when we're on the tourist buses and horse-drawn carriages. Christ, they offer us tips. We can't offend them by saying no."

Davie and I didn't say anything. The commander put his head in his hands. It was obvious he was on a percentage.

"But Rory," Anderson continued, "Rory was something else."

"What do you mean?"

"He always had a lot more in his wallet than the rest of us, even though his roster was the same as everyone else's." The co-ordinator shrugged. "I've often wondered where he got it."

"Those tips you mentioned – how much do you make from them?"

"Say five US dollars, maybe ten of those Chinese things . . ."

"Renminbis," said the fat commander hoarsely.

"Ever get anything from the Greeks?"

Anderson smiled. "Oh aye, they're very generous. They'll give you five thousand of their currency on a good day."

I wrote the numbers down in my notebook. "What could a driver expect to make from tips every year?" I glanced at the man behind the desk. "Net of what he pays your boss here."

The driver grinned. "No one works the tourist routes more than two months a year and often the guard stop us accepting tips." He scratched his chin. "Say three hundred dollars US."

Or around three hundred thousand drachmae, I calculated. Still a lot less than Baillie's wife had flushed away. I turned to Ferguson 73. "Right, here's how we're going to do this. Personally I don't give a shit that you've been taking a cut. As long as you tell me everything that's been happening in this facility and go through the files with us, I'm prepared to forget about your financial arrangements. If you're good, you might even get your magazine back."

The commander's face lit up and he started simpering like a trainee auxiliary at his first sex session.

I raised my hand. "But remember, my colleague here is in the Public Order Directorate. If he thinks either of you is holding out on us, expect tackety boots and thumbscrews."

The threat seemed to work. We spent hours in the mess but

there was nothing that cast any light on the source of Rory Baillie's wealth. The only interesting thing we discovered was about the night shifts Jean Baillie said her husband often worked. There was no reference in the duty rosters to him having driven any vehicle after eight p.m. for over six months. So what was he doing at nights?

Back on Melville Street it occurred to me that Katharine Kirkwood lived less than five minutes' walk away. Like her brother lived a few minutes walk from where Rory Baillie was murdered. Coincidence?

As I was closing the Land-Rover door, Anderson appeared round the corner. He was panting from the short run.

"Just a minute, gents." He looked over his shoulder. "Something I didn't want to say in front of the fat shite. Rory, he caught me eyeballing the wad he was carrying . . . must have been a month or so ago. He told me he had a friend he helped sometimes." The driver leaned further into the cab. "He said the friend was in the Finance Directorate."

I didn't have to rack my brains for long to come up with an idea of who that could be.

Chapter Nine

Thursday evening. After a few sunny days, the fog had returned and was settling over the city as thickly as the mustard gas in a Wilfred Owen poem. I trudged up the Mound, the prospect of another Council meeting with nothing much to report weighing on me more heavily than the concrete overcoat worn by the ENT Man. B.B. King once sang about outside help – he didn't want any, but I could have done with some. I'd just spent the afternoon in the archives and I kept losing track of the time. That's always a bad sign during an investigation. If my mind starts wandering, I know the trail's going cold.

Then, out of my favourite colour, the idea came to me. I ran up Mound Place and sat down in the vestibule of the Assembly Hall to scribble some notes. Shortly afterwards a pair of gleaming brogues appeared in front of me.

"Come on, Dalrymple, you'll be late. Again."

At the sound of Hamilton's voice I closed my notebook hurriedly.

"Working on anything interesting?"

"Are you?"

The guardian shook his head. "But I don't have to, do I? You're the special investigator."

I followed him up the stairs and wondered about the old sod. Hamilton's involvement with the hangings still nagged me, but it had nothing to do with the murders. I'd like to have nailed my former boss, but that was another obsession from the past I had to forget.

"Your report, citizen," said the deputy senior guardian brusquely as the meeting came to order. As the days went by, she, along with most of her colleagues, had become noticeably sharper under the strain. The city's intellectuals, who prided themselves on their deep knowledge of the human condition, were finding the killings harder to live with than ordinary citizens. Most of the latter found Baillie's murder fascinating, a source of endless speculation and gossip.

"Perhaps you could give us a recapitulation of all the evidence you have collated to enable us to gather our thoughts," the speaker added wearily, her command of the guardians' tortuous syntax apparently unaffected.

I started off slowly, trying to spin out the little I had to report. "Well, guardians, extensive research has revealed little of significance. Sarah Spence had an exemplary service record and the only unresolved matter is where she was on the Saturday night twelve days before her death. The rosters of all directorates have been examined and no reference to her has been found."

"But you reported yesterday that the guardsman at her barracks remembered seeing an official authorisation," said Hamilton.

I'd told them about that to pad out an even more vacuous report. "True enough. So we're left with two possibilities. Either Taggart" – I heard the public order guardian's intake of breath – "I mean Knox 31 was mistaken, or somebody removed all traces of that authorisation from the records."

"No doubt you favour the latter," Hamilton said ironically. "You were always keen on conspiracies. I'd be more inclined to think the guardsman confused the dead woman with someone else."

"What, one of your men made a mistake?"

The speaker looked at me sternly. "Continue, citizen."

"Right. Rory Baillie. Twelve fifty thousand drachmae notes and thirteen US hundred dollar bills were recovered from the sewers outside his flat." I glanced along the row of stony faces. "This raises more questions than it answers. For a start, none of the serial numbers on the banknotes tallied with the currency records at the airport and Leith docks."

"Meaning that some of our visitors bring in more than they declare. That's quite normal, citizen." The scratchy voice was that of the finance guardian, Billy Geddes's boss.

"The problem isn't only the existence of undeclared foreign

currency in the city," I said to the wizened old economist. "Though if you ask me, it doesn't seem to be in line with Enlightenment principles. The significant point is the amounts. Even the most generous tourist is hardly likely to tip a driver fifty thousand drachmae. So what was Rory Baillie doing to earn that sort of money?"

No one came up with an answer. I could have asked the same question about Adam Kirkwood, but I'd kept him out of my reports; I didn't think Katharine's case had anything to do with the Council. But I'd checked Adam's banknote. It hadn't been declared either.

"Is that all, citizen?" the speaker asked.

I shook my head. "We've been trying to track down some of the women Baillie spent his time with, but no one was willing to talk." I gave them a bitter smile. "It isn't only in the barracks that speaking to strangers is discouraged."

"Thank you for that observation. Kindly confine yourself to reporting the facts." The deputy senior guardian looked at me like a hassled schoolmistress who's just been pushed over the edge by the class smartass.

I felt a bit sorry for her. "All right. A final point about Baillie. I've double-checked all the records and there's no reference anywhere to him working nights. That contradicts what his wife told us."

"Maybe he was lying to her to cover up his extramarital activities." Robert Yellowlees gave a brief but unusually sympathetic smile for a guardian. His colleagues didn't look too impressed.

"Maybe. But we're assuming he was murdered after curfew, when the lights were out. If he was with a girlfriend, wouldn't he make sure he was at her place by then?"

"He would," put in Hamilton. "The chances of him avoiding all the patrols are minimal."

I was less sure about that than he was – after all, the murderer had managed to get away twice – but I didn't argue. The likelihood was that Baillie had an authorisation and everyone in the chamber knew it. I gave them a couple of minutes to think about the fact that someone was manipulating the city's precious bureaucracy.

Then I hit them again. "There's more bad news. There was no forensic evidence pointing to the killer on the clothing found in the Water of Leith – only blood and other matter from the victim. Either the murderer was very lucky not to leave traces or he was very careful."

"We're assuming the latter, of course," said Yellowlees with a humourless smile.

"Of course." I looked around the guardians. They looked about as bereft of ideas as a 1990s cabinet. Time to give them a nudge with the cattle-prod. "I had a thought on the way up here. Both the victims were killed in the early hours of a Friday morning."

"So?" said Hamilton.

"So maybe there's a pattern. This is Thursday evening."

The guardians' eyes were all wide open now.

"What odds will you give me on another killing in the next twelve hours?"

Davie drove up Ramsay Lane towards the castle. The fog was very thick now. Just what we wanted, especially tonight. Burke and Hare conditions.

"What are we doing up here?" Davie asked.

"I need something from Hamilton."

"Round six of fifteen."

"Have you been counting?"

"Got to do something while I'm hanging around." He accelerated through the checkpoint and on to the esplanade.

"Tell me, Davie," I said, watching him closely. "What do you know about the directorate's undercover operations?"

He looked like I'd just punched him in the balls.

"Not much," he said quietly. "Why do you ask?"

He was a lot paler than he had been when we were next to Baillie's body. "What is it, Davie? What's the matter?"

He looked away to the damp tarmac, then turned back to me. "You remember I told you I had a girl. She . . ." He didn't finish the sentence.

"She was selected to go undercover?"

He nodded slowly. "Two years ago. I haven't seen her since."

"Christ."

His chin jutted forward. "You know what's the worst thing about it?"

I did, but I let him tell me.

"It's the uncertainty. She could be dead, could have been dead for a long time and I just don't know." His hands were clamped to the steering wheel.

I wasn't proud of the pain that my question had etched into his face, but at least I'd found an auxiliary who could pass for a normal human being.

Hamilton hadn't got back to his office yet. I flashed my authorisation at his secretary, a thin young man with grey lips, and went into the guardian's private bathroom. I hadn't had a chance to visit the public baths for a week. The water temperature would have struck even a Spartan as low and the soap was as carbolic as Hamilton's temper, but I felt better afterwards.

Hamilton ambushed me in his outer office. "Dalrymple, what the—" He broke off and led me into his sanctum. "You're pushing your luck, laddie. What do you want?"

"I've got a problem."

The guardian sat down behind his broad Georgian desk and started looking through the files in his in-tray. "Really? Don't tell me you need my help? I thought you preferred to work independently." He raised his eyes. "Not that it's got you very far."

As Davie said, time for the next round. I tossed my authorisation on to his pile of papers. "You remember what that says about co-operation, don't you, guardian?" I tried hard to make his title sound like an insult. "You choose. Either comply with the request I'm about to make or explain your refusal at the next Council meeting."

Hamilton's eyes were colder than the water in his shower. "That rather depends on the request," he said, his voice taut.

"One of the people I'm checking has a file that's classified Restricted. You keep those in the directorate archive here, don't you?"

"You want to see a Restricted file," he said slowly. "Why?"

"That's not a question I have to answer."

He picked up a pen. "Name of the subject?"

"Katharine Kirkwood." I watched his reaction, but I couldn't tell if the name meant anything to him.

"Very well. Wait here."

I raised my hand. "I want the complete file. Don't forget, I spend half my life in the archives. There's no way you'll be able to pull any pages without me noticing."

Hamilton shot a ferocious look at me and walked out. I was surprised how quickly he came back with the maroon cardboard folder.

"There you are." He seemed to have calmed himself down. "So, do you think the precautions we've taken for tonight are adequate?" After my idea about the killer working to a pattern, measures had been approved to monitor movement around the city centre even more than normal.

"Look at the fog," I said, pointing outside the leaded windows. "There could be a massacre without anyone noticing."

"Don't be ridiculous. We'll catch the bugger." He looked at me. "Remember, the contents of that file are confidential."

Large black letters to that effect were stencilled on the cover. "I can read, you know."

"Which means that the subject is not to be given any hint of what we have collated."

"Why?" I headed for the door. "Do you know something she doesn't?"

William Street, once the location of fashionable bistros and sandwich shops patronised by lawyers and their weak-kneed secretaries, is now occupied solely by female citizens who work in the nearby West End hotels and shops. There was less than half an hour till curfew. I sat in the Land-Rover under the streetlight and read the file.

"That's hers, isn't it?" Davie said, keeping his eyes off the typed pages. "What's she got to do with the murders, Quint?"

"God knows. Have you got that carving knife? I'll give it back to her."

"Mind she doesn't use it on you."

"I'm planning on keeping my hands to myself, don't worry."

Davie grinned. "I wasn't thinking of your hands. You know what they call this street?"

"I do, guardsman." The large number of women residents have led to it being referred to as "the Willie" in common parlance. "I thought auxiliaries kept themselves above that kind of thing."

"Did you now?"

I left the maroon folder on the seat. As I went over to number 13, I wondered if Davie would resist the temptation to have a look. That would be a test for him.

"Quint." Katharine stood in the doorway wearing a dressing-gown. "Have you found Adam?"

I shook my head. "I've made some other discoveries though."

She looked at me then turned quickly. I followed her in, my eyes drawn to her bare feet. They were unusually long and thin and I could see the networks of tiny veins around her ankles. I wasn't aware that hotel maids were required to paint their toenails.

Katharine sat down on a pile of cushions on the floor and motioned me to the sofa.

"We didn't finish our conversation the other night." I glanced around the small flat. It was no more than a bedsit with a door off to the toilet in the corner. The sofa I was sitting on converted into a bed and the only other furniture was a small table with a couple of rickety chairs, a kitchen cabinet and a chest of drawers. The Supply Directorate wasn't particularly generous to single female citizens, especially those with the kind of record I'd just been reading. Katharine had tried to put her own stamp on the place: she'd hung rugs made from scraps of different coloured material on the walls and stuck up pages copied from the large number of books that lay around the room. The extract nearest me was from one of Eliot's Sweeney poems.

I took the carving knife out of my jacket pocket, watching her face. It remained impassive. "This is from your brother's flat. Can you take it back?"

She knew I was putting her on the spot and she didn't like it. Her lips were set in a tight line. But she was curious too. "What were you doing with it?" She sat up straight. "You were running tests, weren't you? Why didn't you listen to me? Adam couldn't have killed that man in the gardens."

"I can't take your word for that, Katharine."

She nodded slowly. "No proof."

"Not only that." I pulled out my notebook. "You've been behaving like a civil servant before the Enlightenment."

"What do you mean?"

"You've been economical with the truth."

She stiffened even more. "Like you said, we didn't finish our conversation. You were called away."

"I was. I seem to remember that you offered your help. You can do that by telling me more about yourself and your brother." I handed her the knife, pushing Davie's comments to the back of my mind. Katharine took it nonchalantly and laid it on the floor.

"Haven't you checked us out by now?"

"The archives don't contain everything." I'd been through Adam Kirkwood's file, which wasn't restricted. Davie and I had also questioned his workmates, who'd assumed he was in the mines. He seemed to be an adequate worker who kept himself to himself. None of them saw him out of work hours. There remained the question of the foreign banknote. Katharine was another puzzle. I'd been to the hotel and checked the duty roster. She was off duty on the nights of both murders. I was wondering how much of her past she would reveal voluntarily.

"What happened when they transferred you to the Prostitution Services Department?"

She looked at me curiously. "I still don't understand what that's got to do with Adam or with the killing."

"Any chance of you letting me be the judge of that?"

She laughed. "All right. I refused the transfer, of course. They kept on at me for days. If they'd offered me something else I might have agreed, but they have that rule about auxiliaries never refusing duty. You know all about that. So I was demoted."

So far, as per her file. "What next?"

"I was assigned work as a cleaner in one of the hotels down in Leith. That was someone's idea of a joke, I suppose. I spent more time fighting off drunken Scandinavian tourists than mopping floors." She smiled bitterly. "If it was a joke, it backfired. It was in the hotel that I met the contact from the dissident group."

I knew from the file that his name was Alex Irvine. She had what was referred to as "sexual involvement" with him.

"They had links with the democrats in Glasgow, who used them pretty cynically. We blew up a few buildings."

"And got caught."

"Naturally. Even at that time the Public Order Directorate was good at planting informers." She looked at me coolly. "As you know very well."

I lowered my eyes. "I wasn't involved with that kind of operation." Hamilton became a great advocate of undercover work during the drug wars. I always preferred the investigative approach. "What was your sentence?"

"Three years on Cramond Island." Her voice was flat. "I was lucky. They put the cell leaders up against a wall."

She hadn't concealed anything. I should have been pleased, but her apparent frankness disturbed me. Maybe three years on the prison island, connected to the mainland by a causeway submerged at high tide, was enough to make anyone talkative. One of the few outbursts of resentment against the Council led to the facility being renovated two years ago. Conditions had been even worse than those in UK prisons before the breakdown of central government.

"Must have been tough."

"I read a lot of books," Katharine said impassively. "The Council chose them, of course."

"And when you were released, they gave you no choice of work?"

"I would have done anything." She shivered violently. "It was so fucking cold on that island. I still have it in me." She curled herself up into a tight ball. "I don't think I'll ever feel warm again."

"How was Adam affected by what you went through?"

"It didn't turn him into a murderer, if that's what you're thinking. It just made him give up the idea of becoming an auxiliary."

I had to be sure about one thing. My mother's words about motive were ringing in my head. "How do you feel about what they did to Alex Irvine?"

I realised as soon as I said it that I'd cocked up badly. She hadn't mentioned the dissident's name.

Katharine's whole body went rigid. "You bastard." She stood up and looked down at me like I was something that had crawled out from between the floorboards. "You knew all this already, didn't you? You've been giving yourself a hard-on listening to me cough it all up."

Fortunately she'd forgotten about the knife. There was no need for her to answer my question. It was obvious what she felt about the people who'd killed her lover. But that didn't mean she was capable of murder, and there wasn't much point in asking her that. I felt my fingers trembling. From self-disgust more than anything else.

"Get out!" she shouted, striding towards the toilet.

I wasn't too shaken to miss the sight of her body, naked from ankle to throat, as her dressing-gown parted. Her pubic hair was a thick brown mass and her breasts firm and hard-nippled.

"Out!" she repeated, catching the direction of my gaze but too incensed to bother covering herself.

I left red-faced, like a schoolboy caught spying on matron. As I was halfway down the stairs, the lights went out.

Davie was talking to a guardswoman in the Land-Rover. He had moved the file so she could sit on the passenger seat. There was no way of telling if he'd read about Katharine. For some reason that disturbed me.

Chapter Ten

I was in the Bearskin, strange wailing music from the jazz band rising and falling like someone was playing with the volume control. The bagpiper was on duty this time. While the crowd was cheering, I looked at Billy Geddes and then at the woman he acknowledged: Patsy Cameron from Prostitution Services. She didn't flinch as she stared back at me. Her eyes were the cold fire of a star that burned up a long time ago.

The slam of a Land-Rover door in the street below woke me up. Boots that sounded like auxiliary issue number tens came up the stair. I parted the curtains and was greeted by the first grey tinges of an Edinburgh dawn. The fog had lifted.

I opened the door. "Jesus, what happened to you?"

Davie's face and uniform were blackened, his beret shoved back on his head.

"Fire!" he gasped hoarsely. "Fire in the Independence. Didn't you hear the sirens?" He grabbed the jug of drinking water and gulped down its contents. "Every fire engine in the city was called out."

"In the Independence Hotel?" I thought of Katharine and wondered if she'd been working overnight. "What about casualties?"

"Amazingly few. Every auxiliary in the central barracks was mobilised." He grinned ruefully. "Including me. We got the guests out pretty quickly."

"What about the staff?"

He looked puzzled for a moment. "Most of them got out

themselves. Oh, you mean the Kirkwood woman." He gave a shrug. "I didn't see her."

I stood in the middle of the room, my legs tingling in the chill. Had the murderer suddenly turned arsonist?

"The blaze started somewhere near the kitchens," Davie said, raising his head from the kitchen sink where he was dousing himself. "I heard the hotel manager telling the fire chief that there have been some problems with the electrics recently. By the time I got there – about half four – it had spread all over the building. It's still burning at the south end but they've got it under control in the other parts. Christ, you should see the place. It looks like the photographs of Sarajevo they showed us in modern history classes."

I went to dress. "You'll need to get me down there."

"Why?" Davie followed me into the bedroom. "I thought you were expecting someone to be murdered last night."

I sat down and pulled on my boots. "You should have called me, Davie. A major fire on the night we were expecting our friend to strike again doesn't sound like a coincidence to me."

"Bloody hell."

"Find out where the public order guardian is, will you?"

Davie picked up my mobile and asked the castle for Hamilton's location. "He's at the hotel."

"Amazing." I picked up my jacket and went towards the door. "Don't tell me he's had the same thought as me. The case isn't that weird. Yet."

The great mass of the Independence stretches a hundred and fifty yards up Lothian Road at right angles to Princes Street. Before the Enlightenment, when it was called the Caledonian, its façade was brownish red. Since we started using coal again in the city, it's gone sooty grey. Now it was marked by great smudges of black around windows shattered by the heat. Glass covered the road in a glittering carpet and smoke was billowing from the hotel's southern end. The guard had erected roadblocks. Beyond them fire engines, dwarfed by the giant building, were spraying thousands of gallons of Edinburgh's precious water on the flames that flickered round the window-frames.

"I see what you mean," I said as Davie pulled up at the barricade below Stevenson Hall. "This is a disaster area."

We walked down on the opposite side of the road from the

blaze. Bad move. Even there the heat was enough to make the air blister your throat. We had to push our way through a crowd of exhausted firemen and women.

As we got nearer to Princes Street the temperature began to come down. That end of the hotel was less damaged. A group of auxiliaries had gathered around Hamilton and Yellowlees. They stood on the horse-drawn carriage rank outside the main entrance like a gaggle of schoolkids on an excursion, scribbling notes on their clipboards.

"Bureaucracy even when Rome burns," I said.

Davie smiled. "Especially when Rome burns, we were taught."

Hamilton caught sight of me and exchanged glances with the medical guardian. Then he strode over. "What are you doing here, Dalrymple?"

"What a relief. I was wrong about his mind working like mine," I said under my breath. "Morning, guardian. What's the story?"

"The story," he said, eyes boring into mine, "is that this has nothing to do with you. Why don't you go back to ferreting around in the archives? This is a job for professionals."

Yellowlees walked up. He looked less hostile.

"Let's be civilised about this, gentlemen." I moved them further away from their subordinates. "I don't want to have to start flashing my authorisation around, but if that's the way you want it . . ."

"What's your interest here, exactly?" the medical guardian asked.

"Hasn't it occurred to either of you that there may be a connection between this fire and the killer we're looking for?"

"Come on," Hamilton scoffed. "This was an accident – a pretty horrendous one, I grant you, but these things happen."

"Hold on," Yellowlees said, putting his hand on his colleague's arm to shut him up. He suddenly looked seriously worried. "You think the fire might have been started deliberately?"

"Given what the murderer's done so far, you have to admit the possibility."

"Rubbish." Hamilton made to turn away. "I've got more important things to do than listen to conspiracy theories."

"Wait," Yellowlees said imperiously. "This could be important." He looked at me. "What do you want from my directorate?"

"Full casualty lists, current locations of all the injured, plus a list of any injuries which might not be a result of the fire." I turned to Hamilton. "Are you in on this?"

He bit his lip, then nodded.

"Thank you. I need to know how and why the fire started, whether any suspicious activities were witnessed. I also want full lists of all residents and staff, as well as where they are now."

"Is that all?" the public order guardian demanded sarcastically.

"No. I need the barracks numbers of all auxiliaries involved in fighting the fire and in the rescue operation."

"There are hundreds of them, man." Hamilton's eyes opened wide as the coin dropped. "Why do you want this information? Are you still obsessed by the idea that the killer's an auxiliary?" He jabbed his finger into my chest. "If you're wrong, I'll have your hide."

I faced him, then glanced at Yellowlees. "And if I'm right?" I asked quietly.

"I've found her," said Davie, lowering the mobile from his mouth. "She's in the infirmary."

I'd asked him to locate Katharine while I went through the papers that auxiliaries were bringing in continuously. "What happened to her?"

"They said a piece of burning wood fell on her arm. It's not serious. She's been given a sedative."

So she had been on the night shift. "Thanks, Davie. Come and give me a hand here."

We were in the Public Order Directorate's mobile operations unit, a broken-down caravan which had been parked outside the hotel entrance. Beyond the guard cordon, crowds of tourists stood watching what was going on, gazing up at the clouds of smoke that were gradually being reduced. I was surprised the Tourism Directorate hadn't started selling tickets.

"What are we doing exactly?" Davie asked, peering at the piles of paper I'd made on a fold-down table.

"Looking for a needle in a very large haystack."

"But we've got nothing to go on," he said with a groan. "And not to put too fine a point on it, I'm fucking knackered."

I was at the window, straining forward. "Don't worry. I think my hunch just paid off."

We watched as a firewoman staggered out of the hotel and fell to her knees in front of the caravan. She leaned forward on to her hands, the breathing apparatus dangling from her abdomen like exoskeletal entrails. Even under the layer of grime, her face had the pallor of a corpse. Before anyone could reach her, she vomited copiously on the tarmac.

"What the . . ." Davie yelled as I pushed past him and jumped out.

"Let me through!" I shouted as auxiliaries crowded round. I reached the firewoman and knelt down beside her. "What is it? Take a deep breath and tell me." I rubbed the muck from her barracks number, aware for a second of a soft breast. "Come on, Cullen 212, it's a matter of life and death."

She managed to control her breathing. "Death, citizen," she said with a gasp. "Definitely a matter of death." She started to laugh, then sobbed. "Man in a linen store on the third floor at this end of the hotel. The fire had nothing to do with what happened to him."

"Can you show me?" I took her arm and pulled her up.

Cullen 212 nodded slowly. "I'll take you to the corridor, but I'm not going in that cupboard again." She was staring at me, her face taut with horror.

"Jesus, Quint," said Davie as we followed her inside. "Some bloody hunch."

A guardswoman passed us in the hall. Her face was blackened and her tunic torn, but I recognised her immediately. It was Mary, Queen of Scots.

There was a strong smell of smoke in the passage on the third floor but we didn't need the breathing gear we'd been handed on the way up. Open doors to guests' rooms revealed the panic caused by the fire – covers thrown back from beds, drawers and wardrobes with clothes hanging from them. A trail of paper led from one room into the corridor, typed pages that some desperate resident had tried to save. Another room had heaps of expensive clothing on the floor, as if the owner had tried to decide what to take with her. What struck me most of all was the eerie silence in this part of the building. The sounds of the firefighting at the other end were muted, almost inaudible, like the creaking from the hullplates of a stricken ship that scarcely got through to the first-class smoking room. Our heavy boots sank into the thick pile of the carpet.

Cullen 212 stopped abruptly at a corner. "It's down there, at the far end on the left." She pointed ahead, her arm shaking.

"Right." I felt a dull ache in my stomach. "Let's go, Davie."

The two of us went on, sticking close together. My breathing was rapid and it rasped in my throat. Davie seemed unperturbed though a nerve twitched on his cheek.

"Okay, let's take this slowly," I said as we reached the door. "We've both seen worse."

"Speak for yourself. The worst I normally see is drunken tourists in Rose Street."

"That bad?" I put my fingers on the handle of the storeroom door. It was the only one closed in the whole corridor. I took a deep breath and opened it, then reached for the light switch. Nothing. We both shone our torches in.

In the flashes reflected from the piles of sheets and pillowcases, the small room took on the appearance of the sacred inner chamber of an ancient temple – one belonging to a civilisation that performed human sacrifice. The naked victim was in a seated position, his legs and arms wide and his head flung back on a stack of linen. There was a lot of blood on the right side of his face and, as I looked more closely, I made out the scored line left by a ligature on his neck.

I fumbled in my pockets for rubber gloves, pulled them on and examined the man's face.

"The right eye's been removed," I said. "There's extensive laceration. Christ, I think the bastard used his fingers." I lowered the torch and studied the throat, straddling the body. "Strangulation by ligature." I looked over my shoulder at Davie. He was leaning against the doorframe, his eyes bulging. Then I heard the faintest of croaking sounds and pressed my ear against the man's bare chest.

"Jesus, I don't believe it. He's still alive. Get on the mobile, Davie." I felt for a pulse. It was feeble and irregular, but it was definitely there. I piled blankets over the man and stepped back, running the torch around the closet. Apart from a pair of silk pyjamas and the slippers near the victim's feet, there was nothing.

I heard a stampede in the corridor. A team of medics barged in and took charge. I ran into Hamilton as I came out.

"Why wasn't I informed of this?" he demanded, peering into the storeroom. "Oh my God."

"It's our man all right," I said. "Same strangulation method, an organ removed. I think he ran out of time."

The victim was brought out and laid on a stretcher. Before they strapped him down, I took hold of his left wrist.

"Take a look at this."

The public order guardian bent over, then quickly looked up, his face ashen. "He's a foreigner."

"Exactly." The mutilated man was wearing a Swiss watch that not even Billy Geddes would risk being seen with. He had also cultivated a long nail on his little finger.

The public order guardian looked like a condemned man who'd just seen the scaffold come into view. "A tourist," he mumbled. "This is getting beyond a joke."

His understatement might have made me laugh if the implication hadn't grated – the situation only became critical when foreigners were killed. I could see how his mind was working. In the years since independence, the security of tourists has become one of the Council's priorities. There had never been any incident affecting the volume of visitors to Edinburgh. As the guardian responsible for crime prevention, Hamilton was in an ocean of shit.

"We need to identify him as soon as possible," he said, still in a partial trance.

I nodded. "Shouldn't be difficult. Obviously there's no ID on him, but the staff will recognise him." I saw the guardian's mouth open. "Don't worry. I know the Council will have to decide on whether to go public on this. I'll make sure I only talk to auxiliaries at this stage. They'll keep their mouths shut, won't they?"

Hamilton walked off without replying.

Davie shook his head. "You never give up, do you, Quint?"

I caught his eye for a second. "No, my friend, I don't."

As it turned out, there was no need to involve anyone else in the identification. After I left Davie in charge of the forensics team in the linen store, I found the intended victim's passport in the third room I checked down the passage. It was tricky recognising a face with one eye missing and blood over half of it, but the thick, curly black hair and dimpled chin helped.

"In here, Davie," I shouted. I took the passport out of the drawer of the dressing table. "Andreas Roussos," I read. "Born

11.12.80, Athens." I'd seen Greek tourists with long nails on their little fingers before. You don't have to be a detective to know why they grow them.

"How long's he been in the city?" Davie asked.

The maroon stamp with the heart motif showed 4.1.2020.

"He can't have been an ordinary tourist," I said. "See if you can find out whether he was a guide. There'll be a file in reception if the fire didn't get to it."

Davie nodded and left the room. I closed and locked the door after him. Searching rooms is hard enough without interruptions.

Andreas Roussos had a dressing-gown that a Byzantine emperor would have been proud of – purple and gold with a double-headed eagle motif. There was a diamond-studded bracelet on the bedside table too. It looked like he was a major player in some very lucrative business. I smelled something rotten under the eau-de-cologne.

The wardrobe was full of Parisian suits and shirts, as well as Italian shoes. What have you been up to in our fair city, Mr Roussos? I wondered as I lifted up the mattress. Nothing. The chest of drawers was equally devoid of interest, unless you happened to be a connoisseur of G-strings and thongs. I crawled around the edges of the thick carpet – no expense being spared by the Supply Directorate when it comes to the city's hotels – but I found no gap between the closely positioned tacks. Then I squatted down in the middle of the room and let my mind go blank. I often get inspiration doing that. Andreas Roussos appeared before me in one of his well-cut suits, admiring himself as he knotted one of the garish ties from the wardrobe.

Got you. I jumped up. It had to be the mirror. I lifted the gilt-framed glass down from the wall. The back was plastered with tape. I ripped it off and discovered four brown envelopes. From three of them came wads of brightly coloured banknotes. They were US dollars and Greek drachmae, all of high denominations, including plenty of fifty thousands. That left one envelope. It was larger and had a stiff insert. Photographs. I pulled them out. And found masturbators' paradise. Dozens of pictures of naked bodies, male and female, from all angles. I spread them around me on the floor and sat in the middle of an island of black and white flesh.

There were two unusual things about the photos, both

contesting the idea that Roussos was a purveyor of dirty postcards. They all had what looked like serial numbers stencilled on them – AT231, HF76 and the like. And although the major features of every torso appeared in close detail, not a single one of the photos showed a face or head. The people these were intended for were obviously only interested in serious sexual activity, without the distraction of a pretty face.

"What can you tell us then?" Hamilton's voice was almost back to normal. Maybe he was relieved he'd escaped another post-mortem.

The medical guardian finished rinsing his hands at the sink recessed into his office wall and turned to us. His face was sallow and he looked unusually nervous.

"The man was lucky. His assailant thought he'd held the ligature tight long enough to strangle him. Not only did the Greek survive, but it looks like he's escaped brain damage too." Yellowlees shook his head. "His right eye socket's a hell of a mess though. The butcher dug his fingers in and pulled the eye out with his fingers, would you believe? Then he slashed around to sever the ocular muscles." He glanced at me. "With a suitably sharp blade. I can't tell you anything more about it this time."

"When will I be able to question him?" I asked.

"Not till tomorrow at the earliest. He's heavily sedated."

"Was there any penetration of the anus?"

Yellowlees shook his head.

I turned to Hamilton. "You'll remember the ENT Man never showed any interest in eyes."

"Doesn't prove anything. He's our man. And don't tell me the fact that there was no sodomy here is significant. He was interrupted by the fire alarm."

I let him stay in his own little world.

Hamilton glanced at his colleague, then at me. He looked like a little boy about to try and talk his parents into letting him stay in their bedroom on a Saturday night so he can improve his education. "Em, how exactly are we going to frame our reports to the Council?"

I wasn't going to play this game. "How about telling them what we know?"

The two guardians stared at me like I was an impossibly naive trainee auxiliary.

"It may not be quite as simple as that," Yellowlees said. "This thing is getting out of control, citizen." He smoothed back his silver hair. "We need to – how shall I put it? – protect our interests."

"You mean cover your arses?" I said. Even as much of a drop-out from the system as me knows that there are internal politics under the calm surface of the Council. But I couldn't see why Yellowlees was worried. Hamilton was another story, but I wasn't going to lose any sleep over him.

"Don't push your luck, Dalrymple," said my ex-chief. "You haven't exactly covered yourself in glory either. What pearls of wisdom are you going to give them?"

I shrugged. "The Greek's been in residence at the Indie for eleven weeks. According to the business card I found in his wallet, he's an insurance consultant."

"He's been earning some hefty commissions," grunted Hamilton.

"In cash, too," I said. "We've started checking on who he's been meeting and what he's been doing. I'm also looking to see if the serial numbers on any of the banknotes are close to those we found in the sewer outside Baillie's place." I didn't say anything about the photos. It wasn't just that I was worried about the guardians suffering a collective heart attack at the sight of so much naked flesh. I wanted to do some research of my own first.

Yellowlees came up to me. "My God, Dalrymple, you've got to do something about this lunatic. Who knows who his next victim will be?"

I'd never seen the medical guardian so emotional.

He realised we were staring at him. "Sorry. Not enough sleep recently."

"Come on." Hamilton moved towards the door. "We'll be late."

"You haven't told us what you're going to report." I said. "Are you going to ask for another news blackout?"

He looked at me icily. "I'm going to tell the Council that the city is in grave danger and that we need to declare a state of emergency."

"You're joking." I groaned, knowing the likelihood of the old jackass being deliberately humorous. "How can we investigate with citizens confined to their homes except for the hours of work? The City Guard marching around carrying firearms is hardly going to make people co-operate, is it?"

Hamilton had already left the room. As I followed him, I almost collided with the nurse who'd attended the post-mortems, Simpson 134 of the staggering chest. She didn't even notice me. Her expression softened when she saw Yellowlees, but she still looked like a woman who's just spent Hallowe'en in a particularly lively cemetery.

The Council meeting went on for hours. The Greek consulate had been informed about the attack on Andreas Roussos and had insisted that it be kept confidential. That made Hamilton very happy. Edinburgh locals probably wouldn't have been interested; they were engrossed by the fire and the death toll from it, which rose to eight during the evening. There were over a hundred detained in the infirmary.

I got off lightly since my prediction about the killer working to a pattern had been right. Hamilton was given a hard time by the speaker because of his failure to advise me about the fire. He was then told to report to the senior guardian later on. I tried not to laugh. That wasn't the end of his troubles. The Council threw out his demand for a state of emergency because of its potentially catastrophic effect on the city's finances from cancelled bookings. Holidaymakers like armed auxiliaries in the military tattoo, not on every street corner.

After the meeting Davie drove me to the infirmary. He looked so worn out that I sent him back to his barracks, telling him I'd walk home.

I found Katharine in a ward full of casualties from the fire. She was asleep. For a few moments I studied her features in the glow from the bedside lamp. The deep auburn of her hair contrasted starkly with the pallor of her face, which had a softness that I hadn't been aware of when she was awake. Suddenly she seemed to sense my presence and her eyes opened. They weren't as hostile as I'd expected.

"I wanted to see you," she murmured.

I smiled. "Good." I sat down carefully on the bed. "I wanted to see you too."

She looked at me then shook her head. "That's not what I meant." She lifted her unbandaged arm and motioned to the jug on the bedside table. "Thirsty."

I filled a glass and held it to her lips, feeling the warmth of the skin around her mouth.

"Thank you," she said. "What happened at the Indie?" She spoke so softly that I had to lean close to hear.

"There was a fire. Don't you remember?"

She shook her head violently and winced. "Of course I remember the fire. I mean, what happened on the third floor? I was on duty there."

"What?" I slid my arm behind her back and helped her into a sitting position. "Did you see something?"

"Not enough to help you very much." She looked into my eyes. "There was another murder, wasn't there?"

I shook my head. "Not quite. The bastard tried his best."

She shivered and twitched her hands. "No, it wasn't a—" She broke off and turned away, stifling a sob.

I put my hand on hers. "Calm down, Katharine. Just tell me what you saw."

She took a deep breath and started to speak slowly. "It was a few minutes before the alarm went off. I was at the end of the corridor near the stairs. Down the other end I saw a dark-haired guest in his pyjamas. He went into the linen store." She shook again briefly. "With a woman."

"With a woman?" I had difficulty getting the words out. "What did she look like? Come on, think."

Katharine pulled her hand away, blinking in pain with the movement of her injured arm. "I only got a glimpse. Then the bell rang and people started coming out of their rooms. I got caught up in them." She paused. "There was an old man in the middle of the crowd, you know. They almost pushed him down the stairs . . ." She began to sob, then gradually controlled her breathing.

"The woman, Katharine," I said, squeezing her hand again. "What did the woman look like?"

She sat motionless, her eyes fixed on the wall opposite. "She was tall, wearing high heels, quite well built. Her hair was very blonde. I didn't see her face." She stopped abruptly, her mouth staying open. "My God, Quint. I don't think it was a woman. It looked more like a transvestite. There are always some on duty in the hotel."

I sat back, my head spinning. Hamilton and Yellowlees reckoned things were getting out of control but they didn't know the half of it. I needed to get my mojo working. Fast.

Chapter Eleven

I walked away from the infirmary into the night. The breeze still carried the smell of smoke, though the fire at the hotel had been out for hours. I tried to make sense of what was going on. In the afternoon I had checked Adam Kirkwood's flat and found it exactly as it had been. Was he the transvestite his sister had seen? I had no evidence, but I had bugger all evidence for anything. That's why I was reduced to following up marginal leads.

A car braked and stopped just in front of me on Lauriston Place. It was Billy Geddes's Toyota.

"Get in, Quint."

"What are you doing around here?" I got in without any show of enthusiasm. "No sex clubs in this part of the city."

Billy accelerated away. "Looking for you." His hands gripped the steering wheel hard.

"Oh aye." I was instantly curious. "Need to get something off your chest, maybe?"

"You don't make things easy, do you?" He shook his head. "Fucking smartass. As it happens, I have got something to tell you."

"Come home for a nightcap. I've got some unusually good whisky."

"Wonder where you came by that. Spare me your pit. I'll take you to my place."

"Great, Billy." At least it would be interesting to find out if his years in the Finance Directorate had left him with any understanding of what telling the truth entails.

*   *   *

I wasn't much the wiser after my first hour in Heriot Row. Billy had led me up the ornate Georgian staircase to his apartment on the first floor. From the high windows I looked out over the lights in the street below. The voices of a group of auxiliaries jogging on the all-weather track in the gardens beyond floated up in the still night air. Well, it wasn't that still. From the gaming tents in Charlotte Square came the pounding of music, interspersed by the raucous yells of the winners.

Although even senior auxiliaries are supposedly issued with the same furniture as us ordinary citizens, their residences in the streets near Council members' accommodation aren't checked by Supply Directorate inspectors. I recalled the Latin question my father came up with all the time in the early years of the Enlightenment: "Quis custodiet ipsos custodes?" It didn't look like anyone was keeping an eye on the next generation of guardians.

"Look at this." Billy nudged me and took me over to the polished Regency table that stood in the centre of his large sitting room. "It's a first edition of Hume's *Treatise*."

"Bloody hell." I ran my hands over the stiff pages of the old book carefully. "Where did you get it?"

Billy raised a finger to his nose. "Contacts, Quint. That's what it's all about." He went over to the drinks cabinet by the Adam fireplace and raised a decanter. "This is from Jura."

I was seriously tempted to taste the whisky. Brands like it had disappeared from the city when relations with the unstable states in the north and west were cut after independence. The whisky available to ordinary citizens was a low-quality blend from the few distilleries around Edinburgh. Only the tourist shops stocked the few expensive brands that remained in the bonded warehouses.

"No, thanks." I didn't fancy being bribed. "I suppose you got that from one of your contacts."

Billy smiled and shrugged. "That's the way things work."

"Is it fuck." I poked him in the chest with my left fore-finger. "That's exactly the kind of thieving the Enlightenment was formed to fight. Remember all those corrupt bastards in London?"

"Grow up, Quint. Things are different now."

"Bollocks. You're the one who's different. You used to go on about how people in power had to be above suspicion."

Billy drew back his thin lips. "I *am* above suspicion," he said quietly. "Let me teach you about the reality of life in Edinburgh." He gave me a bitter smile. "Unlike you, I've actually applied myself to working for the city ever since the Council was set up."

That's the problem with old friends – they know how to get to you. What Billy said was true enough. I'd dropped out, failed to honour the commitment I made to the Enlightenment when I was eighteen. Maybe I didn't have a right to criticise those who'd remained in harness.

Billy was standing in front of the carved fireplace. His voice was calm and self-assured, which pissed me off even more.

"Even if I were to come under suspicion, no one would investigate me very carefully." He glanced over to me. I'd taken refuge in a Charles Rennie Mackintosh chair that was even more uncomfortable than it looked. "I'm worth more to the city than just about anyone else in it. Without me, Edinburgh would be full of citizens rioting for bread, and the Council knows it."

"Come off it, Billy," I said wearily. "Nobody's that important. The structure of guardians and auxiliaries is supposed to ensure that individuals can't become indispensable."

He choked on his whisky and almost spilled the contents of his glass over his immaculate grey suit. "Fucking hell, Quint," he gasped. "You of all people should know what a pile of crap that is. Why did you become an outsider? Because you rate your precious ego higher than anything else."

I glared at him. "We're talking about you, not me. What makes you so important?"

Billy opened his hands like a magician producing doves from a handkerchief. "I make the deals that keep this city solvent. Like I said, it's all a question of contacts. Personal contacts. I've got them in the countries we trade with, in the companies we buy from, in the embassies we work with, in the foreign police forces we send auxiliaries to train, even in the neighbouring states we technically don't recognise." He grinned. "The finance guardian signs the contracts, but I negotiate them. I make the decisions."

I believed him. So far. Although Billy had always been a smooth operator, he never bothered boasting about it. I only had to look at the opulent room to be convinced. That's why he'd brought me here.

"What exactly was the nature of your relations with Andreas Roussos, Billy?" I asked quietly.

He looked up from his glass and smiled. "Sharp, Quint, very sharp. Not much gets past you."

Flattery from Billy was the last thing I'd set my heart on. "Just about everything this psycho's done has got past me so far. Answer the question."

"I'm going to. That's why I had the infirmary advise me as soon as you left." He pulled open a drawer. "Want a cigar? I've got some Havanas here . . ."

"Answer the fucking question."

He stopped fumbling with the illegal box. "All right. You would have found witnesses in the hotel who saw me with the Greek, so I thought I'd get in first. There's nothing much to it. He represents an insurance company which looks after its clients' welfare while they're on holiday in the city." He ran the tips of his fingers across his forehead. "Your murderer – I assume it's the same guy?"

"Looks like it."

"Your murderer picked a good one to attack. We'll probably lose a lot of customers."

I stood up and walked over to him. "Is that it?"

Billy shrugged. "What more do you want?"

It was time for the third degree. "I'll tell you what more I want," I yelled, holding up the fingers of my left hand and counting them off. "One, why did Roussos have a stash of what I'm sure will turn out to be undeclared foreign currency hidden in his room?" I didn't mention the photos. I had a feeling Billy knew something about them, but I didn't want to show my hand. "Two, why did my murderer, as you call him, try to kill this particular foreigner? Three, why have you been chasing after me ever since the first killing? That'll do for a start."

"You mean there's more?" he asked with a wan smile.

"Bloody right there is." I moved right up to him. "What kind of an investment have you got in the Bearskin?"

It didn't work. He wasn't scared of me. Even if I'd thrown him around the room a bit, he'd still have kept quiet. After all, he reckoned he was the Council's favourite son. At least I'd let him know I was on his trail. Wherever that might lead.

"What kind of a friend are you?" Billy said as I headed for the door. "I offer you help and all you do is shout at me."

I followed his example and declined to answer, giving the front door a good slam on the way out. The worst thing about growing older is seeing how your friends turn out. All is flux, an ancient philosopher said. I don't suppose I bear much resemblance to my former self either.

As I approached Darnaway Street a thought struck me. Who informed Billy Geddes that I'd left the infirmary? I couldn't think of any reason why he should have a contact in the city's main medical facility.

A wave of exhaustion swamped me as I was passing the charred walls of the Independence. It was easy to flash my authorisation and get a guardswoman to drive me home. Billy would have found that minor abuse of power highly amusing.

Saturday morning was warm and sunny. That was about all that could be said in its favour. I went round to the infirmary to question Roussos and found Hamilton deep in conversation outside the Greek's room with a distinguished-looking guy in a herringbone tweed coat. He had a moustache thick enough for a barn owl to roost in.

"Ah, Dalrymple," the public order guardian said in a nervous voice that made me immediately suspicious. "This is Mr Palamas from the Greek consulate."

The diplomat eyed my unofficial clothing and decided against shaking hands.

"Mr Palamas has been visiting his compatriot to check on his progress."

"Fortunately for you, guardian, he is making a good recovery." The Greek shook his head theatrically. "That such a thing should happen in your city . . ."

"When can I interview Mr Roussos?" I asked.

Hamilton started shaking his head before I finished my question.

Palamas looked down his long, fleshy nose at me. "As I have just explained to your superior, Mr Roussos is not to be interviewed by any city official."

I looked at Hamilton. He opened his hands helplessly.

"Mr Roussos has told me he saw nothing of his assailant. There is therefore no point in interviewing him. The guardian has agreed to this. Good morning." Palamas walked away with his nose in the air.

"Are you out of your fucking . . ."

"Quiet, man. This is nothing to do with you. The senior guardian is aware of my decision." He paused to let that sink in.

"Since when do attempted murder victims get let off making statements? How the fuck am I supposed to catch this maniac?"

"It's out of my hands, citizen." Hamilton twitched his head like a fly was annoying him. A fly named guilt. He knew he should never have agreed to exempting a witness from questioning. If what Katharine had told me was right and the attacker was dressed up as a transvestite, Roussos must have hired him and obviously must have seen him close up.

"It's because of commercial considerations," Hamilton said in a low voice. "The Greeks are worth a fortune to us. If they don't want one of their people to be bothered, what can we do?"

I knew exactly what he could do and I told him. He didn't look too impressed.

So then I went to see the city's chief prostitute. I got a surprise on the way into the Tourism Directorate building on George IVth Bridge. Simpson 134, the buxom nurse who spent her time making eyes at Yellowlees, came out, a well-stuffed briefcase in her hand. She pretended she didn't see me but I was sure she did. What the hell was she doing there? A bit of moonlighting in her off-duty hours?

The Prostitution Services Department is on the second-top floor of the building. That shows how important it is to the Tourism Directorate. Men come all the way from the Far East to have a good time with Edinburgh's finest. No doubt they find the experience very enlightening.

The sun was streaming in the large windows. I sat in the office of the controller and waited for her to come out of a budget meeting. Her desk was clear and all her filing cabinets locked. I began to get bored.

"Hello there, Quint," Patsy Cameron said, bustling in eventually and taking off the jacket of her pinstriped suit. She looked a lot more pleased to see me than she had in the Bearskin the other night. "Sorry I'm late. Financial planning seems to be how I spend all my time these days."

"Beats lying on your back with your legs open though."

She looked across at me, eyes cold, then laughed. "Really, citizen, what kind of way is that to speak to a senior auxiliary?"

"Sorry, Patsy." I looked across to the barracks number on her ample bosom. "I mean Wilkie 164."

"Never mind that nonsense. I was Patsy Cameron when you took me in during the anti-whoring campaign fifteen years ago and I'm the same person now." Although she was over fifty, the controller's hair was blonde and her face surprisingly free of wrinkles. Only the remains of a heavy accent hinted at a less than typical background for a person in her position.

I used to like Patsy, but I hadn't seen her since I dropped out. She was one of the Enlightenment's success stories, an ex-prostitute who'd gone through the adult education system and done well for herself. I often worked with her during the Public Order Directorate's campaigns to keep women off the street. I hadn't realised then that most of them would end up doing the same job in the service of the city. Now that the Council was in open competition with Amsterdam and anywhere else you can think of, Patsy must have got a job for life.

"I'm told you're back doing what you're best at, Quint," she said, opening one of the files she'd brought in.

"I'm not doing it too well now. That's why I need your help." I also needed to con her and I wasn't too sure if I was up to that.

The controller put on a pair of standard-issue glasses, the plain plastic frames clashing with her luxuriant coiffure. "Fire away," she said with more enthusiasm than I'd expected. Maybe she wanted something from me in exchange.

"First, I need to check out the transvestites who work the Indie." I told her a witness had spotted one, without mentioning Katharine.

"I'll give you everything I've got on the boys who were on the roster on Thursday night." She pursed her lips. "Won't necessarily prove a lot – most of them freelance in their spare time."

"Freelance?"

Patsy laughed. "So to speak. I'll give you the full register of t-vs." She looked across at me. "What else?"

Now came the tricky bit. I needed a way into the department's main archive to see if I could find any other photos like the ones I'd found behind Roussos's mirror. I could only think of one name to use.

"Katharine Kirkwood. I need to go through her file."

Patsy eyed me cautiously. "Let's have a look at that authorisation of yours."

I handed it over and watched her scrutinise it.

"Aye, well, it looks like I can't refuse you anything." She gave me a practised tart's leer, her lips parting to show gleaming and even teeth – dental work obviously done before private practices were abolished. "You know she has a security file?"

"I've seen it."

"Have you now? Well, the files we keep aren't always the same as the ones those idiots in the Public Order Directorate have." She shook her head and quickly regained her senior auxiliary's air. "Sorry. The old prejudices die hard. What's your interest in our fair Katharine?"

I had the sudden feeling I'd bitten off more than I could comfortably get through in a single dinner sitting. When I'd used Katharine's name I hadn't expected Patsy to know her. I mumbled some garbage about how I was checking everyone who'd been injured in the fire.

Patsy caught my eye. "You know, we play hard in this department. You might not like everything you read in our files."

"I can take it."

She raised her eyebrows sceptically then pressed the button for her secretary. "You'll be locked in the archive. And Quint, nothing leaves the building, all right?"

"I'll mention your co-operation in my report, Patsy."

The controller was already engrossed in her papers. It seemed she didn't want anything from me in return. "Screw you, citizen," she said, without much sign of humour.

I suppose I was just another man to be satisfied and shown the door.

Things got worse as the day went by. The transvestite lead didn't get us very far. I went through the roster and had Davie check the boys out. There had been three on duty in the hotel when the fire started. The logsheets showed that two of them had been in rooms a long way from the scene of the crime when the alarm went off, and the other had been in the staff messroom with several female prostitutes. The clients, a Norwegian and a Chinese, weren't too keen on providing alibis, but Hamilton twisted their arms. There were seventeen other t-vs on the department's register and they were being traced, but I had a feeling the trail was cold.

The photos were a waste of time too. I didn't find any similar ones in the random sample of files I pulled in the archive and none of the serial numbers matched. Either these particular naked bodies had nothing to do with Patsy's department or efforts had been made to keep them secret. Of course, I could have asked her about them but where would that have got me? If she was involved, she'd make sure I didn't get a sniff – she knew everything there is to know about tricks.

Katharine's file was the perfect end to a shitty spring day. I decided she *was* worth talking to Patsy about. On several counts.

"Do all your operatives fuck as much as she does?" I asked, holding the maroon file up as I walked into the controller's office in the late afternoon.

Patsy shrugged. "I suppose she does have a bit of a talent for it."

"I like the auxiliary-style understatement, Patsy. This woman makes Catherine the Great look like an under-achiever. What do you do with all this information she gathers about her clients?"

The controller went coy on me. It didn't suit her. "Oh, you know, it pays to know about clients' needs – in case they come back."

"It would never occur to the Tourism Directorate to blackmail the ones who get out of hand, would it?"

"Is that an accusation, citizen?" she asked. An Arctic fox's eyes would have been warmer.

"Just an observation. I get the impression you know her pretty well. Fill me in."

"I hope this is relevant to your investigation."

"Trust me."

"Ha." Patsy loosened up a bit. "Actually, I do know her quite well." She shook her blonde mane a couple of times. "If you can really know someone as cold-blooded as her. She's one of our stars. A year ago I even asked her to give up the hotel and come to work with me here." She laughed. "She told me right where I could go. Our Katharine doesn't think much of the Council and its works."

"I noticed." I was trying to come to terms with my client's activities and failing abysmally. What difference did it make to me if she serviced every tourist in the city? I wondered if her brother had any idea of all this.

Patsy gave me a knowing look. "I told you we played hard."

I didn't want to be left on the touchline. "I saw you enjoying the show in the Bearskin the other night. Does your department supply it with boys and girls?"

For a split second the controller looked nervous. "No. The word is that Heriot 07 and his pals are running that place themselves."

"Any idea who his pals are?"

"He's a friend of yours, Quint. Ask him." She went back to her files.

Patsy was good, very good. If I hadn't known her in the past, I'd probably have believed her. But what I was certain wouldn't happen just had – she'd let her guard drop. That was all it took to make me very sure that the key to the investigation wasn't the t-v Katharine said she'd seen, nor was it Katharine herself, despite the doubts her file had raised. It was the city's deputy finance guardian, William Ewart Geddes.

"We can't do it, for fuck's sake." Davie sat in the stationary Land-Rover outside my flat with his head bowed. "He's a deputy guardian, not some poxy dissident."

I watched him as the last of the twilight drained away and scrabbled around for another way to convince him. "He's involved with the Greek who was attacked a sight more than he's admitting. That means he's also linked to the killings."

"You're guessing, Quint." He turned to me, the cheeks above his beard pale. "I'll get demoted. Unauthorised action against an ordinary citizen is bad enough, but against a senior auxiliary . . ."

I let his words trail away unanswered. I'd decided to go ahead with surveillance on my own if I had to. I'd have liked to follow Katharine when she came out of the infirmary too, but Billy had priority.

Davie realised I was set on it. "You're all right. When you get caught they'll just send you back to the Parks Department."

I reckoned I might as well have a go at steamrolling him. "You've forgotten that my Council authorisation gives me the power to demand anything of you."

He didn't buy it. "They didn't mean you to use it like that. I want confirmation from the Council."

"Which they won't give. Billy Geddes is their favourite human being." I glanced at him. "Anyway, what do you mean *when* I get caught? *If* I get caught."

"Don't kid yourself. Hamilton will be on to you soon enough. He's watching us like a hawk." Davie's voice had lost its usual confidence.

"Has he said something to you?"

"Nothing specific. Dropped a hint or two about my future career."

"Bastard." I grabbed his arm. "Look, if these murders go on, you won't have a career. The city's getting restless. What'll happen if there are more killings?" I went for the jugular. "Don't tell me you're frightened of that stiff-necked old cocksucker?" I sat back and waited for the explosion.

Nothing happened. I might have known. Davie let his muscles go slack and breathed in deeply. Auxiliaries are trained to withstand every kind of mental and physical pressure – at least that's what it says in the survival manual.

"I could take you in, you know, Quint," he said calmly. "Abusing a guardian is a serious offence. Your authorisation doesn't give you immunity."

"I don't think your boss would win a slander case. If such a thing could be brought in the city nowadays."

Davie laughed. "Maybe not. I've heard worse said about him." He scratched his beard thoughtfully. "I doubt he's into fellatio though."

"I didn't mean it literally." It looked like he'd capitulated. Badmouthing Hamilton was obviously a good tactic. "Are you looking forward to dressing up as a tourist?"

"You don't really think Heriot 07's the killer, do you?"

I shrugged. "Anyone can wear size twelve boots. Billy's cunning enough to dress himself up as a t-v and then feed me a load of horseshit to distract me." I remembered how feeble he'd been in PE classes at school. Maybe he'd started weight-training. It wouldn't be the only thing he'd changed in his life. "No, I can't see any motive. I reckon he's involved in something the killer's targeting."

Davie looked across in the near darkness. "All right, I'll do it." He raised a hand. "On one condition."

I owed him at least one. "Whatever you like."

"Under no circumstances am I dressing in drag."

I put a brave face on it. "Okay. See you tomorrow." I jumped down from the guard vehicle and went up to my flat.

The absence of Katharine's perfume was almost as overpowering as its presence had been before.

Chapter Twelve

I slept badly and the tramp of workers heading for the assembly points woke me. I stood wrapped in a blanket at the window, watching the first light of dawn filter into the street below. The last Sunday of the month is when the shifts are changed in the mines and on the farms. The lucky ones coming off duty would be on their way to the pubs that open early for them, while their replacements, grim-faced and shivering, boarded the buses in silence. I remembered the times I stood in line and was surprised to find that I felt nostalgic about them. At least then I hadn't always been dreaming of mutilated corpses and a killer who vanished into the mist. I had a bad case of the ghost blues.

Davie arrived carrying a hold-all. "I scoured the barracks and managed to find some casual clothes that look a bit like a tourist's." He held the bag open.

"A pretty poor tourist," I said. "They'll do." I went over to the kitchen area and rooted around for my scissors. "But first we'll have to sort out your facial hair."

His jaw dropped. "Wait a minute. You didn't say anything about that yesterday. I'll get thrown out of the guard."

"Don't worry. I'm not going to cut it all off. Just a trim. You look like bloody John Knox." I pushed him down on to the sofa and set to work.

"Mind you don't cut anything vital." Davie was sitting very still.

"Relax. It took me a few years, but my left hand can do

everything my right hand used to do before I lost my finger."

"Everything?" Davie asked with a grin.

"Everything, guardsman. There you are. Women will be queuing up."

"That'll make a change." He got up and brushed away the thick curls.

"Hang on," I said. "Does Heriot 07 know you?"

"Not unless he's seen me with you." He peered at himself in my small standard-issue mirror. "He won't recognise me even if he has. I look like a chicken that's in the middle of moulting."

"Drop your shoulders a bit, for Christ's sake. You've got to lose that guardsman's purposeful walk." I went to dress. "First stop Hamilton's office to fix up the paperwork. We won't get far without that."

Davie followed me, a thoughtful expression on his face. "We're going to the castle?"

"Yes, why? Got a girlfriend there?"

He nodded slowly, but it didn't look like he had a furtive grope on his mind.

The public order guardian leaned back in his chair and drummed his fingers on the desktop. "Why exactly do you need these undercover clearances, Dalrymple? What are you up to?" He turned to Davie and looked with distaste at his trimmed beard.

"It's a long shot," I said nonchalantly. "I'd rather keep it under wraps at this stage. It probably won't come to anything." If Hamilton discovered I was trailing a senior auxiliary, the blades of the fan would be permanently clogged with excreta. But I had to have the undercover passes – "ask no questions", as they're known in the directorate. Without them our surveillance activities would be interrupted all the time by curious auxiliaries.

The guardian's expression softened. "Oh, all right." He scribbled a note. "Give this to my assistant, guardsman." He fixed Davie with his eyes again. "I hope you're not getting yourself into anything which demeans your rank."

"I'll make sure regulations are observed, guardian," Davie said compliantly, avoiding my eyes.

"Sit down, man," Hamilton said to me wearily. He shuffled the papers on his desk with the look of a man who can't decipher the clues of the crossword, let alone have a go at the answers. "How on earth are we going to find this" – he pushed the papers away – "this savage?"

I was surprised at the change in his bearing. Maybe the Council's rejection of his demand for a state of emergency had knocked the certainty out of him. It struck me that the guardian actually had little experience of this kind of crime. He was an organisation man, an administrator at heart. And like all administrators, a plotter. The question was, how far did his plotting go? Was he just protecting the interests of his directorate or had he got involved in something a lot dirtier? Now I was the one who didn't have a clue.

Davie was waiting for me in the outer office. An attractive red-haired guardswoman lowered her head as I came out, but I saw the smile on her lips.

"Let's go," I said to Davie. "Got the 'ask no questions'?"

He nodded, looking extremely pleased with himself.

Although it was a Sunday morning, senior auxiliaries like Billy Geddes are expected to make an appearance at the office. Davie changed into his tourist clothes and went off to keep an eye on the Finance Directorate in Bank Street. I didn't expect Billy to go anywhere revealing during daylight, but there was a chance he might meet someone during his lunchbreak.

I walked across the esplanade and down to the infirmary. There was a lot of noise in the ward containing the fire victims, patients garrulously comparing experiences and nurses clattering around with trolleys. But the figure in Katharine's bed was inert. I was a few yards from it before I realised that the occupant had grey hair and fleshy shoulders.

"She discharged herself an hour ago, citizen," said a familiar voice. "She shouldn't have. The doctor didn't have a chance to examine her arm again. But I couldn't stop her."

Simpson 134, the senior nurse I'd seen the day before on my way to the Prostitution Control Department, was standing in the centre of the ward. Her subordinates moved around her like drones in the service of a queen bee. I paid less attention than I might have to her chest because I was cursing myself for not putting a guard on the door. She heard some of the words I came out with and looked about as impressed as the former king did when the mob told him where he could put his crown.

"Any idea where she went?" I asked.

"She said she was going home."

The nurse's mordant tone puzzled me. "Is something troubling you, Simpson 134?"

She eyed me coldly. "The city is being terrorised by a lunatic and you ask if something's troubling me? Why aren't you chasing the killer instead of that female citizen?" She turned away abruptly and walked out.

There was a guard vehicle by the gate. I flashed my authorisation and got the guardsman to take me to Katharine's flat. I felt uneasy. It seemed unlikely that she could have met anyone or that anything could have happened to her in the short time since she left the infirmary. A worrying thought came to me. If she had seen the killer from the far end of the corridor, then it was very possible that he had seen her too.

"You look like you've seen a ghost." She stood at the door, her hair wet and a towel round her shoulders.

I felt a wave of relief dash over me, then recovered the power of speech. "Are you all right? They said you shouldn't have left the infirmary."

"Checking up on me?" Katharine asked, her eyes wide open and ice-water cold.

"You're a witness, for God's sake."

Her expression slackened. "I suppose I am. Sorry." She let me into the flat.

"Is your arm okay?"

She flexed it slowly. "A bit sore but I'll manage." As she sat down on the sofa, her dressing-gown parted to reveal a length of thigh.

I gulped and tried to look elsewhere. "Why did you discharge yourself?"

"It's a madhouse there," she said, shaking her head. "Even in the middle of the night there are porters running up and down the corridors with patients on trolleys."

I pulled out my notebook and flicked through the pages. There was no need to remind myself of what I was going to ask her, but I was looking for a way to put it off.

"What is it?" Katharine asked with a smile that made my heart beat faster. "You've got that faraway look again."

No point in delaying any longer. "Andreas Roussos in room 346: did you provide sexual services to him?"

She didn't turn away. Only the disappearance of her smile suggested that the question might have had some effect. "You've been checking up on me, haven't you?" she said quietly. "I was hoping you wouldn't get around to the department's files."

"Answer the question, Katharine."

"All right. Why do you think I was so sure it was a t-v I saw with him? He wasn't interested in women, Quint."

I thought about the fact that the murder victims had been sodomised. Maybe there was a link there with the Greek's sexuality. I didn't fancy it much. I had a feeling we were supposed to think the killer was a sex freak like the ENT Man.

Katharine sat up and leaned over to me. "I want to help, Quint. Why won't you let me? You've forgotten all about Adam."

I hadn't. It was just that he was missing while she was right in front of me. He didn't have her track record either. "Why do you do it? No one's forcing you to fuck all those men."

She looked down at me without flinching. "What's that got to do with your investigation?"

"I'll tell you. From the start you've held things back from me. I had to ferret out your dissidence conviction and the fact that you whore for the Tourism Directorate. How do I know you haven't got more secrets?" I piled on as much indignation as I could. "On top of that, you expect me to accept your help? Christ, Katharine, you're not living in the real world."

"And everyone else in Edinburgh is?" she asked ironically. "Anyway, I thought you knew everything about me from the moment we met. Remember that little demonstration you gave?" The smile disappeared from her lips. "I told you, Quint. After my time on Cramond Island I do what I'm told."

That was bullshit. It was clear from Patsy's file that Katharine wasn't being coerced. I kept on at her. "Does that include throttling the guy in the linen store?"

Her mouth opened slightly and I heard her breathing quicken. "What do you mean?" she asked in a whisper.

I stood up and faced her. "Why should I believe your story about the transvestite? Maybe you ripped the Greek's eye out with those long fingers of yours."

The next few seconds would be crucial. She was about the most enigmatic person I'd ever come across, but I was still confident I'd be able to tell if she was lying.

"You've made your mind up already, haven't you?" she said, holding my gaze. "There's no point in me saying anything."

I waited for a bit, then snapped my notebook shut. If she'd started to weep or plead, if she'd opened her legs and offered me sex, I'd have been seriously suspicious. As it was, she convinced me that she hadn't been involved in the attacks on Roussos and the others simply because she didn't care about them. Or about anyone else except her brother, it seemed.

"I want to assign a guardswoman to you," I said on my way out. "The assailant might have seen you."

"Forget it," she said, her voice harsher. "I can look after myself."

I didn't press the point. Suddenly the idea of arguing with her took on the aspect of Everest's south-west face from below. I went downstairs to the safety of the street.

"Dead ends," said Hamilton laconically.

I looked out from the window of his office in the castle. The city looked unreal in the late afternoon sun, a thin layer of mist hanging over the buildings like the last exhalations of an intelligent but slow-moving species of dinosaur. "Looks that way," I said.

"Do you think we can rely on the official t-vs' alibis?" The guardian pronounced the initial letters with distaste.

"Yes. We'll have to look elsewhere for the butcher."

"But where, for God's sake? My people have checked all the gaming tents and nightclubs. Some of the staff remembered Roussos, but no one could say if he'd been with anyone else. The same in the hotel."

"Did the consulate confirm his job?"

"He's an insurance consultant all right. Unless the contract they showed me was a fake."

That wouldn't have surprised me, but there was no way of proving it. I walked towards the door. "Keep up the good work, guardian."

"Where are you going?" he demanded.

"To follow up my long shot. Looks like it's our only chance."

*   *   *

I leaned my bicycle against the front of the tourist shop opposite the Finance Directorate and went in.

Davie was behind a curtain. "She's seen my 'ask no questions'," he said, glancing at a middle-aged auxiliary in a tartan plaid behind the counter who was studiously ignoring us. "And I showed it to the guardsman in the checkpoint." He shrugged apologetically. "Had to – I did my auxiliary training with him. Don't worry, he'll keep quiet."

I looked over at the imposing building, formerly the head-quarters of a bank. It stands on a prominence overlooking the gardens and is about as close as you get to architectural opulence in the city nowadays. The Council would claim that they've just left it as it was, but I wouldn't buy that. Money still talks, whatever they say.

"Is he still in there?"

Davie nodded. "Been there all day, apart from when he went for a wander on the Royal Mile at lunchtime. He didn't meet anyone."

"Or hand over anything?"

"I don't think so. It was pretty crowded. I suppose he could have slipped a note to someone. There were a lot of foreigners around."

"How many of them were Greeks, I wonder?" I frowned at him. "Next time stay as close as you can to him."

"Easier said than done. The High Street's like a wheelchair track. Have you noticed how many of them there are these days?"

"Yeah, it's . . . hang on . . . here we go."

Billy Geddes had appeared outside the Finance Directorate. He stopped and exchanged a few words with the guardsman at the entrance.

"I'll take him now," I said, jamming my woollen hat over my ears and wrapping a scarf round the lower part of my face.

"I thought you might have dressed in drag," Davie said with a grin.

"Not on my bike. That would be a bit of a giveaway."

Billy's Toyota was driven up by a porter. He got in and moved off down the Mound, followed by a Supply Directorate lorry that was pumping out clouds of fumes. I took a deep breath and dived into the smog. There was no getting away from it. Billy Geddes was a lucky bastard to have his own car and I was jealous as hell.

Not that I was going to let that prejudice my handling of the investigation.

Either Billy wasn't really a bad boy or he was being very careful. He went straight back to his flat and stayed there. I took cover in the bushes lining the lower edge of Queen Street Gardens. Twice I was approached by track-suited auxiliaries. They backed off when they saw my "ask no questions". Twilight deepened and the lights from Billy's high windows shone out over the street. I caught a glimpse of him moving past, a mobile phone to his ear. There was no way of finding out who he was talking to.

Later the lights were dimmed, though not extinguished completely. I was shivering in the gloom, trying to convince myself that I wasn't wasting my time. Even the unchanged sheets and coarse blankets on my bed began to tempt me. I forced myself to concentrate on the elegant Georgian façade across the road. Nearby was number 17, where Robert Louis Stevenson lived as a boy. Perhaps he had the first intimations of Dr Jekyll here when the mist was swirling around, swallowing the drumming of horses' hooves from passing carriages. The doctor and his sinister doppelganger seemed very close. Then I thought of the Ear, Nose and Throat Man's hulking figure, a knife glinting in each hand, and felt a tingling in the stump of my finger.

I was so caught up that I hardly heard the dull click of the door closing behind Billy. I looked over in time to see his small figure move quickly down the steps and along the street. There was no sound from his feet – he must have put on a pair of well-worn shoes – and that made me wonder what he was up to. I stepped away from the bushes and ran along the grass by the all-weather track, hoping he'd think I was a jogger. It was too late to vault the fence. I'd have to wait till Billy was off Heriot Row and use the nearest gate. The question was, where was he heading?

When he got to India Street, he turned and walked downhill rapidly. I sprinted to the gate then froze as I saw Billy stop and look round. Fortunately I was obscured. He carried on. Then disappeared.

My heart skipped a couple of beats. I went down India Street cautiously, looking at all the basement flats and the steps down to them. Nothing. Then it came to me. I'd forgotten about the narrow entrance to Jamaica Street. There was a bar patronised by senior auxiliaries further down. The lights were low, curtains covering most of the window space. A buzz of voices was audible despite the heavy door. Billy must have gone for a pint. I got my breathing back to normal and wedged myself behind a large rubbish container to see if he came out with anyone interesting. If I'd been spotted by a resident, the guard would be along any minute. They weren't.

Half an hour later I heard high-heeled footsteps coming from the darkness beyond the bar and swore under my breath. My geography was all screwed up. Jamaica Street looked like a cul-de-sac, but there were actually a couple of lanes leading on from it. They were unlit by streetlamps. Billy could have met someone there or kept going and shaken off a tail as incompetent as me. The footsteps came closer. I crouched motionless, wondering if they were a woman's or a transvestite's. As they passed, I looked out and got a clear view of the straight body and unmistakable chest of Simpson 134 from the infirmary. Except instead of a nurse's uniform, she was dressed up in a flashy wool coat, black stockings and shoes that didn't come from the Supply Directorate. She was also carrying the briefcase I'd seen her with outside Patsy's office. She turned the corner and vanished.

Jigsaw pieces began to come together in my mind. She must have been Billy's contact, the one who told him when I left the infirmary. But what was she doing meeting him in a pitch-black backstreet?

A faint noise came from the lane. Billy turned the corner and pulled open the bar door, to be greeted by raised voices.

After a few minutes, I decided to leave him to it and set off home. My long shot had hit an interesting target but I couldn't say I was much further on. None of what I'd seen was worth reporting to the Council. To confront them I needed evidence and that was in shorter supply than Danish bacon in the city's foodstores.

As I crossed Heriot Row I had another thought. I'd completely forgotten to make the Sunday visit to my father. There was definitely something wrong with my memory.

Chapter Thirteen

When Davie arrived at six the next morning I was already working on the lists Hamilton had sent over.

"What's all that?" he asked.

"Auxiliaries who were involved in the fire and the rescue."

"Have you found me there?"

"Don't worry, you're not a suspect." I glanced at the faded labourers' fatigues he'd dressed himself up in. "Your feet aren't the right size."

"What a relief."

I threw down my pencil. "This is a waste of time. There were hundreds of your lot at the Indie. Even if the killer is an auxiliary, he could have been off duty on Thursday evening and gone to the hotel earlier."

"To start the fire, you mean? What did the fire chief's report say about arson?"

"He's still investigating, but there's a good chance it was started deliberately. The heat around the kitchens was so intense that there's not much evidence."

Davie scratched what remained of his beard. "You know what I think? If he was dressed as a t-v, he already had the freedom of the hotel. So he didn't need a distraction."

I looked up at him. "What are you getting at?"

He shrugged. "Maybe he set the fire just to show us what he can do."

I shivered and pulled the blanket tighter around my shoulders. "Bloody hell, Davie, that's an idea which makes me look forward to the rest of my life." It was also one with a definite ring of truth. I told him about Billy Geddes and the nursing auxiliary.

"Why don't you take her in and interrogate her?" he asked.

I shook my head. "That would make Billy run for cover. Anyway, he'd just say he was giving her a knee-trembler against the wall."

"Very likely. That woman would crush all his ribs."

I laughed. "I'm going to ask Hamilton to put a guard on her. We can say it's for her safety. Then at least we'll know where she is all the time."

"You want me to stay on Heriot 07?"

"Yes. Hide yourself in the bushes opposite his flat till he comes out then tail him."

He looked unusually anxious.

"What's the problem? You've got your 'ask no questions'."

"It's not that." His cheeks reddened. "I've got something I have to do in the castle."

"Something to do with that redhead in the guardian's office, guardsman?"

"You could say that."

"I'll try to spare you later on." I looked at my watch. "Let's get going. I want to see my father before the fun starts." I knew Hector would be unimpressed that a mere double murder investigation had stopped me visiting. Besides, I had something to tell him.

The door on the top floor was half open. I looked in and saw the old man bent over his desk. I could hear the rasp of the fountain pen he always used. It was a mystery where he found the ink for it – the city's stationery shops provide only pencils and cheap ballpoints. He didn't look up when I went in. I took in his worn cardigan and the loose skin on his neck. His characteristic wheeze came regularly, like the revolutions of a decrepit but still serviceable pump.

"Hello, old man."

Hector sat up and swung round with surprising speed. "Ah, there you are, failure." He gave me a smile that was both ironic and welcoming. "Let me finish this page."

I went over to the window and looked out over the waves that were dancing away in the sunlight. My father had started writing again.

"I saw her last week," I said when I heard his pen stop.

He put the cap on the pen and laid it carefully on the desk. "The standard view of Juvenal is that he hated women." He put his hand on a pile of books, all containing slips of paper covered with minuscule notes. "That's what the experts say." He got to his feet, hands spread on the desk for support. "What I say is bollocks to that. The old bugger was so obsessed with women that he spent all his time abusing them and . . ."

"I said, I saw Mother."

Hector turned to me, his eyes wide. "I'm not deaf," he shouted. Then he asked more quietly, "Why do you think I'm spending my dotage trying to make sense of this Roman misogynist? There must be more to life than despising women." He lowered his head. "Or in my case, one particular woman."

I moved closer. "She looks terrible. The lupus is much worse."

"And what the hell can I do about that?" he demanded, clutching at my arm as I went to close the door. "Did you come down here just to tell me her condition's worse? Surely she's not asking for my sympathy?" He suddenly looked his age.

I led him to the sofa. "You know Mother. Sympathy's not something she's ever needed." I kept my hand on his fore-arm.

"Are they looking after her properly?"

"I think so. Apparently the medical guardian's treating her himself."

"Is he?" My father looked at me curiously. "But even the great Robert Yellowlees hasn't found a cure yet?"

I shook my head, remembering that the old man was one of the few people in the city with a poor opinion of the medical guardian. He thought his loyalty to the Enlightenment took second place to his research interests.

"He's working on a new approach, Mother said."

Hector twitched his head impatiently. "And what about your investigation? Did your killer have something to do with the fire at the hotel?"

"I think so." I gave him a downbeat report, keeping Billy Geddes out of it. That didn't escape him.

"What about your friend in the Finance Directorate? Did you find anything more out about his activities?"

"Sort of," I answered, remembering too late how much he loathed vagueness.

"What the hell does that mean?" he raged. "You went to university, didn't you? Express yourself properly."

"Sorry," I replied lamely. At least Hector was back to his normal self. "What I meant was that I've discovered things, but I can't link any of them to the murders." I glanced at my father, who was studying me through his battered spectacles. "I'm sure there is a connection though."

He smiled broadly. "At least there's one thing you're sure of." He got up and moved purposefully towards his desk. "You'll work it out," he said, picking up his pen. "You always did." His face clouded. "Until Caro was . . ."

"I thought we agreed we wouldn't talk about her again."

He raised his hands placatingly. "Mea culpa, Quintilian." He frowned. "It's just that the city has needed you these past five years. You might have stopped things going the way they have."

I walked to the door. "I'm an investigator, not a political philosopher."

"What's the difference?"

"I'll see you next Sunday."

"She's much worse, you say?" Hector's voice was almost inaudible.

I nodded then turned away. Before I reached the stair, I heard the scratch of his pen start up again.

"Hume 253, advise your location," I said into the mouthpiece of my mobile, using Davie's barracks number because of the severe guardsman in the driver's seat.

"My location?" Davie demanded. "Up to my knees in the hole you told me to dig."

"Subject's still in his hutch then?"

"Correct. Maybe he thinks he can have the day off after working on Sunday. When are you coming to relieve me?"

"As soon as I pick up the relevant vehicle."

Davie grunted. "Try and get here before I strike oil."

"A piece of advice. If you want to avoid blisters, keep spitting on your hands."

The driver gave me a sidelong glance.

"Now you tell me," moaned Davie despairingly.

The fat commander of the drivers' mess peered at the ancient

Ford Transit like an ornithologist who's just spotted a dodo in his back garden. "We can't give him that," he said.

All around us mechanics in heavily stained overalls were tinkering with vehicles ranging from ten-year-old taxis bought on the cheap from Slovakia to minibuses with more rust on them than the German High Seas Fleet in Scapa Flow.

Anderson touched the crack that ran down the centre of the windscreen and laughed. "It'll be fine." Although it was hot in the garage behind the drivers' mess, he was still wearing his leather jacket. "It hasn't been used for a few years, mind." He leaned into the cab. "Only 148,000 on the clock. You'll not be planning on doing too many more, will you?"

"I shouldn't think so." I looked at the Parks Department stickers that had been fixed to the doors. "Where is there to go?" I sat behind the wheel.

"Citizen Dalrymple," the auxiliary said, "you do have a driving licence, don't you?"

"Of course," I replied, trying to remember how the controls worked. "I took my test when I was seventeen."

"Could I see it?" the fat man asked officiously.

I turned the key. To my surprise the engine fired immediately. I closed the door. "You'll just have to take my word for it." I stirred the gear lever and produced a grating cacophony.

Anderson jumped in from the other side and found first for me. "Just out of interest, when was the last time you drove?"

I lifted my foot cautiously from the clutch pedal. "Six or seven years ago, I suppose." I saw the leather jacket exit rapidly. "It's like riding a bike, isn't it?" I shouted after him. "You never forget."

The van juddered its way out of the garage. I wasn't sure if Anderson had wished me good luck or something else that rhymes with it.

I parked fifty yards from Billy Geddes's flat and walked through the gardens towards the pile of earth that was being heaped up by a broad-backed labourer.

"Hit bedrock yet?"

"Hours ago." Davie wiped his forehead with his sleeve.

"Any sign of our man?"

"He's still inside. I saw him through the window a few minutes ago."

"And there's no rear exit, unless he's prepared to shin down a rope." I looked at Davie. Without the heavy beard and guard uniform he was very different. "Christ, you look almost human now."

"Thanks a lot." He tensed. "There he is."

Through the bushes we watched Billy Geddes come down the steps, resplendent in a light blue suit and pink tie. He obviously wasn't bothered about sticking out from the crowd. He glanced up and down Heriot Row, paying no attention to the Transit, then got into his Toyota.

"Time to knock off here," I said.

We ran to the van. I jumped into the driver's seat and started the engine.

"When did you learn to drive?" Davie asked suspiciously.

"Not another one." I accelerated away, narrowly missing a couple of track-suited guardswomen. "I learned before the Enlightenment, if you must know." The lights changed and I had to brake sharply. "Haven't had much practice recently."

"So I see." Davie's knuckles were white.

Fortunately the Toyota stayed in sight. It went round St Andrew Square, turned left on to Princes Street and headed up Waterloo Place, past the former main post office which is now a video game centre for the tourists. Then Billy drove up the road behind the old Royal High School and stopped.

"What's he up to?" I said. "Going for a walk during office hours? What kind of example is that to set?" I parked on the pavement and climbed over my seat into the back of the van. "Keep an eye on which way he's going."

Davie got out and watched the short figure start off up Calton Hill.

When I was ready, I opened the back door and walked over to Davie. "Hello, big boy."

"Christ, Quint, is that you?"

It looked like my disguise worked.

"Do you get a kick out of wearing women's clothing?"

"Not really. I'm just trying to get an insight into the transvestite mentality."

Davie didn't look convinced. I'd put on the uniform of a certain kind of female American tourist: mauve slacks tight over the arse and baggy everywhere else, crinkly showerproof jacket, sneakers, baseball cap pulled low, shoulder bag and camera. The yellow bouffant wig I'd ordered from the Theatrical Productions Department was set off by an excess of rouge and glistening purple lipstick.

"Do you think I'll get picked up?"

Davie stifled laughter. "No danger of that. Does the camera work?"

"You better believe it, lover boy. One of the directorate's finest." I set off up the hill. "I've taken my mobile, but don't call me in case he hears it."

Over my shoulder I heard Davie muttering, "Madam, there is no way I'll be calling you."

Billy was standing by one of the National Monument's ten columns. The tableau in front of me was loaded with symbolism. There was the city's financial genius dressed up in non-regulation clothes silhouetted against the tourist-ridden, soulless state he'd helped create. Not that Billy was the only long-standing member of the Enlightenment on the hill at that moment. Despite my demotion, I'd never actually handed in my party card.

A group of Filipinos came past, chattering and taking photographs of the sights their guide pointed out. The clicking of their cameras reminded me that I should be capturing Billy on film. I wondered what he was doing up here. One thing was certain – he wasn't simply taking the air. Even at school he never had any time for activities that didn't provide some tangible benefit.

Time dragged by and I began to feel conspicuous. Amateur theatricals are all very well in the local church hall, but you've got to be a hardened female impersonator to hang around on a windswept hilltop.

Then Billy moved away from the pseudo Parthenon towards the Nelson Monument. There was a rattle and a thud as the time ball dropped from the top of the inelegant Gothic tower, provoking a round of applause from the Filipinos. I took up position behind the column where Billy had been standing and checked my watch. By the time I looked up again, he'd met someone I knew.

It was Palamas, the Greek diplomat with the moustache Nietzsche in his moments of sanity would have been proud of. He was wearing the same herringbone coat and carrying a black leather briefcase. I raised the camera and shot the pair of them repeatedly before they went into the Nelson Monument and disappeared.

I called Davie. "He's made contact – with a guy from the Greek consulate."

"What are they doing?"

"They're up the tower. I'll wait for them here then tail the Greek. You take our man. Out."

I fancied trying to eavesdrop on their conversation, but I wasn't confident enough of how I looked to risk meeting Billy in the narrow confines of the building. After half an hour he reappeared, carrying the briefcase, and headed down the hill towards his car. As he passed me, he didn't even turn his head.

Five minutes went by before the Greek came out. This time I had a narrow escape. He gave me a long glance and seemed to be weighing up making a move on me. He must have been short-sighted. Either that or his taste in sexual partners was a matter for serious concern. Then he saw the error of his ways and stalked off to the consulate.

I went back to my flat to change. That was enough of life from the other side of the great sexual divide.

Davie called not long after I got home.

"Subject returned to his place with the briefcase, then came out empty-handed and went to the Finance Directorate."

"Care to hazard a guess at the contents of the case?"

Davie grunted. "Why don't we search the flat and take him in?"

"And do him for accepting bribes?" I thought about it for a moment. As well as all this, I was pretty sure Billy was behind the authorisations Sarah Spence had to leave her barracks after midnight. But he'd have made sure all reference to them in Finance Directorate records had been expunged. I shook my head. "We've nothing that'll get us any nearer to catching the murderer yet."

"Listen, Quint, there's something I want to do. Can you take over in Bank Street for a bit?" His voice was suddenly breathless.

"The redhead?"

"Aye."

"All right. I'll give you an hour."

"As long as that?" He didn't sound too disappointed.

I hadn't been behind the curtain in the tourist shop opposite

Billy's office for more than twenty minutes when Davie burst back in. He had a large brown envelope in his hands and the wide-eyed look of a man who's just struck very lucky in the draw for the weekly sex session.

"That good?" I asked.

He ran over to the counter and pulled the female auxiliary out. "Early closing," he said firmly.

She was out in a flash.

"What is it?" Now he was pulling me to the counter, having locked the shop door.

"Look what I've got hold of." He pulled a buff folder out of the envelope. On it was embossed the city's heart emblem. The words "Guardians' Eyes Only" were stamped in large black letters above and below it. Considering the fact that possession of this file constituted guaranteed grounds for demotion, Davie was looking very pleased with himself. I didn't think I'd had that much of an influence on him.

"You realise the risk you're . . ." I stopped when I saw the file's title. "'Citizens Reported Missing as of 1.1.2020'. Bloody hell. Let's have a look."

There was a thick wad of City Guard Missing Persons forms. What grabbed my attention was the cover sheet. Forty-eight people, twenty-eight female and twenty male citizens, had gone AWOL in the last three months. All of them were under twenty-six years old. Underneath the front page was a list of the names. I felt my heart race. One of them was Katharine Kirkwood's brother Adam. There were six others that clients had asked me to find.

"Do I get a coconut?" Davie asked with a grin.

"If Hamilton finds out you took this, you'll get a whole lorry-load of them dumped on you. The redhead?"

"She made sure she was out of the office long enough for me to have a look at the guardian's personal files. This one was on top. I saw Adam Kirkwood's name and thought you'd go for it."

"But why didn't you tell me what you were up to?"

He shrugged and looked awakward. "Well, you know, I wanted to show you I could do something on my own initiative."

I laughed. "Christ, Davie. Not even I would have gone through Hamilton's confidential files."

He chewed his lip, as if the significance had finally struck him. I had plenty more bad news for him.

"Well done, pal. But I haven't got a clue how this fits in to the rest of what we're investigating. If it fits in at all."

"All these people missing while there's a psycho on the loose? Course it fits in." He was looking pleased with himself again.

"Maybe. But there's another problem we have to solve first."

"Hit me. I can handle anything."

"Uh-huh. After you've copied the file, you'll have to figure out a way to get it back without anyone noticing."

He wasn't beaten. "Good enough. I thought you might be going to walk into the chief's office with this in your hand."

I shook my head. "No chance. For the time being this is our little secret, guardsman."

The Council meeting that evening was a bit difficult. I got my head in my hands for not being available throughout the day. I got my own back by telling them exactly what I thought about the fact I hadn't been allowed to question Roussos in the infirmary. Hamilton looked embarrassed about that. So much so that he forgot to mention that I was working on a long shot. Just as well.

I went back to my place after the meeting, having arranged to relieve Davie outside Billy's at midnight. I sat outside in the Transit trying to work out what to do about the missing young people. I knew one thing for sure. There were far too many for them just to be deserters – and the fact that the Council had a file on them meant that they weren't in the mines or on the farms. Christ, I'd even noticed an increase in my own workload before the killings started, but I'd forgotten all about it till now. Davie had remedied that. But what about Adam Kirkwood? What was I going to tell Katharine?

Then I saw her come round the corner. She had on a skirt that stopped about six inches above the knee. I noticed that because she was wearing red stockings and high heels that made her legs as striking as a smiling face in a philosophy seminar. I watched as she drew nearer. In the gloom she didn't see me. She went in the street door.

I didn't get out straight away because I was still wondering whether to say anything about her brother. Then I chickened out, decided to keep my mouth shut and followed her in. Her scent lingered in the musty air. By the time I reached the third floor, she was on her way down. Her legs looked even more stunning from that angle. There was the hint of a smile at the corners of her mouth. We stood looking at each other.

"I thought I'd missed you."

"You were lucky."

"I should say so." She gave a light, mocking laugh then turned back up again.

"What a surprise," I said, my eyes fixed on the back of her thighs.

She didn't answer, waiting for me to open the door. Then she walked in and dropped her jacket on the end of the sofa. The white blouse she was wearing was almost transparent. I could see the points of her breasts. She caught me staring.

"I'll have a drink," she said coolly. "Before we get down to business."

I poured whisky into a glass, wondering what she was after. I knew very well what I was after.

"Thanks." She raised the glass. "Are you not having one?"

I sat down in the armchair opposite her and shook my head. "I've got to work later on."

"He works nights too," she said with a smile. "The dedication." She put the glass to her lips and touched the rim with her tongue, unwavering eyes locked on me.

I suddenly felt breathless, like an astronaut, in the old days before space travel became too expensive, whose safety line has broken. "What is it you want, Katharine?" I asked weakly.

"What is it I want?" she asked, taking a sip of whisky. "I'd have thought that was obvious." She opened her mouth, the tip of her tongue glistening as it protruded for a second. "I want you." Then she moved over, stood in front of me and lifted her skirt up. She was wearing the full tart's get-up, suspender belt and knickers matching her stockings. I hadn't forgotten what I'd read about her in Patsy's file. I just didn't give a damn.

"Kath . . ." I began, then lost the power of speech as she straddled me, knees against my abdomen.

She knew exactly what she was doing. Lowered a hand to the bulge in my groin and squeezed, leaning back as I ran my hands down her buttocks. I slid my fingers under the elastic of her knickers and pressed them forward. To my surprise I found she was wet.

"Come on," she whispered, "I want you now." She unfastened my belt, unzipped me and touched my cock. Before I could move she rolled a condom over me with practised skill. And pushed down, directing me into her. My hands were on her breasts, which became taut as she leaned back again. I felt the dark brown nipples harden even more. Looking at her face, I saw that she had her eyes closed. I kept mine open.

As in all the best erotica, we came together. At least it seemed that way to me. When I spurted, she shuddered then slumped over me, her breath warm in my ear and the scent of her in my nostrils. I floated off into deepest space.

But she wouldn't let me go. Clenched well-exercised muscles and held me inside her.

"Actually," she murmured, "there is one other thing I want."

"To help find Adam?" I gasped, my breathing still all over the place.

"You're way ahead of me," she said, sitting up straight and looking down at me. "Well?"

If she's working with me I'll be able to keep an eye on her, I told myself. It wasn't a difficult decision.

"All right," I said, pushing her off gently. As she stepped back I caught sight of Caro's photograph.

There was the sound of water being splashed around in the toilet. Eventually Katharine emerged, shaking her head.

"You can tell the city's washing facilities were organised by men. Have you any idea how difficult it is for a woman to wash herself in a basin?"

"I suppose you've got used to the bidets in the Indie."

She sat down and looked at me curiously. "What's the matter?"

I turned away, but not before Katharine saw the photo.

"Who is she, Quint?" she asked softly.

It was the tone of her voice that did it. Hoarser than usual, somehow suggesting a capacity to understand that I suddenly needed badly.

So I told her about Caro – about the law lectures we attended together at the university, about her belief in the Enlightenment and about our time in the Public Order Directorate. She didn't interrupt or comment, didn't show how she felt at all. Until I got to the last operations against the drug gangs and stopped. I couldn't go on.

"You have to share it with someone, Quint." Katharine was looking across at me with eyes that had none of their usual steeliness. "You've kept this bottled up for years, haven't you?"

I nodded slowly. "You're the first person I've ever spoken to about Caro's . . . about what happened."

"I've had a lot of experience of confessions."

"Is that what this is?"

"Of course." She smiled to encourage me.

It worked. I found that I could go on. "It was five years back. The leader of the worst gang was holed up with about twenty of his men in a farmhouse on the northern slopes of Soutra."

"Just beyond the city's borders."

"Yes. We bent the rules – it was my decision. Caro was in charge of the scouting group and I was with two other squads to the rear, waiting for her signal." I stopped to get my breath. Usually my heart pounded like a piston engine when I woke up after dreaming about that night, but it was beating normally now. "Then everything went wrong. Their sentries must have spotted Caro's group. They grabbed them before we realised what had happened. We'd had problems with the mobile phones earlier. We didn't react quickly enough."

"These things happen," Katharine said. "It wasn't your fault."

"Then we heard screaming, men's voices, and afterwards a high-pitched shriek that seemed like it would never stop. I didn't recognise it. We went in then. They were waiting for us, they knew exactly how many of us there were. A lot of my people were taken out. Not me, though. I had a charmed life. Ran right through the centre of their line and reached the barn. By the time I got there the screaming had stopped." I had to stop, swallow saliva. The same thing had happened that night too.

"I was on my own. The guard were still fighting their way through the outer defences. The bastards had fortified the place. And all I had was my service knife. My pistol had jammed on the way in."

Katharine moved round the table and sat on the arm of my chair. She didn't touch me.

"There was nothing else for it. I burst in the door and headed for the light in the centre of the barn. I had to jump over the bodies of a couple of guardsmen from Caro's group. There were four men in a huddle round the hurricane lamp. When they heard me, they broke up and . . . and I saw her." I looked round at Katharine. "I thought she was all right at first. Except . . . except her foot was jerking crazily. Then I saw the blood round her mouth."

Now Katharine put her hand on mine for a few seconds. It was cool, absorbed some of the heat.

"I put my arm under her shoulders and tried to find a pulse. I was too late. She'd been strangled. I put my fingers into her mouth to try to clear her throat. She'd . . ." I turned to Katharine again, suddenly not wanting to spare her anything. "She'd bitten through her tongue. It came out on my fingers. Like a little fish."

Katharine gripped my hand hard. "Oh my God."

"Then I was hit over the back of the head. I came round in the infirmary." I pulled my hand away and slumped back in the chair. I was totally drained.

She was silent for a time, then nodded at my right hand. "You got that injury then?"

"Soon afterwards." I wasn't going to tell her about the Ear, Nose and Throat Man, about how I'd seen him break away from the group first, a length of rope dangling from one hand. I had to keep something secret. For Caro.

Katharine got up and moved over to the sofa. "You've never forgotten her, have you, Quint? But you have to. It's finished."

"You want me to let myself become a soulless robot like everyone else in Edinburgh?"

She shook her head slowly. "No. You just have to stop caring so much."

"Like you stopped caring for that dissident – what was his name?" I remembered it perfectly well, but I wanted to shake her.

"Alex." She looked at me without animosity. "I think I've got over him. He's out of the Council's reach now."

I envied him. For all my pathetic attempts at independence, the Council still had its claws deep into me.

Chapter Fourteen

The buzz of the mobile phone woke me. I fell out of the chair and crawled over to my jacket.

"What the hell's happened to you?" asked Davie in a caustic whisper.

"Good question," I replied. "What time is it?" I fumbled for matches and lit a candle. Katharine was asleep on the sofa.

"You took my watch, didn't you?"

"Christ, half one. Sorry, Davie. I'll be down right away. Out."

Katharine stirred, then sat up and stretched her arms. "Going to work? I'll come with you?" There was no trace of sleep in her voice.

I nodded. An extra pair of eyes would be useful during the surveillance. She was pulling on her short skirt.

"You're not exactly dressed for what we're going to do. I'll see if I can find you something warmer." The first clothes I came across in my bedroom were the American tourist outfit. I didn't bother giving her the wig.

On the way downstairs I made the decision. "There's something I have to tell you about Adam."

She pushed me up against the wall, almost knocking the candle from my hand. "You bastard," she hissed. "You've waited all this time?"

I put my hand between her breasts and shoved her backwards. "Calm down, Katharine. It isn't bad news." I shrugged. "It isn't really any kind of news."

"What the fuck are you trying to say?"

"Look, this is seriously classified. If the Council finds out we know this, we'll both be in Cramond Island before you can blink."

"If you don't tell me right now, you'll be in intensive care before you can blink."

"All right." I led her down the stairs and out into the street. There was a moon so we managed to get to the Transit even though the candle was immediately blown out. "The guard did register Adam as missing."

"I know that, for Christ's sake. I more or less filled the form in for them. The problem is they haven't done anything about finding him."

"I think they tried." I opened the door and let her in. "He's not the only one though. Forty-seven other people have gone missing in the last three months. The weird thing is, they're all under twenty-six."

Her face was yellow in the dull light from the dashboard. "What does it mean?" she asked slowly. "I don't understand."

"Me neither. But it makes you wonder. Forty-eight citizens missing and a killer on the loose." I heard her sharp intake of breath. "Shit, sorry. I didn't mean . . ." I glanced at her. Even in the unflattering clothes she looked striking, her high cheekbones prominent in the glow.

"Where are we going?"

"Heriot Row." I started the engine and drove down to Tollcross. "We're tailing someone." It suddenly occurred to me that Katharine might have seen Billy in the hotel with the Greek. "An auxiliary." I watched her out of the corner of my eye. She didn't react. "Heriot 07. Know him?"

"I know him." She sighed. "He's around the hotel all the time, playing God. He must be on the take." She turned to me, a faint smile on her lips. "I think I'm going to enjoy this."

I knew the feeling. No one likes catching auxiliaries out more than demoted auxiliaries.

When I parked the van at the end of Heriot Row, she was out like a shot. I took the opportunity to make a quick call on the mobile.

The moon was casting long shadows from the bushes in the gardens. We kept to them as we approached Davie's position.

"I've brought reinforcements," I whispered. "Well, one reinforcement."

Davie looked up from his hide and examined Katharine. He didn't make any comment.

"What happened to your beard?" she asked quietly. "I can hardly tell you're an auxiliary."

He shook his head with what looked like disbelief and turned to the front again. "He's inside – fast asleep if he's got any sense. I saw him against the bedroom light not long before he switched it off." He looked down at his notebook. "At twelve eleven." He stood up and stretched his legs. "I'll be back at 0800. Good hunting."

Katharine watched him move away stealthily. "I'll take the first watch, if you like." She patted her thigh. "You can put your head here."

I tried not to accept the offer with too much alacrity. "Wake me if you see anyone go in or come out."

"Yes, citizen."

I was only going to doze but I'd forgotten what the road to hell is paved with. Besides, my pillow was unusually soft.

Birdsong started up like a battery of tuneful road-drills. The virtual disappearance of vehicles from Edinburgh's streets has led to a massive increase in the number of birds and that morning it seemed like they were all gathered on the branches directly above me. For a moment I thought the ceiling had been removed from my bedroom. Then I remembered where I was.

My head was resting on a shoulder bag. Sitting up quickly, I caught sight of Katharine. She was watching the windows of Billy's flat, her back against the trunk of a rhododendron.

I looked at my watch. "Bloody hell, six thirty. You should have woken me hours ago."

She turned and smiled. "Good morning to you too." She stretched her arms, wincing as the bandage on her burn moved. "You were sleeping so sweetly that I decided to leave you to it."

"Well, I did have a tiring evening."

"As I remember, you never got off your backside."

I had a look through the binoculars. The curtains were still drawn across Billy's bedroom window. The Toyota was exactly where it had been. "I take it you saw nothing?"

"No one went in or came out."

"Good." I touched her knee. "You should get some rest."

"I'm all right. There'll be plenty of time for rest when this is all finished."

"Don't hold your breath. It might take weeks."

The pounding feet of an early morning jogger came towards us. We both froze and waited for them to pass, but they slowed down. Looking through the foliage, I saw legs in a maroon track suit and auxiliary-issue running shoes. I reached into my pocket for my "ask no questions".

"Raise your hands and come out slowly. You have five seconds to comply."

Katharine licked her lips but remained where she was. The auxiliary came nearer.

"Fuck you, Davie," I said in disgust. "Get down before you're spotted."

He joined us in the small clearing, removing the scarf he'd wrapped round his face. He had a Thermos of coffee and a loaf of barracks bread.

"What are you doing here so early?" I demanded.

"Just out on my morning run." Davie grinned. "I reckoned you'd been in the bushes long enough with this female citizen."

Katharine looked at him sharply. "I thought guardsmen were supposed to be above that kind of innuendo."

"Pardon me," Davie said ironically. "I forgot you were a lady of high moral standing."

"Shut up, you two," I said. "We're supposed to be a team."

"Is that right?" asked Davie. "I'm glad someone told me."

Katharine stood up and glanced around. "I'm going for a pee. Keep some coffee for me."

"What's the matter with you, Davie?" I pulled out my mobile. "I want to keep an eye on her. The killer might have seen her." A thought struck me. "You looked at her file that time I left it in the Land-Rover, didn't you? That's why you're down on her."

"She was a dissident, for Christ's sake." He looked guiltier than a kid who's been caught with his telescope trained on the neighbour's bedroom. "Sorry."

"Forget it." I made a couple of calls.

"What was all that about?" Davie asked when I finished.

"Katharine's in the clear. I put a sentry at each end of the street

164

overnight – just in case she tried to wander off." I kept my eyes lowered.

"What a way to treat a member of the team."

"Thank you, guardsman. Now piss off back to Hume and get changed. There's something else I have to check up on."

When Davie came back, Katharine and I left in a guard vehicle. She didn't seem too bothered when I told the driver to take us to the castle. When we got there, I asked her to wait in Hamilton's outer office. I didn't want her to see the file I needed yet.

The public order guardian's reaction when he saw me was strangely muted. He listened to what I had to say about Katharine with about as much interest as an atheist forced to have dinner with the Pope.

"I suppose you know what you're doing, using a convicted dissident," he said dully. He looked anaemic, his movements sluggish. Remembering the suspicions I had about him, I suddenly felt like an idiot. On the other hand, maybe he was guilty about something. He didn't object when I asked to see Alex Irvine's file.

The first page got me going. He was a big man, six feet two in height, and he took a size eleven boot. That was near enough the murderer's. I ran through the record of his interrogation. Under the strongarm methods of one of Hamilton's expert headbangers, Irvine had admitted killing three auxiliaries, one with a knife and two with a length of rope. Better and better. My suspicion that he'd somehow escaped the execution squad and come back to take his revenge against the city was getting out of hand. Then I came to the death certificate. There was a close-up photograph of a face with the entry wounds from three bullets. But I had to be sure.

I went to the outer office. "Katharine, come in for a minute, will you?" I tried to keep my voice level. I was not having a good time.

She looked briefly at the guardian, her face impassive. Then looked even more briefly at the photo I showed her. And closed her eyes once, long enough for me to make out moistness at the corners.

"It is Alex Irvine, isn't it?" I prompted, touching her arm.

She pulled away like I was a leper. "I suppose you're going to tell me you had to be sure he was dead." She didn't wait for me to confirm that. "It's Alex," she said as she headed for the door. "The first photo I've ever seen of him."

The phone on Hamilton's desk rang. His expression livened up after a few seconds. "Something strange, Dalrymple," he said, his hand over the receiver. I saw Katharine stop in the doorway. "It's your father. Apparently he's disappeared."

We followed the guardian's Land-Rover down to Trinity. Katharine sat beside me, her face blank. It was almost as if she'd forgotten what I'd done to her in the castle. Or perhaps finding her brother was all that mattered and I was her best option on that score.

The resident nurse in the retirement home was convinced that Hector had wandered off with a book to enjoy the spring morning. It wouldn't have been the first time. But regulations required her to report any absentee immediately and as my father was a former guardian, the local barracks commander had informed Hamilton. I was surprised the guardian had come down himself – he never got on with the old man. Then I thought of the top-secret missing persons file. Surely he didn't think Hector had any connection with the forty-eight young people? I suddenly felt uneasy.

I went up to the third floor. Hector's room looked the same as it had the day before, apart from his desk. The books on Juvenal that he was working on had all been tidied away. The bed was as neatly made as ever. My father insisted on making it himself. He'd always been an early riser and he might have let himself out before the main door was unbolted. But someone would have seen him.

The nurse, Simpson 172, shook her head impatiently when I asked her. "No, I've already checked with all the residents. And the door was bolted too."

"How about the back door?"

"That too."

"And all the windows were locked?"

"Of course."

I lost my patience with the woman. She was the kind of lazy and unimaginative auxiliary that somehow slips through the selection net. "That only leaves one possibility, then," I said, giving her a rancid smile. "Unless you do conjuring tricks in your spare time."

"That'll do, Dalrymple," Hamilton said from behind me. "What is this possibility you're talking about?"

"It's obvious. Somebody let my father out, then bolted the door after him."

It didn't take me long to find the guilty party. The only resident Hector spent any time with was an old guy called Joe Bell. He was in the lounge, playing dominoes. He got up when he saw me and came over, his back bent from years working on the roads.

"Hello, son. I was wondering when you'd turn up." His rheumy eyes opened wide as Hamilton came over.

"It's all right," I said. "Come into the office."

The nurse was sitting stiff-necked at her desk. She stood up when she saw the guardian, then cast a disapproving eye over Joe Bell and Katharine.

"Joe, you can tell us what you know," I said, nodding at him. "We have to be sure that Hector's disappearing hasn't got anything to do with the killer we're looking for."

"Jesus Christ," the old man said.

"What kind of language is that, citizen?"

"Do you mind?" I asked acidly. I remembered my father saying that Simpson 172 was called Florence Nightingale behind her back.

Joe Bell smiled at the nurse's affronted look. "Well, I suppose it's all right. Hector wouldnae mind me telling you, son . . ." He paused, licking his chapped lips.

"Well, go on then, man," said the guardian impatiently.

Joe Bell looked at me and raised an eyebrow.

I got the message. "Is there anything you'd like in return for this information?" I asked with a grin.

Hamilton looked like he was about to do an impression of Mussolini with a hangover. I waved a finger at him.

"Well . . ." Joe pointed shakily at the nurse. "She doesn't give us our whisky ration. Says it's bad for us . . ."

"Which it is," the auxiliary said primly. "I always have to clean up afterwards."

"Perhaps you could make an exception today," I said. It wasn't a request.

Simpson 172 pursed her lips then nodded.

"Thanks very much, son," said citizen Bell, his face a picture of bliss an icon painter would have been canonised for.

"So you let Hector out and closed up after him this morning?"

"Aye."

"He didn't say where he was going?"

Joe shook his head, then glanced at the guardian. "Just before I shut the door I looked out. I saw a vehicle at the end of the road. Hector seemed to be going to it."

"What kind of vehicle?" Hamilton asked.

Joe found the question very amusing. He laughed until he began to choke. "What kind?" he repeated. "It was one of your lot's. It was a bloody guard Land-Rover."

Considering Hector's feeling about the guard, I couldn't see him asking for a lift.

"Did you see him get in?" the guardian demanded.

Joe shook his head. "Florence here finally woke up and started down the stairs. I had to close the door sharpish."

"It's a pity you didn't come on duty when you should have," Hamilton said scathingly to the nurse.

"Will you check if there were any patrols around here at that time?" I asked him.

He nodded. "I've already circulated an instruction to all barracks to look out for your father."

My mobile buzzed. I turned away.

"There's movement here," Davie said. "Subject's coming out. I'm off to the van. Out."

Hamilton was curious. "What's going on?"

"I'll keep you posted." I beckoned to Katharine and we moved off.

"Dalrymple," the guardian called. "I'm sorry about all this. We'll find Hector."

I was surprised by how sincere he sounded.

A middle-aged female auxiliary with sad eyes drove us down Inverleith Row.

"So, another one goes missing," Katharine said. "I can't see what your father's got to do with the murders. Or with Adam."

"Join the club." I shook my head, unwilling to talk in front of the driver. Then my mobile rang again. It was one of my mother's assistants requiring my presence immediately at Moray Place.

"Shit," I said under my breath, then redirected the driver. "You'll have to contact Davie and find out where he's heading," I said to Katharine. "I can't get out of this."

She nodded and reached for the Land-Rover's mobile.

"Aren't you exhausted?" I asked. "You hardly slept."

"I'm fine." She smiled bitterly. "I'm used to all-night performances."

I couldn't think of an answer to that. At the Darnaway Street barrier I jumped down.

"I'll catch up with you as soon as I can." In the second it took the auxiliary to engage first gear, I looked at Katharine. I was letting her loose on the investigation without any supervision. When she'd gone, I put in a call to make sure Davie kept an eye on her, but his mobile was engaged.

They were on their own.

"Mother, what's happened to you?" I stood on the landing outside her study and stared.

She walked towards me with no awkwardness, the pain apparently gone from her joints. "I feel twenty years younger," she said, her voice strong and unwavering.

I walked around her. She allowed me to examine her, an almost coquettish smile on her lips. Although her hair was still devastated, her face was no longer so moon-shaped and her skin had fewer blemishes. She led me into the room, stepping out like a model on a catwalk. The sudden change in her character was about as likely as the existence of teetotallers in the House of Commons before independence.

"You remember I told you that the medical guardian was working on a new approach?" my mother said. "This is the result."

"He's actually found a cure for the lupus?"

She raised her hand, more to restrain her own excitement rather than mine. "Not yet. But this treatment substantially neutralises the effects of the disease." Her face was glowing. "I'll be able to go on working for years."

I frowned at her. "You know Hector's disappeared, don't you?"

She nodded, avoiding my eyes. "The public order guardian has informed me. It's hardly the first time."

I considered bringing up the forty-eight missing young people but decided against it. She would insist on knowing how I'd found out. "It's the first time when there's a murderer at large."

"Do you really imagine the killer has any interest in your father,

Quintilian?" She ran her fingers slowly down her cheeks as if to ensure the smoother surface really belonged to her.

"You don't care, do you?" I leaned over her desk. "Why should you? After all, it's years since you've seen him."

Her eyes flared and she opened her mouth like she was going to argue about that. Then she looked away. "Stop it," she said softly. "This is of no benefit to either of us."

"No benefit!" I shouted. "You always think about who benefits, Mother. Christ, this isn't a philosophy tutorial. Aren't you even slightly concerned?"

She moved over to the fireplace, her eyes fixed on the marble fluting. "What I feel, Quintilian, is no business of yours." She gazed at me sternly. "What's important is that you find the murderer. You are not to allow your father's disappearance to distract you."

As usual when I'm told to do something, my inclination was to do the opposite. But in this case I couldn't fault my mother's reasoning. Her lack of feeling for Hector was nothing new. I turned to go.

"One other matter," she said. "Heriot 07."

I stopped in my tracks. Surely she couldn't have discovered we were tailing Billy Geddes.

"Have you seen him recently?" Her tone was neutral.

"Yes, I have." I watched her carefully. "Why the interest?"

Her expression gave nothing away. "As I'm sure you know, he has been allowed to handle certain activities with a free hand."

I wasn't sure if I was really hearing this. My mother in league with the city's chief fixer? "I know he parades around like a semi-reformed drug gang boss."

"Don't be ridiculous," she said sharply. "He has been permitted certain privileges, but he's worth them. Without the income he provides, the city would be insolvent."

"He's on the take, Mother."

"Rubbish. We tolerate his car and his clothes, that's all."

I looked at the Renoir and shook my head. "I don't think it stops there."

She looked at me without twitching a muscle. "Then find out and report. To me, though – not the Council."

I headed for the door.

"And Quintilian?" She waited for me to look back. "Be careful.

Heriot 07 has some powerful friends." She turned to gaze into the mirror above the fire.

I went down the stairs slowly, trying to work out exactly why the senior guardian had called me to Moray Place.

I called Davie on the mobile as soon as I got outside. It seemed Billy Geddes had just walked into the former Royal Scottish Museum in Chambers Street. Whatever he was after, I was bloody sure it wasn't culture.

Chapter Fifteen

I got the guardsman who answered my call to drop me where the Transit was parked at the corner of George IVth Bridge and Chambers Street. Through the window I saw Davie slumped forward over the steering wheel. He was so still that for a few panic-stricken seconds I thought something had happened to him. When I pulled the door open, he stirred.

"Wakey fucking wakey, Davie. God, you gave me a shock. It looked like you were murder victim number three."

"Sorry." He rubbed his eyes. "Not enough sleep recently."

"I know the feeling. Where's Billy?"

"Still in the museum. Katharine's on him." He punched me lightly on the chest. "Hey, she told me about your father. Don't worry, he'll turn up."

"That's what everyone's saying." I nodded at him. "Thanks, Davie." I was touched by his concern. "I hope Katharine's keeping her distance."

"She seems to know what she's doing. She made me requisition a scarf and a horrendous tartan jacket from one of the tourist shops. She looks like a mobile carpet."

"Is that right? I'm obviously out of my depth. I'll just go as I am." I pulled my scarf up over my mouth.

"She's got a mobile, by the way. I had one sent down from the castle. Shouldn't she have an 'ask no questions' as well?"

"I wouldn't worry," I said as I got out. "She seems to be getting on fine. Wait for me here. Awake if you can manage it."

"Yes, sir."

I turned into Chambers Street. There were signs on every available wall advertising the exhibits in what's now called the Museum of Edinburgh. As I ran up the broad steps below the main entrance, I remembered going up them countless times with my grandfather – he loved the place.

The buzz of my mobile made me stop.

"Quint, where are you?" Katharine's voice was low.

I told her.

"You'd better get inside. Subject's been giving a man with a dark complexion the eye and I don't think it's because he fancies him. I'm in the natural history hall, under the whale's tail."

I flashed my "ask no questions" at the ticket clerk. The museum was free when my grandfather used to take me but the Council changed that years ago. I went into the east hall where the blue whale's skeleton hangs from the roof arches. Looking around cautiously from behind a pillar, I saw Billy Geddes at the far end. A stocky female in a virulent red and yellow jacket was examining a display case full of monkeys. I strolled over to her.

"Heriot 07 just nodded to the other guy," Katharine whispered. "They're getting closer."

"Stay down here. Billy might recognise me. When they split up, I'll follow the other guy. You stick with Billy." I glanced at the jacket. "Couldn't you find anything a bit less conspicuous?" She must have padded it out with a lorryload of pullovers.

"I like to be centre-stage." She pouted like a vamp who'd turned to fat and moved away, showing interest in a gruesome exhibit about the craft of taxidermy.

I went back into the main hall and ran up the curved staircase to the first floor. From the balcony I could see Billy and his contact clearly. I had the camera in my pocket but I didn't want to risk attracting their attention with the flash. The other man had greasy black hair and was wearing a tan leather jacket that Anderson in the drivers' mess would have killed for. He was younger than both Andreas Roussos and Palamas, the diplomat Billy had met on Calton Hill, but I was pretty sure he was the same nationality. Unfortunately, I couldn't make out his fingernails.

The two of them were carrying on an animated conversation, oblivious to Katharine who was about twenty yards away. Then Billy looked around. I felt my stomach turn over and tried to disappear behind a supporting column. Billy caught sight of the skinned otter in the taxidermy display and wrinkled his nose in disgust. His contact tapped him on the chest impatiently and Billy produced an envelope from his pocket. It was secreted in the man's jacket before I could blink.

The olive-skinned man turned and walked quickly away. I went down the stairs three at a time, assuming that Billy would be hanging back to let him get clear. By the time I got out of the museum, my man was heading right towards the South Bridge. He seemed to be on the lookout for a cab. I called Davie and told him to pick me up. By the time the Transit arrived, the man had stopped a taxi.

"Follow that cab," I shouted as I jumped in.

"Very funny," Davie growled, accelerating away.

"I've always wanted to say that."

"How sad."

The taxi driver ahead went through the checkpoint at the top of the North Bridge, drove down to Princes Street then turned left.

"Which hotel do you reckon?"

Davie's chin jutted forward. "He looked foreign, right enough. Maybe he's heading for one of the consulates."

"Doubt it. He's hardly dressed like a diplomat."

"True enough. How about the Boswell?"

"Too full of geriatrics for this specimen. I go for the Waverley. Bottle of malt on it?"

"How am I supposed to talk the barracks steward into giving me one of those?"

I grinned. "That's part of the fun."

The taxi slowed down then drew up outside the Waverley. It was built on top of what used to be the railway station.

"Shit," said Davie with a groan. "How long have I got to come up with the whisky?"

"I'm a generous soul." This time I had no problem with using the camera. I fired off several shots of the man as he got out of the cab. Now I'd be able to identify him in the archive. "I'll give you twenty-four hours."

My mobile buzzed before he could express his gratitude.

"Subject just went into the Finance Directorate," Katharine reported.

"Right. I'll pick you up at the gallows. Out."

"What's the plan?" Davie asked.

"Katharine's an expert at getting into hotel rooms. I want to have a look at the contents of the envelope Billy passed to our friend here."

"Oh aye?"

"I'm prepared to make another bet. He knows Andreas Roussos. In fact, it wouldn't surprise me to find out that he was staying at the Indie before it went up in smoke." I looked at Davie. "Any takers?"

There was no reply.

I called for a guard vehicle and left Davie watching the door of the hotel. Katharine didn't seem too concerned when I asked her to go home and change into something a bit more seductive than her carpet. I sent her off in the Land-Rover and went into the castle to get the film developed.

While I was waiting, I went to see Lewis Hamilton. He was sitting at the conference table in his office with several mountain ranges of files in front of him.

"Ah, Dalrymple," the guardian said, looking up blearily. "Any news?"

"Nothing concrete yet. Have you picked up any trace of my father?"

He shook his head, avoiding my eyes. "I put my best auxiliaries in charge of collating the reports from the barracks." He stood up and ran a hand through his hair. "None of them had a patrol vehicle near the retirement home this morning."

"Really?" I frowned at him. "Have they all been checked?"

He nodded. "And all the directorates."

"So where the hell did that Land-Rover come from?"

"Maybe the old citizen was mistaken."

I looked out over the city, wondering where Hector was. If he'd just wandered off, the likelihood was that he'd have been picked up by now.

"You're not thinking the killer's involved, surely?" said Hamilton. "His modus operandi hasn't included kidnapping."

But someone's has, I thought. I considered telling him that I knew about the young men and women who were missing, then rejected the idea. Obviously the Council was suppressing any mention of them. Christ, maybe the guardians themselves were all involved in some massive scam. Letting Hamilton know that I'd seen the file might be a good way to end up dressed in eighteenth-century costume on the gallows.

"Look, I'm not going to be at the Council meeting this evening," I said. I saw his eyebrows shoot up. "You can handle the daily report, can't you? After all, there isn't exactly a lot to tell your colleagues." I picked up a file from the table. "What are you doing?"

He shrugged, looking sheepish. "Trying to compile a list of auxiliaries who had Thursday nights off duty and also attended the fire."

I'm sure he was expecting me to comment on the fact that he was even considering the possibility of an auxiliary being linked with the killings, but I couldn't be bothered. Besides, he was carrying out a piece of drudgery that I'd started doing myself but had given up on the grounds that anyone clever enough to commit the murders was capable of covering his tracks by swapping shifts.

"Keep up the good work," I said, unable to resist a dig.

He didn't pick it up. "Dalrymple," he said as I reached the door, "I never wanted Hector to leave the Council, you know. Only . . . priorities changed. The real world was harder than we'd imagined."

The tyrant's excuse through history. I remembered that he and my mother had vetoed the anti-corruption safeguard. You could say they were responsible for all that had happened recently. The question was, how directly?

Katharine looked at me unflinchingly after I sent Davie off to keep an eye on Billy Geddes. We were in the back of the Transit, lit by the streetlamps on Princes Street.

"Let me get this straight," she said. "You want me to pick up Heriot 07's contact and locate the envelope?" Her eyes glinted and stayed on me.

"You can handle that, can't you?"

"And exactly how far do you want me to go?"

I looked out at the hotel, then at my knees. "As far as you have to. This is our best lead."

"All right."

I felt her gaze suddenly move off me. She stood up and undid the buttons of her coat, then lifted her short skirt and smoothed the top of her black stockings. I knew very well that the show was for my benefit. She wanted me to be aware of the potential consequences. Given the thin white blouse and almost transparent bra she was wearing, I had no doubt what they'd be. Unless our man had other inclinations.

I picked up the file I'd pulled on him. "Nikos Papazoglou," I read. "Born 1997, Thessaloniki. Accredited as a resident tour group leader four months ago. Until last week, he had a room on the second floor of the Independence. Staff report seeing him often with Andreas Roussos in the bar and restaurant. Did you ever see him in the hotel?"

Katharine put her compact back in her bag and reached for one of the photographs. "No. How much do you think he earns? That jacket he was wearing's a bit special."

"Maybe he wins a lot on the gambling tables."

"And maybe I'm the virgin Mary." She slipped on a pair of high-heeled shoes and went to the rear door of the van. "See you later, citizen."

I watched her go, not too happy about what I'd given her to do. Or about her acceptance of the job without complaint. Then there was the danger of the situation she was going into. I wanted to go after her; Christ, I wanted to protect her. It was a long time since I'd felt that way about anyone.

I called Davie. He told me that Billy had returned to his flat and was still there. Then I called the guardswoman who'd been assigned to watch Simpson 134. She said that the nursing auxiliary was on duty in the infirmary. There was nothing to do except wait for Katharine.

I sat watching the tourists on their way to the pubs and clubs in Rose Street, then lost myself in a maze of unanswered questions. Where had the guardswoman whose body we found first been going on Saturday nights with the official authorisation I'd never managed to trace? Could there really be a connection between her, the driver Rory Baillie and the Greek who'd lost an eye? What was the significance of the different mutilations? And what about Billy? What kind of scam was he running with the Greeks?

A noise at the rear door roused me. It opened and Katharine climbed in, a broad smile across her face.

"God, that was quick."

She waved two sheets of paper at me. "Look what I've got."

I scrambled over from the front seat and grabbed them. "You took them? Now he knows someone's on to him."

"Take a closer look, Quint."

"Photocopies. You have done well. But how did you get them?"

She had pulled off her shoes and was sitting with her knees apart, completely unconcerned by the direction of my gaze. "Simple. When I didn't find him in the bar or restaurant, I went up to his room. I was going to pretend that Heriot 07 had sent me, but he didn't answer my knock. I could hear a terrible racket coming from the bathroom – he could do with some singing lessons – so I tried the door. The stupid bugger had left it open. I found the envelope in the drawer of the bedside table, ran down the corridor to the photocopier they have for businessmen on that floor, copied the pages and put them back. All before he'd finished treating his dandruff." She shot a glance at me. "No exchange of body fluids required."

I was relieved about that, though I tried not to show it. I examined the photocopies. They looked like balance sheets – there were a lot of numbers, most of them strings of zeroes. But there were also combinations of letters and numbers which I recognised. I pulled out my notebook and found the references I'd copied from the headless photographs in Roussos's room: LR462, AT231, PH167 and so on. All thirty of them were on the pages. Some of them had numbers without many zeroes against them, others had plenty. A column on the right wasn't too hard to decipher. It showed dates. Some were in February, some in March and the last six were in the middle of April.

"Some sort of code," Katharine said.

"Brilliant."

"What does it all mean?" she asked, watching me carefully. "Do you think the letters could be initials?"

I told her about the photographs. Katharine grabbed my leg hard. "You bastard. You should have shown them to me. I could identify Adam. These are the missing people, aren't they?"

"Calm down," I said, prising her fingers from my thigh. "The photographs don't show anything except torsos and limbs. There are no scars or marks on any of them." I squeezed her hand gently. "You're right, these letters probably refer to people. But I already checked the initials of the ones who've gone missing against the references on the photos. They don't match."

"So it's a code, like I said." She was looking at me like I was shit on her stilettos.

I felt my face go scarlet. "Look, I'm sorry I didn't show you the photos. They're a bit gross and . . ."

"Fuck you, Quint," she shouted. "You're happy enough to send me off to lick the guy in the hotel's balls but you get all coy when it comes to giving me a chance to find Adam."

"All right, I'll let you see . . ."

My mobile buzzed.

It was the guardswoman in the infirmary. She was scarcely able to identify herself. "Citizen . . . it's Simpson 134 . . . I went . . . to the toilet . . . she . . ."

"Take a deep breath," I said, trying not to scream as I climbed into the front of the Transit. "Tell me what happened."

"She was attacked. I don't know if she's alive or . . ."

"Call the public order guardian. And make sure there's a guard on every exit. I'm on my way."

"What's going on?" Katharine joined me in the front.

"Either the killer's changed his timetable or we've got another one on the loose."

"I'm coming with you."

"No, you're not. I need you to stay here and watch Papazoglou, Katharine."

Again, she didn't demur. "Keep in touch."

"I will, pretty lady."

She raised an eyebrow and got out of the van.

Hamilton was getting out of his Land-Rover when I arrived at the infirmary.

"It doesn't stop," he said despondently.

"It might if your directorate did its job."

He looked ahead. "Don't worry. I'll have the guardswoman's head."

"That'll be a great help." I pushed through the knot of auxiliaries at the main entrance and found a tear-stained girl whom the others were ignoring.

"How long were you away from her?" I asked, giving her an encouraging smile. She couldn't have been long in the guard.

"No more than five minutes, citizen. She was working in her office and I thought I could . . ."

I raised my hand. "Where is Simpson 134 now?"

The guardswoman pointed. "In intensive care. The medical guardian got her there straight away."

I wondered how Yellowlees was taking it. "Show me the scene of the crime."

She walked away quickly, avoiding the public order guardian's glare. I motioned to him to keep his distance and caught her up.

"Simpson 134 went down to one of the storerooms. That's where she was attacked." The guardswoman glanced at me, her face white. "One of the porters heard something but the attacker got out of the window before he saw him."

She led me into a gloomy corridor. At the far end I could make out a guardsman and a short figure in grey overalls.

"I'll be all right from here," I said.

The guardswoman stopped, clearly reluctant to face the guardian. There was nothing I could do for her.

"What's your name, citizen?" I said to the balding, middle-aged hospital porter.

"Gregson," he said, keeping his eyes lowered.

"Your first name."

Now he looked up, puzzled by my last question. When he saw I wasn't in uniform, he replied, "Andrew."

"Mine's Quint."

"Citizen Dalrymple," supplied Hamilton from behind me. "He's in charge of this investigation."

The porter nodded, then began to speak rapidly as if he wanted to get his story out as soon as possible. "It was like this. I'd just wheeled an old fellow into geriatrics and I was on my way back to reception. Then I met my supervisor and she says to me, 'Go down to the stores and get me a socket set so I can fix the wheel on that trolley.' When I was halfway down the corridor, I heard this noise. I couldn't place it at first. It was a bit like one of they big clocks that tick really slowly. A kind of croaking, then a long-drawn-out gasping that fair made me shiver."

"What did you do?"

Andrew Gregson wiped beads of sweat from his forehead. "I started to run." He looked down ruefully at his heavy boots. "That's what let the bastard know somebody was coming. By the time I got to the door the choking noise had stopped. Then I heard the pounding on the window. I tried the door but he'd taken the key and locked it from the inside." He shrugged. "It took me a good few shoves with my shoulder to break it down. By then he was out of the window and away."

"You nearly got him, Andrew."

"Judging by the state of her, I'm bloody glad I didn't." He took me by the arm and led me through the broken door.

The room was lit by fluorescent strips. It was full of floor-polishers and vacuum cleaners, buckets, half-dismantled trolleys and general maintenance stores. In the centre was a space between two piles of mattresses.

"She was leaning against them," the porter said hoarsely. "Her head was at a funny angle and she was still making a noise, but it was very faint." He gulped. "Her skirt was up . . . over her thighs and her . . . her stockings were ripped." He stopped and stared down at the place where Simpson 134 had been. "She was almost gone but she must have realised I was there."

"How do you know?"

Andrew Gregson's eyes met mine. "Because she spoke to me."

I felt my heart jump. "She said something to you?"

"Well, she tried. Poor woman. I couldn't stand her but no one deserves to be throttled like that."

"Andrew," I said insistently, "what did she say?"

He bit his lip then shook his head. "I couldn't really understand it. It sounded like she was saying 'sick'. Three or four times she said it, then she slumped over. And the medical guardian came rushing in and pushed me out of the way."

"Sick"? It meant as little to me as it did to him. But in terms of the body politic, it was certainly appropriate.

The fingerprint squad dusted all over the storeroom, but I wasn't surprised when they found nothing on the window and door except smudges. Obviously the nurse's assailant had worn gloves. Outside, all I found were scuff marks on the grass, suggesting socks had been worn until he got to the tarmac road. Those indications, along with the fact that a ligature had been put round Simpson 134's throat, made me quite sure it was the killer – even though it was Tuesday, rather than the Thursday evening he'd preferred until now.

Yellowlees appeared in the shattered doorway as I was getting ready to leave. He looked around with wild eyes for a few seconds, then stared at me dully.

"She died five minutes ago," he said.

I felt as hopeless as the medical guardian sounded.

Chapter Sixteen

Yellowlees led Hamilton and me back up the corridor, the limbs hanging from his tall frame like an unstrung marionette's. "You'll want to see her, I suppose," he said in a faint voice.

Simpson 134 lay on her own in a small room. The medical guardian pulled the sheet down carefully, holding his eyes on the body. Her face was bloodless, white as chalk, in contrast to the livid line around her neck. The ligature had been twisted with enough force to break the skin. It was surprising she'd lasted long enough to say anything.

"Any idea what she was trying to say?" I asked.

Yellowlees shook his head then replaced the sheet. He stood there like a statue. If I hadn't taken his arm and led him out, I think he'd have been there for hours.

In his office he sat down heavily at his desk and watched Hamilton close the door with staring eyes.

"There are some things I have to know, guardian."

"Is this really necessary, Dalrymple?" The public order guardian seemed strangely protective of his colleague.

"It is." I gave Hamilton a glare that would have warmed Katharine's heart and turned to Yellowlees. "What exactly were Simpson 134's duties?"

"Margaret . . ." The medical guardian shivered as if saying her name was an act of betrayal. "She was one of the infirmary's most senior nurses. She assisted me in the labs, in theatre, with administration . . ." His head sank down.

"You realise it's the same killer?" I said.

Yellowlees nodded slowly. "At least he didn't have time to—"
He stopped abruptly and took a few deep breaths.

"Why do you think he came after her?"

He raised his hands from the desk and watched the fingers
twitch before rubbing them together. "I don't know." He didn't
look at me. "Maybe she saw him and asked him what he was
doing. She was fearless."

I remembered Simpson 134's angry question about the investigation when I'd been looking for Katharine; she seemed to
have a personal interest in the killer's capture. Had she known
something that Yellowlees didn't? Did he know that she'd met
Billy Geddes that night I'd seen them in Jamaica Street Lane?
I was pretty sure that she and the guardian had no secrets from
each other.

"Do you know if she had any connection with the murdered
guardswoman Sarah Spence? Or the driver Rory Baillie?"

He was shaking his head, eyes still lowered.

"How about the Greek Roussos who lost his eye?"

He glanced up. "Don't be ridiculous. What could she possibly
have had to do with him?" His lips twisted in an odd smile.

Guardians, like all auxiliaries, are supposed to respect the truth.
In my experience that doesn't stop most of them becoming
accomplished liars. Normally Yellowlees was very smooth. Not
now though. He'd tried to brazen things out and I wasn't buying
it. I played what I thought was my ace.

"Tell me, what do the organs that have been taken from the
victims have in common?" I saw Hamilton's eyes open wide.

Yellowlees suddenly seemed more in control. "That's obvious,
citizen. Liver, kidney, eye. They can all be used, in part if not in
whole, for transplantation."

"Which, of course, isn't practised in Enlightenment Edinburgh."

The medical guardian nodded. "It goes against the constitution's directive about the inviolability of the body." He gave
a bitter smile. "Besides, the abolition of private car ownership
has reduced traffic accidents to a minimal level and the supply
of organ donors has dried up." He walked towards the door.
"Excuse me. I have to see to Margaret."

Hamilton and I were left alone.

"You knew they were lovers," I said.

Points of red appeared on the public order guardian's cheeks.
"It was something the Council was aware of, yes. I can't say I

approved, but others regarded it as nothing more than a minor foible."

Others obviously included my mother. As senior guardian, she must have known what Yellowlees was up to. I wasn't sure what to make of that. I wasn't sure what to make of anything. I resorted to my usual fallback position. When in doubt, hit the archive.

It didn't get me very far. I got the supervisor to open the building for me despite the late hour and sat at a huge table with the photos from the Greek's room on my left and the files of the forty-eight missing young people on my right. I was trying to link their ID card mugshots with the headless torsos. It was a waste of time.

Well, not completely. All that naked flesh made me think of Patsy and the Prostitution Services Department. And then I remembered something. I'd seen Simpson 134 coming out of the building as I was on my way in to see Patsy. With a large briefcase. What the hell was she doing there? What was in the briefcase?

I wondered about Patsy. Could she be the connection? I'd got the impression that she was nervous about Billy's involvement in the Bearskin. But maybe she'd actually been nervous about my interest. Maybe she was in business with Billy.

And that was where I got stuck. I already had the Council's golden boy under surveillance. It would be a struggle for Davie, Katharine and me to keep a trace on Patsy too. Unless I went to the Council and told them about my suspicions. Which I didn't want to do. Some individual or individuals on the Council were in this up to their necks. I needed conclusive evidence if I wasn't to become the forty-ninth missing person. Or fiftieth including my father.

So I went back to thinking about the killer's modus operandi – it was *like* the ENT Man's, but not exactly the same. That was significant, I knew it was. Everything came back to the ENT Man, but I just couldn't work out how. This time even the archive failed me.

It was after one when I got to the Transit. Katharine told me the Greek had stayed put all evening so I spoke to the hotel's senior auxiliary and asked him to call me if Billy's contact moved that night. Then Katharine and I went back to my place.

I should have got as much sleep as possible before relieving

Davie outside Billy's flat, but things didn't work out that way. Afterwards we lay sprawled on my bed and Katharine dropped off. Sleep wouldn't come to me though. I was thinking about my father, still unaccounted for. Surely there wasn't any link between his disappearance and the killer's latest strike? I was getting nowhere. I got up and tiptoed out of the bedroom, overcome by an irresistible urge to listen to the blues. But even looking through my tapes didn't provide any escape. I came across my Leadbelly recordings and thought of the convict I'd promised them to. There I was, back at the ENT Man.

And suddenly my heart took off like one of the intercontinental ballistic missiles the last UK government had threatened to launch at its fellow European Union states. The Ear, Nose and Throat Man. Two things that Leadbelly said about him came back to me: that the butcher had mentioned a younger brother and that he had never showed much interest in the gang's music. It was the second that struck me most. I remembered how the ENT Man looked as I came up behind him in the gardens, the way he held his head. Cocked to one side, like he was straining to hear. Christ, he cut his victims' ears off; maybe the bastard had something wrong with his hearing. In which case there would be records. I knew exactly where to look.

Katharine woke as I was pulling my clothes on.

"Stay here and keep your mobile on," I said. "It's going to be a busy day."

The Council had concentrated all the city's facilities for the treatment of the deaf in what had once been a school for children with hearing problems. I drove past the Haymarket and into the total darkness outside the central area. The great grey turreted building lay beyond an expanse of lawn but I had to use my memory to find it. The place was as lost in the mist as a fairy castle. Or a vampire's. I stopped the Transit in a shower of gravel outside the main entrance.

A startled guardsman appeared at the door. "It's three in the morning, citizen. What the . . . ?"

I stuck my authorisation into his face. "The records room. Take me there."

He hesitated, glancing at the mobile phone on the table beside him.

"Now, guardsman!" I shouted. "Call your commander afterwards."

"Yes, citizen." He set off down the corridor at speed, his nailed boots echoing around like the dying fall of shotgun pellets fired out of range. At last, deep in the guts of the building, he skidded to a stop outside a heavy door.

"Let me in and lock the door after me," I ordered. I didn't fancy being disturbed by anyone the guard commander might advise of my presence.

Inside there was the familiar archive smell: dry paper and cardboard, dust in places where the cleaner's broom never reaches and the still-acrid tang of sweat from the poor sods who spend their lives shuffling files. I'd already decided where I was going to start. I estimated that the ENT Man was in his mid-thirties when he died. So he could have been treated from the early 1980s, but there wasn't time to trawl through that many files. There was a fair chance that when he was an adult he deliberately kept himself out of the Enlightenment's bureaucracy so I went for the 1990s. It took me fifty-eight minutes to nail him. The photograph was of a fourteen-year-old boy but I recognised the misshapen features and empty eyes immediately.

His name was Stewart Duncan Dunbar. Knowing it suddenly made him seem even more real than when I saw him in the flesh – like a vengeful ghost made corporeal, an evil spirit made human. I skimmed through the details, my fingers catching on the edges of the documents. Born 6.7.80, admitted to the school for the deaf 7.1.94, expelled 24.6.95. Surprise, surprise – he'd been a seriously disruptive pupil and was eventually kicked out for trying to rape a girl in the toilets. What was interesting in a worrying way was the nature of his deafness. Severe damage to the tympanic membrane caused by the insertion of pointed objects. I hazarded a guess that he'd injured himself in pursuit of some desperate sexual thrill. The last tests performed on him showed that he retained some vestigial hearing and that he'd made progress with lip-reading. Good enough progress to conceal his condition from the others in the Howlin' Wolf gang. And from me. Not that I had much of a conversation with the animal.

Then I found a couple of other things, one I'd been hoping for and another which made me shiver. The first was that he had a brother, one Gordon Oliver Dunbar – Leadbelly was right about that. The second was that their family address had been 18 Russell

Place. That was less than a hundred yards away from my father's retirement home.

In the castle, the guardsman on watch leaped to his feet as I pushed open the door to Hamilton's outer office.

"You can't go in there, citizen. The guardian's . . ."

I pushed past him and turned the lights on.

Hamilton sat up on the couch, a blanket slipping down to reveal pale skin and a surprisingly grubby standard-issue singlet. "What the hell . . ."

"Sorry to disturb your slumbers. I need to use your computer."

"Why?" He started buttoning his shirt quickly.

"I've found out the ENT Man's identity." I went round to the screen and keyboard behind his desk.

"You've what?" His mouth gaped like an idiot's.

"Don't get too excited. That doesn't mean he's the killer."

Hamilton sat down and reached for his brogues. "Well, don't ask me how the bloody thing works. I always get my assistants to handle it."

I started to tap away. "Don't worry. I think I can manage." Only guardians and senior auxiliaries are provided with computers; the Council limits the number of machines ostensibly because of the shortage of electricity but in reality to control the flow of information. "I need your entry code."

"Oh." The guardian looked sheepish. "It's 'Colonel'."

"Uh-huh." I entered it. "Right, we're into the main archive. Let's go to the index of citizens' names."

"What are you after?" Hamilton was leaning over my shoulder.

"The ENT Man's brother. How much do you want to bet that he's an auxiliary?"

"Are you still obsessed by that idea? Anyway, what makes you so sure the ENT Man himself's not the killer?"

I was tempted to come clean but a picture of Leadbelly came to me, not for the first time that night. I didn't want to join him carting stones on bomb sites and sleeping in a cell on Cramond Island. Hamilton would have done me, accident or not; after all, I'd kept quiet about it for five years.

"Here we are. Gordon Oliver Dunbar. Barracks number Scott 391." I looked round at the guardian. "Just as well you didn't put your shirt on it. Or your singlet."

"I don't understand the point of all this. What's this auxiliary supposed to have done?"

"He might well be the butcher we're looking for." I went back into the main archive and called up details on Scott 391.

Hamilton was slow but he got there in the end. "How did you find this name?"

I felt his breath on the back of my neck. "That doesn't matter just now. It—" I broke off as words came up on the screen.

"'No reference found'," Hamilton read. He gave a dry laugh.

"Shit! That can't be right." I tried again, hoping I'd made an input error. Same response. I stood up in frustration, jamming the back of the chair into the guardian's midriff. I went over to the window without apologising. A few pinpoints of light were dotted about the city centre. Dawn was still an hour away and the outer reaches were plunged into a darkness denser than in any Edgar Allan Poe tomb. That was it. I rushed back to the keyboard.

"The main archive only has files on the living." I called up the "Auxiliaries – Deceased" archive and typed in the barracks number. "This has got to be it." The cursor stayed where it was as the computer searched. "Come on, you bastard, come on." I smelled Hamilton's sour breath. Even if Scott 391 was dead, he might still be the connection I needed.

Then the cursor jumped and the file came up.

"Scott 391," I read. "Date of birth 28.5.85, registered date of death 5.3.2020."

"He died over three weeks ago," said the guardian.

"Before the first murder," I added, not giving him the satisfaction of pointing that out.

"Exactly. Now will you tell me exactly what this is all about?"

"Cause of death," I continued. "Bullet wound to head during operations against scavengers near Soutra border post." Everything came back to Soutra, I thought, seeing Caro's body at the farm for a second.

"Oh yes, I remember the report about that," said Hamilton. "Bloody dissidents. They got away as well."

I motioned to him to be quiet. I needed to work out what to do. Scott Barracks where the dead auxiliary had been based is in Goldenacre and its territory includes both my father's and the ENT Man's family home. I remembered the guard vehicle Hector was seen walking towards. Was there a connection? Then there was Patsy. What was I going to do about her? What could she have to do with all of this?

"Where are you going, Dalrymple?" Hamilton asked uneasily as I headed for the door.

"I'll let you know as soon as I make my mind up."

It was six in the morning. I didn't think Billy Geddes was likely to make an early start, so I called Davie and told him to meet me at my flat.

He arrived looking like he'd been dragged through a bush backwards. "Where have you been all night?" he demanded. "I couldn't get through on your mobile."

"Shit." I pulled it out of my pocket. "I turned it off about three. I didn't want any interruptions." I turned it on again.

"Lucky for you that Heriot 07 didn't do anything naughty." Davie glanced at Katharine. She'd emerged from the bedroom with her hair sticking up like a bomb had gone off under it. "Oh aye." He looked at me knowingly.

"I've been out all night, guardsman."

"Oh aye." He rubbed his eyes with muddy fingers. "Any chance of me getting some sleep?"

"Of course." I gave him a tight smile. "When the investigation's over."

"She looks like she's been in bed all night," he complained.

Katharine was ignoring him. "Have you made some kind of breakthrough?" she said to me.

"Sort of." I wasn't going to tell them about the ENT Man, so I was vague about his brother and concentrated on the other angles. "There might be a connection between Billy Geddes, Patsy Cameron and the medical guardian."

"Patsy Cameron in Prostitution Services?" Katharine asked, her eyes locked on me.

I nodded. "I'm pretty sure the nursing auxiliary who died last night was involved." I filled Davie in about events in the infirmary.

"Simpson 134 and the medical guardian were more than just good friends," he said.

"You know about that?"

"Christ, everyone in the guard knows about that. So you reckon they were doing more than just screwing?"

I shrugged. "We need evidence. I'd like to keep an eye on

Yellowlees, but right now I've got other priorities. Davie, you'll have to watch Geddes again. Katharine, can you . . ."

"Tail Patsy Cameron?" She didn't look like she was too bothered by the prospect.

"You'll need a less conspicuous disguise, I think. Make sure she doesn't spot you."

Katharine nodded impatiently. "I think I can manage that, Quint."

"What about you?" Davie put in. "What are these other priorities?"

"I'm going down to Scott Barracks to do some digging."

"In the gardens? Apparently if you spit on your hands . . ."

I didn't respond to that. It had just struck me that tomorrow was Thursday. The killer was probably getting ready for another attack. Then again, today was April Fools' Day. I wondered how much of a sense of humour the butcher had.

I stood on Goldenacre looking up at the façade of the stand. I had a dim memory of watching a rugby match with my father when I was a small boy: a freezing winter's afternoon high above the pitch, being buffeted by the wind. I couldn't remember anything of the match itself. It probably involved some of Hector's students. He used to follow the rugby before the Enlightenment gave him other things to think about.

Scott Barracks is a custom-built block beyond the rugby field. It stands between the once affluent area of Goldenacre and the outskirts of Leith, where civil unrest was endemic in the first ten years of the Enlightenment. The lack of large buildings in the vicinity forced the planners to erect a dreary three-storey block of mess rooms and sleeping quarters. Auxiliaries from the barracks always had a reputation for being headbangers. I wished Davie was with me.

I flashed my authorisation and went into the entrance hall. The place had the usual institutional smell, the drab paint and scuffed woodwork of all barracks – but there was something else to the atmosphere. The guardsmen and women on duty seemed strangely depressed. There was none of the enthusiastic officiousness encouraged by the Council. I was directed to the commander's office by a young woman who looked like she hadn't slept for a week. I knocked and went in without waiting for a reply.

Scott 01 raised his head slowly and looked at me without blinking. He was hollow-eyed and prematurely bald. He couldn't have been much over thirty and even before he said anything I could see that he was having a hard time holding the job down. His beard was flecked with grey and it was probably a long time since he last smiled.

"Dalrymple," I said, showing him my authorisation. If he knew about me, he wasn't showing it.

"What can I do for you, citizen?" His voice was unusually high-pitched, reedy as a shepherd's pipe on a distant hillside.

"I need immediate access to your records room."

That got a flicker from his eyelashes. "If you need a file, I can have it brought to you here, citizen."

And then you can see which one I want, I thought. "No, thanks. I want you to escort me to the archive personally and I want no one else to know I'm in there."

"Can I see your authorisation again?" he asked.

I'd run out of time. "No, Scott 01. If you've got a problem, call the public order guardian." I beat his fingers to the phone. "After you've taken me."

"Very well." The commander closed the file he'd been working on and stood up.

I wondered if he'd move any faster if I shouted "Fire". Probably not. Auxiliaries are trained to keep a hold of themselves. Or at least to look like they're keeping a hold of themselves.

A group of guardswomen passed us in the corridor. They lowered their voices and their faces when they saw the commander and me. The first two were nondescript but the third wasn't the kind you look away from. I recognised her immediately. It was Mary, Queen of Scots. She gave me a quick glance and was gone. I didn't catch her barracks number.

I waited impatiently as Scott 01 unlocked the records room. In accordance with security regulations its door was steel-plated and equipped with three separate locks. In the early years of the Enlightenment there had been frequent break-ins by relatives trying to discover the whereabouts of auxiliaries after they'd been separated from their families. More recently the Education Directorate has been working hard to explain the need, as the Council sees it, for the city's servants to be anonymous and breaches in security have fallen away.

The commander stood back at last and let me into the windowless room. Then I waited till he'd locked me in. No doubt he'd be haring back to his office to call Hamilton.

Now for the ENT Man's brother. I pulled Scott 391's file, relieved to find that the thick maroon folder hadn't yet been sent to the central archive. The barracks are reluctant to hand over information on their people, even to other auxiliaries. So I sat down and learned all about the dead guardsman.

Or rather, tried to fill in the gaps. Auxiliaries have to write a Personal Evaluation at the start of the training programme. Scott 391's was remarkable because of the complete lack of reference to his older brother. He went on at some length about his parents, who were lawyers and strong supporters of the Enlightenment; he described his feelings about several schoolfriends and filled three pages about a girlfriend; he even wrote about the family house in Trinity and what he got up to as a kid in the area. But about his brother Stewart, not a word.

I went on through the file, tracing the guardsman's life through school, where he was particularly good at biology, to tours of duty on the border after he'd finished auxiliary training, to community service in Leith. He seemed like a conscientious enough guy, without much imagination. He fitted in well. It seemed pretty clear that he'd had no contact at all with his brother since the beginning of the Enlightenment, unless he'd been very clever about it. Auxiliaries get very little free time and they have to ask permission to move outside barracks areas – which, of course, would be recorded in the file. Gordon Oliver Dunbar spent most of his time off pumping iron in the barracks gym or writing seriously dull papers on Plato for the debating society. Then I got to the section about his sexual activities.

I felt a bit guilty. I always do when I go through other people's files. The problem is, I like it. I get a kind of vicarious pleasure from witnessing other lives, the successes and failures, the dreams and unachieved ambitions. No doubt voyeurs get the same rush.

My subject was definitely hetero. All his sessions were spent with female auxiliaries. I took a note of the numbers for the last couple of years, as well as those of his friends – not that they're described as such in Enlightenment-speak. His "close colleagues" amounted to eighteen barracks numbers. Either he was a liar or he was distinctly popular. It would take hours to go through all their files and, anyway, I wasn't sure what I was looking for. The poor sod had died before the first murder.

I went on to the end of Scott 391's file, turning the pages with rapidly decreasing interest. Then I got to the end and sat up like I'd been jabbed with a picador's lance. I tore out the memo that had been stapled in last and hammered on the door for it to be opened.

Scott Barracks is less than two hundred yards from the crematorium that serves the northern half of the city. The night the coffin containing the ENT Man's brother was delivered, something very unusual had happened there.

Chapter Seventeen

I parked the Transit outside the low brick building. The sign said that services, secular of course, were held only in the afternoons. Judging by the state of the place, I reckoned that the mornings were devoted to maintenance and cleaning. The Council had obviously shied away from rebuilding the dilapidated facility.

A thin, balding man with yellowish skin appeared on the steps. He rubbed his hands nervously and came over to the van. "Are you wanting to work in the gardens?" he asked, peering at the Parks Department sticker. "Only, they usually come on a Monday."

I jumped down and showed him my "ask no questions". His lack of beard and uniform showed he wasn't an auxiliary so there was no need to let him know my identity.

"Em, I hope there's no dissatisfaction with my work," the official said warily. "I've always followed the Council's instructions to the letter."

I shook my head. "There have been no complaints. You are . . . ?"

"Douglas Haigh," he said, thumbs on the seams of his worn grey trousers and the upper part of his body bending forward like a heron following a fish. "Haigh with 'g-h'," he added. "I've been here for thirty years. How may I help you?"

"I need to see your records, citizen." I stepped away from him and into the building. I didn't fancy his cadaverous appearance much. It looked like devotion to his work had kept him in a job that would normally be an auxiliary's.

"My records? Certainly." Haigh overtook me and headed down the corridor with long strides. "What precisely do you want to know?" He had started rubbing his hands together again.

"You sent a memo to Scott Barracks on 8 March. It was a Sunday . . ."

"I work seven days a week," he put in.

"What a surprise," I said under my breath, pulling the sheet of paper from my pocket. "'I wish to point out that Scott 477, the sentry on duty on the night of 7–8.3.2020, was guilty of several serious breaches of procedure. One, he . . .'"

"My word, yes. I remember that night very clearly." He led me into a small office set back from the passageway that was echoing from our footsteps.

"You were here during the night?" That sounded promising.

Haigh sat down in an ancient chair that he had bound together with plastic-covered wire and motioned me to the other even more rickety seat. "Indeed I was." He gave a brief, thin-lipped smile. "I don't like the flat I was assigned. Saturday nights are quiet here. There are usually no deliveries. But there was one that night." The joints of his fingers cracked. "And a very curious one it was too."

I leaned forward. "Why was that?"

"Well, first of all, the documentation was incomplete. If I hadn't happened to be here when the delivery was made, I would have had a terrible job chasing up the missing information."

"What exactly was missing, citizen?"

Haigh cleared his throat like a professor about to start a lecture. "The Consignment of Human Remains form must show the barracks numbers of the auxiliary who approves release from the hospital or wherever the death was registered. It must also show the number of the guardsman or woman who accompanies the coffin and the name of the civilian driver." He spread his arms dramatically. "In this case, none of them was filled in."

I suddenly realised that the old ghoul was about to give me something precious. That was what prevented me from grabbing the desiccated bureaucrat by the throat to speed things up.

Haigh turned quickly to the grey metal cabinets behind him and produced a folder. He must have seen the look on my face.

"I took down the guardswoman's and the driver's details," he said proudly. "And I even succeeded in obtaining the nursing auxiliary's number."

I snatched the file from him. The top page was a mass of boxes and numbers, some filled in, others ticked or crossed out. It was what I found at the bottom that made me whistle. The dead guardsman had been logged out of the infirmary by Yellowlees's girlfriend, Simpson 134. The guardswoman accompanying the coffin was Sarah Spence, the murder victim we found first. After that, I wasn't too surprised to see Rory Baillie's name in the box marked "Driver". But what the hell did it all mean?

"Anyway," Haigh continued, "after the coffin was brought in, I went off home, thinking that was enough disorder for one night."

The memo I'd taken from the barracks was making sense now. "And when you came back in the morning, you found all the screws on the coffin loose and the documents strewn across the floor."

"Quite so." He shook his head. "The sentry must have had a look at the body. After all, he was in the same barracks." Now he was rubbing his hands like Lady Macbeth on speed. "I wonder if that's what drove him to kill himself."

"What?" I looked up in astonishment. "The sentry committed suicide?"

Haigh's face turned even paler. "Oh, I . . . I assumed you knew about that. I . . . I didn't mean to . . ."

The constitution is firm about suicide. People who kill themselves become non-citizens without any memorial. No one, not even family and friends, is allowed to talk about them. The rules are even stricter when it comes to auxiliaries. No wonder Haigh was worried.

"I'm s . . . sorry," he stuttered. "I heard it from one of the sentries last week. I . . . promise I won't . . ."

I raised my hand. "It's all right, citizen. You've been a great help." As I left his office I saw a self-satisfied smile creep across the parchment of his face.

The commander of Scott Barracks looked up wearily when I burst back into his office.

"You had a suicide here recently," I said.

That seemed to bring him even nearer to the end of his tether. "Scott 477," he said in a faint voice. "It was a great shock. The barracks hasn't been the same since."

Now I understood the atmosphere of the place. "When did it happen?"

"A week ago today – 25 March."

I checked the barracks number in my notebook. "Scott 477 was a 'close colleague' of Scott 391, the guardsman who was killed on the border."

The commander nodded. "He was. And he was very down about his death. But . . . but he wasn't suicidal. I spoke to him at some length after I received the memo from the crematorium manager." He shook his head slowly. "There was something else. Something happened afterwards."

I thought about the date: 25 March. The news of Rory Baillie's murder had been made public by then. Could there be a connection? Something else struck me.

"How did Scott 477 commit suicide?"

There was a flash of hostility at my question in the commander's eyes. "He hanged himself, if you must know. In the storeroom."

I nodded. "I'll need to see his file. You can have it brought to me here."

Before it arrived, my mobile buzzed.

"It's Davie, Quint. Where are you? Billy Geddes has just left the Finance Directorate. He's heading down the Mound on foot."

"Keep on his tail. He can't be going far if he's walking."

"Quint, he looks pretty bloody keen. I smell big money. Are you coming?"

Did the former king have a predilection for feminine sanitary goods?

Davie, dressed as a labourer, was standing on the concrete path above the racetrack at the west end of Princes Street Gardens. Below, preparations were under way for the twelve o'clock race. Grooms were parading horses around the enclosure and large crowds of tourists were clustered around the Finance Directorate's betting booths.

"Where's our man?" I asked as I joined him.

Davie pointed to one of the refreshment stalls. There were fewer people there in the minutes leading up to the off. Billy was very conspicuous, the only man wearing a suit and an open camel-hair coat. He checked the time and looked around anxiously.

"He's waiting for someone," Davie said.

"You'll make an investigator yet."

"Here we go. Who's this then?"

I recognised the dark-haired figure in the tan leather jacket immediately. It was Papazoglou, looking even more shifty than he had in the museum. One hand was stuffed into his pocket and the other held a briefcase that he seemed to be very attached to – he kept it tight against his leg. The two of them met and exchanged a few words. Then the Greek handed over the briefcase.

"What now?" asked Davie.

They separated, Papazoglou heading towards the Mound and Billy to the right. Suddenly Billy stopped, turned back as if he'd forgotten something – and saw me. He stood stock still for a few seconds, his face inscrutable, then kept going in his original direction.

"Fucking hell. Call the guard on the exit over there and get the gate locked. I think it's time to pull the plug on Heriot 07's deals."

Davie spoke rapidly into his mobile then signed off. "Done."

The voice of the race announcer boomed out from speakers hung on trees and lampposts. There was a rush of bodies towards the fence alongside the track. Billy was caught in the crowd.

"Christ, we'll lose him," said Davie.

"You cover the left." I ran down the slope.

"I can't stand horse-racing," he shouted as he followed me.

The six horses were in the stalls by the time I reached the concourse in front of the track. The spectators fell silent and the chimes of the clocks in the vicinity started to ring out.

Then I caught sight of Billy. He was pushing his way along the white rail, oblivious to the abuse from tourists he was banging into. The tolling of the bells seemed to rise to a crescendo and I realised what he was going to do.

"No, Billy, no!" Then I flinched as the gates of the stalls crashed open.

Billy had ducked under the fence and started to run across the track. He must have thought he could reach the upper exit. He didn't stand a chance. In an instant the horses were on him. Spectators screamed as his body was bundled up like a ball of rags and kicked around the turf by a blur of hooves.

"No, Billy, for fuck's sake, no," I heard myself repeating.

People got out of the way as they turned away from the track. The announcer was keeping quiet and all that could be heard now was the pounding of hooves further down the gardens as the jockeys tried to rein in their mounts.

The first thing I came to on the closely cut grass was the briefcase Billy had received from the Greek. It had been knocked open but none of the banknotes from the large number of wads in it had slipped out. The crowd hadn't even noticed the money. I closed the case and left it where it was, then ran over to where Billy lay. He was still crumpled in a ball, only his left arm extended. The forearm was bent back from the elbow at an angle that was all wrong. His face was pressed into the ground, the single eye that was visible half open and glazed.

Kneeling down beside him, I felt for a pulse. "Why, Billy?" I mumbled. "Why? Couldn't you see it was hopeless?" I knew he couldn't hear me.

Davie ran up. "They've got his contact at the Mound gate." He bent down. "Is he dead?"

I looked up at him in amazement. "No, he isn't. There's a pulse, would you believe?" I pulled off my jacket and laid it over the battered body.

"There's an ambulance on its way."

I stood up slowly. "They'd better be quick."

"Why did he make a break? There wasn't anywhere for him to go."

"I don't know. Panic, the survival instinct." I went back to the briefcase. "One thing's for sure. There's a hell of a lot of money involved."

The ambulance drew up, siren blaring. There was a guard vehicle behind it. Hamilton jumped down and ducked under the fence.

"What happened here?" he asked, peering at Heriot 07.

"The deputy finance guardian may well have made his last transaction," I said slowly.

The medics lifted Billy carefully on to a stretcher and moved him towards their vehicle.

Hamilton was glaring at me. "Have you had Heriot 07 under surveillance?"

I turned away. "He was the long shot," I said over my shoulder. "Pick up the money, guardian. It belongs to the city."

I watched the ambulance drive away.

"This is all foreign currency," Hamilton said. "Where did it come from?"

"Heriot 07's been selling the city's assets," I said. "Come on. Let's see what the medical guardian thinks. I'm sure he'll be keen to treat Billy personally."

Robert Yellowlees finished drying his hands at the basin in his office and turned to face us.

"I've never seen anything like it," he said, shaking his head. "Most of his ribs are broken, one lung is punctured, his left elbow is shattered, his skull's cracked in two places – and he's still alive."

I wondered how important that was to Yellowlees. "How long will he be unconscious?"

The medical guardian shrugged. "Who knows? The brain scan showed remarkably little damage. He may well regain consciousness soon." He didn't sound very optimistic. "You want to question him, I suppose."

Bloody right I do, I said to myself.

"He hasn't got some connection with the murderer, has he?" Yellowlees narrowed his eyes. "With the bastard who killed Margaret?"

I watched him as he walked round his desk. His normally steady surgeon's hands were trembling. Again I wondered what he knew about Billy's activities.

"We'll need to keep a close guard on Heriot 07," I said, turning to Hamilton. "Davie – I mean Hume 253 – will supervise. He'll need a couple of experienced squads."

"I'll see to it." Hamilton came up to me. "Still nothing on your father, I'm afraid." He went out.

Before I could say what I wanted to Yellowlees, my mobile went off. I moved away when I heard Katharine's voice. "I'm in conference," I said.

"Got you. I'll do the talking. I can't speak for long anyway. Patsy Cameron's on the move. On foot. I'll shadow her."

I looked round at the medical guardian. He was watching me, making no attempt to disguise his interest. "Are you sure you can handle it? The subject may have some unpleasant friends."

"I'll be all right. Don't call me in case I'm close to her."

"Don't take any independent action," I said, realising before I'd finished that she'd rung off.

"What was that all about?" Yellowlees asked.

I ignored the question. "I need your help, guardian," I said, walking up to the desk. "There's a medical file I want." His face remained impassive. "An auxiliary who was killed on the border a few weeks ago. Scott 391." Unless the file had been doctored, it might give me an idea of what the sentry saw when he opened the coffin in the crematorium.

Yellowlees was finding the papers on his desk a lot more interesting than my face. Finally he raised his eyes. "I remember the case," he said hoarsely. "Bullet wound to the head."

I heard the door open behind me. It was Hamilton.

Yellowlees looked both relieved and anxious. "Lewis was asking me about it this morning." His gaze dropped again. "Since Margaret . . . died, everything's fallen apart here." He shook his head at me helplessly. "I can't locate the file."

He was treating my mother so I gave him one last opportunity to come clean. It was obvious that the file contained something that he didn't want me to know. "Are you quite sure about that, guardian? There could be serious consequences."

No reaction. Well, I tried. The medical guardian would have to take his chances. I filled them in on what I found out at the crematorium. "It looks like the murderer is working his way through a list of victims. They all had some connection with the dead guardsman except the Greek in the Indie – and I suspect the killer must have seen him with one of the others."

"But what's the motive?" asked Hamilton. "If he's got a list, he must have a reason for attacking these people."

"I'm not clear about that yet." I glanced at Yellowlees. "But I can hazard a guess at who's next on the list."

I left them to think about that. If the medical guardian wouldn't talk, maybe Billy's Greek contact would.

Chapter Eighteen

Interrogating Nikos Papazoglou turned out to be as productive as asking an auxiliary to sing "God Save the Queen". The Greek stared sullenly at the wall in the cell, mumbling over and over again, "I want to call the consulate," in heavily accented English. Eventually I lost my cool.

"All right," I shouted. "I'll let you talk to your people." I slapped down in front of him the copies Katharine had taken of the pages Billy passed him in the museum. "After you tell me what this is all about and why you gave Heriot 07 that case with two hundred and seventy-five million drachmae."

When he saw the papers, the young man gave an involuntary start and his eyes opened wide. "How did you—?" He broke off and went back to stonewalling. "I don't know what you're talking about, mister."

I leaned over and glared at his sallow face. "You know what happened to Andreas Roussos, don't you?" I said, my voice not much more than a whisper. "You know that someone took his eye out? Without an anaesthetic. As I see it, you've got two choices. Either you tell me what these pages mean and I let you out of here in five minutes . . ." I paused and moved in closer to him. "Or I print in the newspaper that you had links with Roussos and the killer comes after you." I sat back and smiled. "I wonder which organ he'll go for this time."

Papazoglou's chin quivered and his tongue appeared between dry lips. Then he raised his hand so quickly that the guardsman at the door jumped forward with his truncheon raised.

"Okay, okay," the Greek jabbered, cowering. "You guarantee I face no charges?"

"Sure," I lied.

He raised his hand very slowly, eyes fixed on the auxiliary, and wiped the sweat from his forehead. "All right. These papers are—"

There was a clang as the bolt was drawn back and the door pulled open. Hamilton came in, followed by a man with a heavy moustache whom I'd been hoping I wouldn't see that day.

"I'm sorry, Dalrymple. Mr Palamas from the Greek consulate insisted on being brought down."

The Greek I'd seen on the Calton Hill with Billy ignored me, standing behind Papazoglou and addressing his lecture to the public order guardian.

"Under Edinburgh law, the prisoner is entitled to have a representative of his country present at all interviews. I am concerned that we were not officially informed that this" – he looked at me like I was an Untouchable – "this interrogation was taking place."

Hamilton opened his arms in a gesture of hopelessness. "I apologise on behalf of the Council for this lapse."

I stared at him in disgust, my arms folded tightly to stop myself offering violence to a guardian.

Palamas nodded brusquely. "What are the charges, please?"

Hamilton glanced at me.

I shrugged; now that Palamas was pulling strings, Papazoglou would clam up. There was no point in holding him.

"Em, no charges will be pressed," the guardian said lamely. "Guardsman, escort these gentlemen to the esplanade."

I watched as Papazoglou left, relief etched into his face like acid. "Couldn't you have stalled him for a bit longer? I almost got what I wanted."

Hamilton was examining his feet. "He got on to the deputy senior guardian. What could we do? You know how important Greek business is to the city."

I wished I knew a lot more about that particular matter. I could either tell Hamilton that I'd found out about the missing young people and that I suspected Patsy Cameron of being involved in some horrendous scam with Billy, or I could hit Billy's flat. The latter would be much less hassle.

"How did Palamas know we had Papazoglou?" I asked on my way out.

"Every Greek at the race meeting saw him being arrested by the gate." Hamilton sighed. "At the rate you're going, there won't be any tourist trade left in the city."

I parked the Transit outside Billy's flat and got the guardswoman who'd been sent down after he was injured to let me in. The hallway was cool and the smell of floor polish filled my nostrils as I ran up the marble staircase.

Inside the flat there was dead silence. I stood motionless for a few moments, breathing in deeply and listening. I suddenly had a premonition that someone was about to appear, someone who didn't care too much about my health. I could have called the sentry up but instead I ran from room to room like a child certain that a monster was lurking. There was no one, of course. I'd been living on my nerves too much recently. Tearing the place apart would be good therapy.

For a senior auxiliary sworn to live according to the Council's ascetic standards, Billy had accumulated an amazing collection of luxury goods. The wardrobes in his bedroom were stuffed with Italian suits and shoes, silk shirts and ties, a couple of leather jackets – even a fur coat which the label showed to have originated from independent Siberia. Billy must have made a business trip there. It wasn't the greed that pissed me off, it was the waste. He could get away with dressing up in flash suits, but not even Billy would venture out wearing a fur coat in Edinburgh. Mind you, in winter most buildings are cold enough to warrant one.

The kitchen was insanely overstocked. There was a full range of French saucepans that would have been worth a small fortune in that country before the Moslem fundamentalists reduced it to a collection of bankrupt city-states. The cupboards were full of tinned foods that are never available in the city's shops: tomatoes, olives, kidney beans, stuffed vine leaves. I even found the components of a pasta machine. I can't remember the last time I ate spaghetti.

After an hour I began to run out of steam. The only documents I'd found were from standard Finance Directorate files and there was no sign of any foreign exchange. I began to suspect that Billy had organised a hiding-place. I squatted down on the carpet in the middle of the sitting room and looked dispiritedly at the heap of his personal possessions that I'd piled up.

"Shit, Billy," I muttered. "What the hell have you done with it all?" Pins and needles started to attack my feet. I got up and went over to the table where he kept the first edition of Hume's treatise. The first creak of the uneven floorboards made no impression on me. Then I shifted my weight to the other foot and the noise came again, this time louder. Eureka.

I ran to the wall. Although the carpet looked like it had been secured with tacks, it came up easily when I stuck my fingers between it and the skirting board. I quickly moved the furniture aside – a couple of armchairs, a coffee table, an escritoire and a Georgian display cabinet that almost broke my back – and rolled up the heavy floor covering. Where the small table stood, there was a two-foot square cut in the underlay. I lifted it and the boards beneath it, thinking how Billy must have been laughing to himself at the idea of me innocently standing there when he showed me the book. And struck gold. Literally.

The hole contained six bars of that metal, over twenty thousand US dollars and so many wads of Greek drachmae that I didn't waste time counting them. There was also a thick folder of statements from a bank in Berne, a file of papers similar to the one Billy had passed to Papazoglou and, right at the bottom, the confirmation I needed to connect the deputy finance guardian both to Yellowlees and to Patsy Cameron. What was Billy doing with a copy of a research report entitled "Towards the Effective Treatment of Systemic Lupus Erythematosus"? Was he bankrolling the medical guardian's research? Or blackmailing him, perhaps?

And what was he doing with Prostitution Service Department appraisals of ten male and female citizens? Their names had been blacked out and replaced with letter and number references which tallied with ten of those on the headless photographs in Roussos's hotel room. The appraisals included physical and mental profiles and aptitude ratings for specific sexual services. They were all initialled PC. Things were falling into place at last.

My mobile buzzed. I had a job finding it under the carpet at the edge of the room.

"Quint, Davie. Subject is leaving the infirmary. Do I follow?"

"Bloody right you do." I put Davie in charge of Billy's security so that he could also keep track of Yellowlees. "What about Heriot 07? Has he come round yet?"

"Negative. I've got three guards in his room and another half-dozen in the corridor outside. That do you?"

"Yes. Let me know where the subject's headed. And Davie?"

"Aye?"

"Don't lose him. The killer's probably after him."

"Christ."

"Exactly." I signed off and looked down at the money and documents around the hole in the floor. Suddenly I had a flash of the gaping wounds the murderer had cut in the bodies of his victims. How did what he was doing fit in with Yellowlees and the ENT Man's brother? How did it fit in with Billy and Patsy? There was something missing from the equation and I couldn't work out what it was.

I ran down the stairs, this time impervious to the smell of polish. Something much ranker had filled my nostrils in Billy's flat and I was sure it was about to get worse.

The cloud had thickened over the city and it began to drizzle as I drove towards the castle. I reckoned it was time to come clean with Hamilton. There was too much going on for me to handle without more back-up. Even if there were some Council members who were bent, it wasn't likely that Hamilton was one of them.

I didn't get the chance to find out. He came on the mobile when I was halfway up the Mound.

"Dalrymple, that female citizen you've got working for you . . ."

"Katharine Kirkwood?" I felt my stomach somersault. "What's happened to her?"

"A tourist found her lying unconscious in Reid's Close off the Canongate."

"Where is she now?"

"She's still there. An ambulance is on its way."

I accelerated out of the corner at the Finance Directorate and drove down towards the ruins of Holyrood Palace. I left the Transit on the pavement behind the ambulance. A guardsman stepped forward, then stopped when he saw my authorisation. A couple of his colleagues were talking to a male tourist who looked shocked. I ran into the narrow close. The high walls were dark grey, the flagstones wet from the drizzle. Round a corner I found the medics. They were bent over a figure in a light blue raincoat. A woollen hat lay on the ground between me and them.

I went closer. "How is she?"

The more senior of the two male medics turned to me.

"Coming round. She took a heavy blow to the back of the head."

"Quint?" Katharine's voice was weak. "Is that you, Quint?"

"What happened?"

"She . . . someone was behind me suddenly . . . hit me . . . I didn't see . . ."

The medic stood up. "She should be X-rayed. She's probably concussed."

I knelt down and took her hand. Her eyes seemed unfocused. "Katharine, you'd better go to the infirmary. They think . . ."

"No!" she said, her voice suddenly back to normal. "I'm staying with you. I was on to something. She must have seen me . . ."

I looked round helplessly at the medics. "Keep an eye on her for a moment."

I went back down the close and found Hamilton questioning the tourist. "Did he see anything?" I asked.

The man had a Korean flag on his baseball cap, jacket and shoulder bag. His English appeared to be Korean too.

"From what we can understand," said the guardian, "he was trying to find his way back to his hotel from the palace."

"Bit of an indirect route," I said dubiously.

Hamilton shrugged. "He's got a copy of *Jekyll and Hyde* in his bag. Maybe he was in search of local colour."

"And he found Katharine in there?"

There was another burst of incomprehensible English from the tourist, accompanied by what seemed to be positive head movements.

"We'll take that as a yes, shall we?" I turned to the Korean. "Did you see anyone else? Was anyone coming out when you went in?"

More yabbering, but the gestures looked negative. I took Hamilton aside. "Get your people to find an interpreter before they take a statement from him. I don't think he's involved in this, but if we stall we can keep an eye on him."

Hamilton looked confused. "Not involved in what? What exactly was the woman—"

He broke off as Katharine came staggering from the close, her face white and her right arm against the wall.

"What are you doing?" I said. "You're not supposed to be walking about."

She pushed one of the medics away. "I told you, Quint. I'm staying with you till we catch her."

"Catch who?" the guardian demanded. "What's going on here, Dalrymple?"

I took a deep breath. Now was the time to tell him about Patsy. So I did. I was a bit vague about the connection with the missing young people, but that didn't seem to bother Hamilton. A tight smile began to show on his face as I spoke.

"So the controller of Prostitution Services has been up to no good," he said when I finished. "I can't say I'm surprised. I never approved of her promotion to senior auxiliary rank."

You sanctimonious old bastard, I thought. Where would the Council be without the income from Patsy's department?

"You didn't see her?" he asked Katharine.

She shook her head. "But obviously she saw me. I followed her from outside her office to a café on the Royal Mile. She sat there for over an hour, then went into some shops. I had that woollen hat pulled down low over my forehead, but she must still have recognised me. Led me down here and hid in one of the doorways and hit me from behind, the bitch."

"She may have had help," I said. "You're lucky you weren't injured more seriously."

Hamilton was desperate to get involved. "Shall I instruct all guard units and barracks to look out for the controller?"

I raised my hand. "Wait a minute. I need to think." I walked back into the dank close, stood in a granite corner and let the stream of images bombard me. The Bearskin, Patsy's office, the Greek's hotel room where I'd found the headless photographs, the hiding-place in Billy's flat with the Prostitution Department appraisals. All those places had links with Patsy. But there was something else, something relevant that I couldn't quite grasp. I put my hands against the damp stone and tried to hatch the idea that had begun to torment me. There wasn't much time. Even if Patsy hadn't recognised Katharine until she was knocked unconscious, she'd seen her close up here. She knew of my interest in Katharine and it would be clear that I was closing in on her. So where would she go? None of the obvious places, I was sure of that. Patsy had been a smart operator before she joined the Enlightenment and I knew she hadn't forgotten any of her old tricks. So where had she gone? I ran my mind back over the places: the Bearskin, her office – Christ, her office. Suddenly

I saw Simpson 134, the dead nurse, the time she came out of the building where Patsy worked. Simpson 134. She was involved with Billy, she'd met him. That was it. I knew where Patsy was.

"Let's go," I said, running back out to the pavement. "To Jamaica Street Lane North."

Katharine came with me to the Transit. As I drove off, Hamilton's guard vehicle in my rearview mirror, I thought of the night I'd hidden behind the refuse bin and waited for Billy to reappear from the lane. He wasn't the kind of guy who would have a meeting out of doors in the dark. He had a hideaway down the lane and I was positive that's where Patsy had gone. I was also positive that we wouldn't find her there alone.

I stopped on India Street, near the bar I'd seen Billy go into that night after he met Simpson 134.

"What's the location?" Hamilton asked.

"I'm not sure," I said, watching his eyebrows jump. I wasn't sure how to go about identifying the building where Patsy was either. If the people I suspected were there too, using the City Guard's stormtrooper methods mightn't be a good idea.

"Quint?" Katharine said. "What if I walk down the street? That would probably bring Patsy out."

"More likely get you killed." I thought about it. "On the other hand . . ."

"Where are you going, Dalrymple?" Hamilton shouted as I reached the corner.

"To talk to Patsy." I smiled at Katharine. "Right idea, wrong person to carry it out. Patsy and I used to be friends." I turned to Hamilton. "Put a roadblock at the other end of the lane. If I don't contact you within five minutes, send in the cavalry."

"Quint . . ."

I faced the front. "Stay here, Katharine."

The buildings in the lane had originally been stables and servants' quarters, two-storey blocks that had been renovated by young professional people in the years before the Enlightenment. Now most of them are set aside for middle-ranking auxiliaries. Most of them. Billy must have managed to get his hands on one. What number was it? Only one way to find out. My palms were wet and I wasn't in complete control of my breathing.

"Patsy!" I yelled. "Patsy! We need to talk!"

I looked around the damp stone façades. Nothing. I walked on a bit further.

"Patsy! I'm on my own. I'm not armed."

No reply.

"Patsy! You're better off . . ."

A window to the left above me rattled open. I stopped and waited. There was no one visible.

"Patsy . . ."

"Will you stop shouting, Quint? I might need glasses, but I'm not deaf." Patsy's head appeared. "Here, you'll need these." She dropped a ring of keys.

Before I used them, I called Hamilton and told him to stay where he was.

I found Patsy on the first floor. It was a small flat but through the rear window I could see a series of low buildings in what would originally have been a garden.

"I'm impressed, man," Patsy said with a slack smile. "How did you find out about this place?"

I tapped the side of my head with my forefinger. "Where are they, Patsy? In there?" I pointed to the outhouses.

"Has Billy talked?" Patsy said, her voice hardening.

I let her think he had.

"That little shite. He swore he'd look after things with the Council," Patsy said bitterly. Then she laughed. "I should have known. Never trust a man. Aye, they're down there. Asleep probably. We've been giving them tranquillisers to keep them quiet."

"How many are there?"

"Six boys and four girls. The rest are all away to Greece. These ones were to leave at the end of the week."

"Is there one called Adam Kirkwood?"

"I knew we shouldn't have taken Katharine's brother. He was too much of a good thing. Maybe it runs in the family." She nodded. "Aye, he's still here."

I took out my mobile and asked Hamilton to put Katharine on. Then we went to find Adam.

Patsy told the two hard men who were watching over the sex slaves to forget about putting up a fight. They hadn't looked exactly keen when they saw the double squad of guardsmen Hamilton sent in. Katharine ran over to the bed her brother was occupying in the makeshift dormitory and tried to bring him round with a tenderness I hadn't expected. It was difficult to rouse him and the others. Ambulances took them to the infirmary for check-ups. Katharine went with Adam after giving Patsy a look that would have made a statue's eyes water.

"I haven't much time, Patsy," I said, waving Hamilton back. "Tell me what's been going on here."

Patsy looked at me quizzically. "I thought you said Billy had talked?" Her lips creased. "Fuck you, Quint. You made me . . ."

"Forget it, Patsy. If you want me to keep the public order guardian off your back, you'd better co-operate. Whose idea was it to sell off citizens as sex slaves?"

She laughed scornfully. "Whose do you think?"

"But Billy couldn't have done it without you."

"I provided the technical know-how." She sat down on one of the beds and smoothed the cover. "He worked the deal with the Greek Roussos in the Indie and found this place." She looked around at the drab walls and shook her head. "The kids were better off on their backs in Athens than in this shite-hole. We told them they were in line to become cultural representatives and gave them some Greek money to impress them. And we told them not to tell anyone else till their jobs were confirmed."

That explained the banknote I found in Adam Kirkwood's flat. "And when you'd run preliminary checks on them, they were picked up. Did you give them any choice?"

She shrugged. "No. After they were picked up, we made sure they couldn't get away."

"Simpson 134 checked their medical records?"

"That's right. The Greeks only wanted young, fully fit specimens. And photographs they could drool over."

"What about Rory Baillie?"

"We used him to drive them around; I trained them with Sarah Spence in different places. Some of them were in the Bearskin that night you were there."

I walked over to her. "Billy's in intensive care."

Patsy looked like a snake had started to glide up her leg. "The killer?"

I shook my head. "He ran in front of the horses in Princes Street Gardens – trying to get away from me."

She stared at me. "Are you proud of yourself, Quint?"

"No." I bent over her. "Christ, Patsy, you knew a maniac was butchering the others in your scam. Why didn't you run earlier? Why didn't Billy?"

She looked up at me. "There was so much money coming to us. I could've got out of this bastard city and started somewhere else." She stood up slowly. "Besides, it didn't make any sense. We couldn't see what the murders had to do with this business. It isn't all just some crazy coincidence, is it?"

"What do you think? Patsy, what about the medical guardian? Did he have anything to do with this?"

I knew before she spoke that the answer was negative. I turned to go.

"Quint," Patsy called. "You'll do what you can for me?"

I passed Hamilton in the doorway. She was his now.

Davie called before I got to the Transit. "Subject went into his residence a minute ago. I'm trying not to look too suspicious in the gardens in Moray Place."

"Right. Keep on him."

So Yellowlees was out of the infirmary. But his files weren't. Time to take a look. The fact that Katharine was there gave me an extra incentive. I was wondering what my payment for finding her brother would be.

Then, as I drove towards the centre through the drizzle, I remembered my father. Like the murderer, I'd lost track of him in this lunatic city. Maybe Patsy had the right idea. Maybe it was time to get out. But first I had a lot of unfinished business.

Chapter Nineteen

In the infirmary a ward had been set aside for the sex slaves. A senior nursing auxiliary told me she'd contacted the medical guardian and told him about the ten tranquillised patients. She was surprised that he hadn't arrived to take charge. I wasn't, but he might still turn up any minute.

Katharine was sitting by her brother's bed holding his hand. Her face was close to his and they were deep in conversation. Adam Kirkwood was pale, but he looked healthy enough. Patsy had been feeding the slaves up. I turned back before I reached them, but Katharine spotted me.

"What are you up to now, Quint?" she asked.

I shrugged. "I've still got a murderer to catch."

She stood up, pulling her brother into a seated position. "*We* have, you mean."

"Katharine, you've got your brother back. You've done your part."

She looked at me like a schoolmistress about to sort out the class villain. "There's a connection between the killings and what Adam's been through, isn't there?"

"It looks that way to me."

"So Adam and I have a right to be involved."

"What are you talking about? This is a murder investigation, not a human rights forum."

Her eyes flashed. "Oh, I see. When it suits you, you take my help. When it doesn't, you dump me."

"What's this all about, Katharine? Adam's back. What more do you want?"

She came up to me. The look on her face almost made me run away. "Look, Quint," she said in a harsh whisper, "I've been fucked by the Council and I don't care about myself any more. But Adam's still young. He didn't know much about what life's really like. Patsy Cameron and the rest of them have seen to that though. I'm going to stick with this to the end, then I'm going to make them pay."

"Personal vendettas don't help."

"Don't they?" she replied indifferently. "Come on, Adam. Citizen Dalrymple needs our help."

I watched as her brother got out of the bed unsteadily. I couldn't see him being much use but the mood Katharine was in, I didn't fancy objecting.

"Lock the door, Adam," I said.

We were standing in Yellowlees's outer office.

"What are we looking for?" Katharine asked.

I started to pull open filing-cabinet drawers. They were all unlocked, which was a bad sign. "The organs that the murderer cut out can all be transplanted."

"But transplantation's illegal, isn't it?" Adam Kirkwood said. For a big guy, he had an incongruously high voice.

"So's selling people as sex slaves," said Katharine.

"Quite." I went over to the door leading into the medical guardian's inner sanctum. It was locked. I put my shoulder to it and the poor quality wood quickly gave way. "I'll look in here. You two see if you can find anything about transplantation out there. And tell me if you find any files about the auxiliary Scott 391. I'll explain later." I hadn't said anything about Yellowlees's lupus research and his treatment of my mother. If there were any papers about that in the infirmary, they would be in his private office.

But there was nothing. We found patients' reports, memoranda on infirmary administration, personnel files on medical staff and a heap of other documentation but not a hint about transplants or about the lupus. And nothing about the dead auxiliary.

Katharine squatted down by the mound of files. "I don't get this," she said, pulling Adam down beside her. "Obviously the organs the murderer removed couldn't have been used for transplantation."

"No, they were hacked out pretty crudely."

"So why do you think there might be transplants going on in the infirmary?"

I told them about Scott 391 – how the sight of his body in the crematorium had affected the sentry there and how Yellowlees had mislaid his file. "It could be that organs were removed from him."

Katharine's forehead was furrowed. "But what's that got to do with the killer mutilating corpses?"

"Search me," I replied. And what's it got to do with the ENT Man? I asked myself. "Whatever the reason, my hunch is that Yellowlees is the next victim on the killer's list. He got the guardian's girlfriend last time and . . ."

"Your hunch?" Katharine said scornfully. "You run investigations on hunches?"

"They've never failed me yet." I nodded at Adam. "My hunch about Jamaica Street Lane was right, wasn't it?"

Katharine stood up. "But you need evidence, even in this city. And you haven't got a thing, have you?"

"If I had, I'd have arrested the guardian."

Her eyes narrowed. "Quint, you're a bastard. You're using Yellowlees as bait, aren't you?"

I shrugged. "My father's still missing. I think there's some connection with all of this."

"I thought you disapproved of personal vendettas," she said with an ironic smile. "God, you're as much of a hypocrite as the rest of them." She took her brother's hand and pulled him to his feet. He was looking pretty queasy.

On the way to the exit I checked with the security squad commander. Billy Geddes was in a stable condition and no one had been near him except the nurses. A stable condition meant that he still hadn't come round. I wished I could have had five minutes with a conscious Billy: he would at least have explained why he had a copy of Yellowlees's lupus research in his flat. But that would have been too easy.

I headed for the Transit and the Assembly Hall. I couldn't shake Katharine and her brother off. It didn't look like I was going to get much of a reward for finding him after all.

I called Davie before the Council meeting started. "Where are you?"

"On the Mound. I saw the medical guardian go in to the Assembly Hall five minutes ago."

"Right. Trail him when he comes out and keep in touch. I'll be close. And Davie?"

"What, Quint?"

"Be careful, my friend. I've got a feeling we're near the end of this caper."

"Not before time. I want my bed. Out."

I laughed then ran over to the entrance as Hamilton's Land-Rover pulled up.

"We'll tell them about Billy and Patsy Cameron, but not about the dead guardsman and the fact that Yellowlees lost his file, okay?"

The public order guardian was looking pleased with himself. No doubt he'd spent a happy time ripping Patsy to pieces. "Very well, Dalrymple. By the way, I had the senior guardian on the line. She was shocked to hear about the sex slaves."

I bet she was. She'd be even more shocked if she knew that Billy had a copy of Yellowlees's research.

"She also offered both of us her congratulations on the out-come of the investigation," Hamilton added with a self-satisfied smile.

I was unimpressed that she hadn't bothered to call me person-ally. "In case you've forgotten, there's still a killer on the loose," I said. Hamilton was an easier target than my mother.

The Council meeting was a ludicrous performance, the guardians trying to outdo each other in expressions of disgust and horror at the news of the sex slave scam. The only one who kept a low profile was Yellowlees. He sat through it all without making any comment, his fingers in the usual pyramid beneath his nose and his mane of hair as tidy as ever. But he didn't look at me once.

I thought about my mother again. A few days ago she had been much better. I'd expected to see her resume her place at the centre of the horseshoe table by now, but the deputy senior guardian was still acting as speaker. Was the treatment losing its effect? Or did she have some other reason for keeping away?

At the end of the meeting, Yellowlees left the chamber without speaking to anyone.

"What now, Dalrymple?" asked the public order guardian. "Did you find out anything more about that dead guardsman?"

"I'm still working on it," I said vaguely. I'd been hoping he'd forgotten about the ENT Man's brother. I should have been down at Scott Barracks checking out his close colleagues and trying to find out why the sentry in the crematorium had committed suicide. But there wasn't time for that. I was sure the killer was about to strike again. I'd given Yellowlees a chance to come clean and he'd rejected it.

Hamilton walked on. "I'm going back to the castle to continue the interrogation." He seemed to be so keen on nailing Patsy that he'd lost interest in the murderer. Maybe he was hoping that we'd scared him off.

"What about my father?" I called after him.

He stopped and turned round. "We're still looking," he said feebly. "What else can we do?"

I didn't respond and went past him to the Transit, hoping that might distract him from his assault on Patsy. That was all I could do for her.

Katharine was waiting for me. Her brother had crashed out in the back of the van. "Well, what next?"

"We wait." I looked at my watch. "It won't be long."

I got that right.

My mobile rang ten minutes later.

"I've lost him." Davie sounded desperate.

"Where are you?" I started the Transit and slammed it into gear.

"Corner of Frederick Street and Rose Street. A bloody great group of Japanese came out of a shop and . . ."

"Stay there," I shouted, slewing round the bend and on to the Mound. "Did you see anyone with him before you lost him?"

"No!" Davie shouted above a babble of foreign voices.

The mobile slipped from between my ear and neck. "Shit." I braked hard behind a horse-drawn carriage that was overloaded with women wearing chadors.

"Quint?"

I felt Katharine's eyes on me as I jumped the lights on Princes Street. "What?"

"If you put me through the windscreen of this wreck, there'll be big fucking trouble."

She wasn't just making polite conversation.

*   *   *

Davie was waving his arms frantically. "The guardsman at the far end of Rose Street saw the guardian a few minutes ago. He was getting into a taxi with a male tourist wearing a pinstripe suit and a baseball cap." He pushed in beside Katharine and peered at Adam Kirkwood in the back.

"Height?" I asked as I turned into the pedestrian precinct.

"Who's this?" Davie asked.

"What bloody height was the tourist?" I shouted.

Davie spoke on his mobile. "About five feet nine inches, he says."

"Five feet nine inches?" I repeated. "But the murderer takes size twelve boots."

"Watch out!" Katharine screamed.

I stood on the brakes as a pair of Arabs squared up to each other in the middle of the road, oblivious to the Transit. As I waited for their friends to separate them and while Katharine was introducing Davie to Adam, I glanced out of the side window. We'd stopped right outside the Bearskin. It was impossible to avoid the photographs of the show. And at that moment it came to me with the shriek of a Hendrix high note and the pounding certainty of a bass riff from Willie Dixon. I understood what Yellowlees's lover had been trying to say about her assailant. I knew who the killer was.

Then my mobile rang again.

I scrabbled around for it on the floor.

"Dalrymple? Is that you, Dalrymple?" The medical guardian sounded like he'd just completed a five-mile run. "I'm . . . I'm to tell you . . . to tell you to come . . . to Moray Place . . ."

The connection was broken before I could say anything; before I could tell him I knew who had captured him. Not that it would have done him any good. I put my hand on the horn and held it there.

"Why the guardians' residences?" Davie asked.

"It's the last act," I said. "All is about to be revealed." I turned on to Heriot Row.

"Shouldn't we tell the public order guardian?"

"He'll have been informed already, I'm sure of it, Davie. This is going to be a performance that all the guardians are expected to attend." I turned to Katharine. "I want you and Adam to wait in the van. Things might get nasty."

She was looking straight ahead. "I told you, Quint. I'm staying with you."

I couldn't be bothered to argue with her.

"Here," said Davie. "You'd better take this." He handed over his knife.

"No, thanks. There's been enough killing."

"You were right." Davie pointed ahead. "The word's out."

Guardsmen and women were swarming around like bees whose queen is under threat.

After we stopped I beckoned to Davie to lean across Katharine and put his ear to my mouth. The murderer wasn't the only one who had stage directions to give.

The commander at the barrier scrutinised my authorisation then looked dubiously at Katharine and Adam. She'd insisted on bringing him along too, God knows why.

"Oh, for fuck's sake, they're with me." I grabbed Katharine's arm and pushed past the auxiliary into Moray Place.

"Where are they?" she asked, wincing. I'd taken hold of the arm she burned in the blaze.

There was a clatter of boots from a squad running to take up position outside the senior guardian's residence. When they'd passed, I walked over to the edge of the gardens that form the centre of the circular street, and gazed into the darkness at the heart of the Enlightenment.

"They're on the grass," I said.

"I can't see any . . ."

The floodlights ignited with a crack and a hum. I was blinded by the white light for a few seconds. I'd rarely seen the gardens lit up. The guardians only use the illuminations when they want to impress foreign dignitaries.

Then I saw the two of them. They were standing close together in the middle of the well-manicured grass. The medical guardian's head was lowered and his shirt was out of his trousers but I didn't look at him for long. It was the figure next to him that I was drawn to, the figure in the pinstripe suit. That individual's head, under a wide-peaked baseball cap, was also lowered, obscuring the face. There was a glint from their wrists and I made out a pair of handcuffs.

"Stay here," I whispered to Katharine. "I've got to go out there."

"Why?" she demanded, her eyes flaring as she turned to me. "Have you got a death wish?"

"Don't tell me you care." I leaned forward and kissed her hard on the lips. I saw her brother grin. "Watch my back," I said, then pushed her gently away.

And stepped out from the line of bushes into the light.

I stopped when I was about ten yards away from them. With a sweeping movement, the figure on Yellowlees's right raised the hand untethered by the cuffs and grasped the peak of the cap. I could read the words around the heart emblem on it. They said "Edinburgh – International City of the Year". I was also able to count the number of fingers as the cap was pulled off.

Mary, Queen of Scots lifted her head and shook it a couple of times. Fair hair billowed out around her perfect features like the aura around a Pre-Raphaelite pin-up.

"So, here you are, citizen Dalrymple. I've been looking forward to meeting you." Her voice was warm and welcoming, very unlike the average auxiliary's. Then again, she wasn't by any standards an average auxiliary. "Stand still, guardian," she said, her voice still friendly. But her hand moved to her pocket quickly and re-emerged with her service knife, which she put to Yellowlees's throat.

"Are you all right?" I asked him.

He nodded, keeping his eyes lowered.

"We haven't been introduced," I said to the woman. "You're from Scott Barracks, aren't you? Close colleague of 391 and 477."

"Very good. I thought you might be getting close." She looked at me and I felt my spine freeze. "Scott 372 is how they refer to me in this festering city." She glanced behind me. "Who's this?"

I turned, my heart missing a beat as I saw Katharine coming towards us. In the background I suddenly caught a glimpse of my mother in the window of her study. Her face looked moon-shaped again. There was a tall figure I couldn't make out at the curtain beside her.

"Come and join us," Scott 372 said with mock civility. "The more, the merrier. Just tell all my fellow auxiliaries to keep back if they want the guardian to stay alive, citizen."

I made the call and saw Hamilton raise his hand in acknowledgement from the bushes.

"Now throw your mobile over here." There was an easy smile on Mary, Queen of Scots' face, the smile of someone who's in complete control. "Let's see what you've got in your pockets."

I tossed over my phone then dropped my notebook, keys and wallet.

"And you," she said to Katharine. "What brought you out here? Don't you trust your boyfriend?" She smiled, this time sardonically.

"Why don't you come over here and empty my pockets yourself?" Katharine asked.

"No, thanks." The auxiliary gave Katharine the imperious look I saw in the Bearskin. "Do it or the guardian dies."

I glared at her too and finally she produced a knife. She must have convinced Davie to give her his. She threw it away to the left.

"Sensible move." Scott 372 turned her gaze back on me. I tried to see beyond the mask of her beautiful, unperturbed face but didn't get very far. Her eyes were vacant, definitely not the windows of her soul. I wondered if I would be able to provoke her. It was worth a try.

"What's your name?"

She laughed. It wasn't a pleasant sound and I saw Yellowlees glance at her nervously. "I don't have a name, citizen. You know that."

"I'm sure Gordon Dunbar didn't call you Scott 372 during sex sessions."

I saw her lips tremble momentarily. It looked like I'd got to her. Now what?

"All right," she said, her voice hardening. "My name's Amanda."

"Well, Amanda, release the guardian. I guarantee you'll be treated fairly. I know there's corruption in the city. You can help me root it out."

She laughed again, this time an even more metallic, pitiless noise that was about as far from humour as you can go.

"Spare me, citizen. I'm an expert at rooting out what's wrong in the city." She looked at me like I was a trainee footman in her court. "I don't need your help."

"What are you going to do now?"

"Extract a confession from this butcher here."

The medical guardian's head shot up as Amanda slammed the

butt of her knife into his solar plexus, then he slumped down. She pulled him upright again.

"You can both witness what he says. Then you'll understand everything that I've done."

"Everything you've done?" Katharine said scathingly. "You're protecting someone. You can't be the murderer . . ."

I jammed my elbow into her ribs.

There was a hint of a smile on Amanda's mouth as she turned to Yellowlees.

"Stop her, Dalrymple," he said, his eyes wild. "This is all a terrible mistake."

Amanda shot a cold glance at Katharine. Then punctured the skin below the guardian's Adam's apple with a lightning-quick movement. A thin jet of blood spurted out. Yellowlees gave a loud gasp and raised his uncuffed hand to the wound.

"I don't understand what you want from me," he said desperately. "I don't know . . . I've . . . I've never even seen you before."

The hesitation was enough for her. "You may not have seen me, but you certainly saw Gordon, Scott 391." Her voice was rising in a crescendo. "Didn't you?" she screamed.

The guardian didn't answer. She stuck her knife into his thigh and pulled it out so quickly that I hardly saw her hand move.

His face twisted in agony. "Oh Christ . . . yes . . . I . . . I know who he was . . ."

"You cut Gordon to pieces," Amanda said, her lips close to his ear. "That nurse of yours wouldn't tell me, but I know you did. Who else but a guardian would dare to carry out transplants in Edinburgh?"

"No, you're wrong." Yellowlees was almost weeping now. Blood trickled between the fingers he had clamped to his thigh. "You're wrong! There were no transplants."

The way he was pleading convinced me. I heard plenty of confessions during my time in the directorate and I learned to tell when bullshit turns into the truth.

"You don't deny you extracted organs from Scott 391?" I said. That was what the sentry had discovered when he opened the coffin in the crematorium.

He shook his head dumbly, cowering from the blow he was expecting. This time it didn't come.

"That's better," said Amanda. "Now tell us how many transplants you've carried out."

She was obsessed by transplants. Suddenly I realised she'd misunderstood what the medical guardian had done with her friend's organs.

Yellowlees was staring at her, his mouth open. He'd realised that if he said the wrong thing now he was dead.

I tried to distract Amanda. "It was your research, wasn't it, guardian? That's what was behind all this."

Yellowlees grabbed the lifeline I'd thrown him gratefully. "Exactly. My research into lupus requires certain hormones and cells. I only extract them from . . . dead tissue." He was avoiding the auxiliary's eyes. "As in the case of your friend."

Amanda turned to me. Her lips parted and the tip of her tongue protruded. She was staring, as if what I'd said was inconceivable. Then she snapped to attention again. She'd dismissed the idea that she'd been mistaken.

"You're lying, guardian," she said sharply. "I know you've been doing transplants."

Yellowlees looked at me imploringly. "Help me, Dalrymple. Your mother's benefited from my work." He tried to step forward, then juddered to a halt like a dog on a lead as Amanda pulled him back. "I was only interested in my research. I had nothing to do with the illegal deals the others were running, you must believe that."

I did, but I wasn't calling the shots. I had a nasty feeling he'd overplayed his hand.

"Others?" said the auxiliary, her features alert. "Which others?"

The guardian swallowed, then dropped his head. "Heriot 07 . . ."

I had a feeling that if he ran through the names of the murder victims he would only convince Amanda he was involved. I tried to muddy the waters. "You realise that your research led indirectly to Margaret's death?"

"I know that," Yellowlees said weakly. "I can't stop thinking about Margaret . . ."

"Which others?" Amanda said inexorably. "Heriot 07 and who else?" She saw me move. "Stay where you are, citizen."

The guardian raised his head as warily as a cow in an abattoir. "The Greek Roussos, the driver Baillie, the guardswoman Sarah Spence . . ."

The auxiliary's chin went up like she'd been electrocuted.

"That bitch?" she hissed, pulling Yellowlees closer. "Well, don't worry about your precious Margaret any longer. Soon you'll be . . ."

Before she finished the sentence I raised the stump of my forefinger to my chin, hoping that Davie had positioned spotters all round the gardens.

For a split second everything seemed to stand still – Amanda with her knife to the guardian's neck, Katharine by my side, the guardsmen lined up beyond the grass – we were all like players on a stage, motionless before the curtain falls.

Then the lights went out with a loud crack and I leaped forward into the blue-black night.

Chapter Twenty

I'd arranged with Davie for the lights to go off for ten seconds. They seemed longer than the slowest-moving episode in the French New Wave films my parents used to watch on their video in pre-Enlightenment times. I reached the spot where I thought the auxiliary and the guardian had been, but found no one. Then I heard a thud and a groan to my right. Before I could move I was hit in the chest by a blow which would have broken ribs if it hadn't struck my sternum. I went down in a heap, winded. At the same time the lights came back on. Someone ran past and dived on to the scrum of bodies in front of me.

By the time I crawled over there, only one of them was moving. It was Amanda. She stood up unsteadily. Beyond her I could see Katharine lying on her side unconscious, her mouth open. Her brother was crumpled on top of Yellowlees. I saw legs in dark blue pinstripe come close and tried to sit up. I still couldn't catch my breath. My heart was pounding. I saw the knife in the murderess's hand, the blood on it. She bent over me. I waited for the thrust of the blade.

"Come on, citizen. I didn't kick you that hard." She put her arm under my back and sat me up. "I don't know about your girlfriend." She looked over at Adam. "Who was that madman? I think I may have killed him." She said the words as if they were a meaningless platitude.

"Yellowlees," I gasped, noticing that she no longer had the handcuff on her left wrist. "What happened?"

"I don't think he'll be doing any more surgery."

"Drop the knife." Davie had an automatic pistol in his hand. "Stand up slowly and put your hands on your head." He glanced down at me. "Are you all right, Quint?"

"I'll live. What about Katharine?"

An army of guard personnel surrounded us. I saw a couple of medics squat down beside her. I managed to stand up, in time to see Amanda's hands being cuffed behind her back. Hamilton was on his knees with more medics beside the medical guardian and Adam. I stumbled over and crouched down.

"They're both gone," the public order guardian said hopelessly. Yellowlees's throat had been cut from ear to ear. If he hadn't been lying face down, there would have been blood everywhere. As for Adam, there didn't seem to be a mark on him. Till I looked at his chest and saw the stain over his thorax. You didn't have to be a cardiologist to realise which organ had been perforated.

"We have failed to look after our young," said my mother from behind me. "The heart of the body politic no longer beats."

I looked up at her. She was leaning against my father, her face a blotched and flaking ruin.

"She's coming round," the medic said. "Heavy blow to the chin, but her jaw's still in one piece."

I kneeled down beside Katharine and helped her sit up. Her eyes rolled then focused on me.

"What happened? Where . . ." She was slurring her words. She started to look around. "Where's Adam?"

"Why did you follow me out here, Katharine? I told you to . . ."

She grabbed my arms hard. "What's happened to Adam?"

There was nowhere to hide. "When the lights went out, he ran out. To help you, I suppose . . ."

"She killed him," Katharine said dully. "The bitch killed him."

I nodded slowly. "She killed the guardian too."

Her eyes flared. "I don't give a fuck about the guardian. He deserved everything he got. But Adam . . ." She let out a single, devastated sob. "Adam . . . never laid a finger on anyone. That's why they all took advantage of him." She pushed me away and got to her feet. "I want to see him."

Hamilton stepped up. "Come with me. He's in that ambulance." I was surprised by the sympathetic look on his face.

"It's over now, Katharine," I called after her feebly.

She turned and skewered me with a glare. "It's not over for me, Quint."

"I'll catch up with you later."

"Where are you going?" she demanded suspiciously.

I squeezed her arm. "Things to clear up. Keep your mobile switched on."

"You're not going to interrogate her now, are you?" She brought her face up to mine. "I want to be there when you do."

I wasn't going to commit myself to that. I shook my head. "I've got some family business to sort out."

She kept her eyes on me. "So have I."

My mother looked like she'd collapsed into the armchair by the fireplace in her study. Otherwise I would have been harder on her.

"You had him here all the time, didn't you?" I glanced at my father. He was leaning against the marble mantelpiece and looking uncomfortable.

She nodded.

"Thanks for telling me. You realise I might have caught the murderess more quickly if you hadn't put that distraction in my way?" I bent over her. "Did you know that Billy was funding Yellowlees's research so he could sell the results?"

"No, Quintilian," she said weakly. "Anyway, you've no hard evidence of that."

I'd seen the look on the medical guardian's face when he mentioned Billy's barracks number. "You must have known that Yellowlees couldn't have made that kind of breakthrough without finance."

"He was . . . reticent about how he'd been able to make such progress," she said, looking away. "I know, I should have pressed him." Her eyes, almost invisible under swollen flesh, moved back to me slowly. "As you see, I've already stopped using the serum."

I didn't feel congratulations were in order. "You sent for Hector, didn't you? Why?"

Her distended cheeks took on an even redder tint. "Vanity. I . . . I wanted him to see how much younger I looked."

I glanced at my father again. He shrugged awkwardly.

"I got what I deserved," my mother said with a faint laugh. "He was horrified by what he called the unnatural reversal of my condition. He wanted to get you to investigate the medical guardian." She shaded her eyes with unsteady fingers. "I couldn't allow that so I kept him here."

I was amazed. I couldn't say I knew my mother well. Over the past fifteen years I'd rarely seen her. But the idea that she was concerned about how she looked seemed almost as much of a betrayal of Enlightenment principles as Billy's deals. Then again, I was an expert in betraying the Enlightenment. Maybe it ran in the family.

"I want all of this to be given full publicity," I said.

My mother raised her head, wincing with the effort. "That is a matter for the Council to decide." Her tone was more like it used to be.

"I want everyone to know that senior auxiliaries were stealing from the city, that they were selling the city's young people as whores. I want the medical guardian's use of illegally obtained organs for . . ."

My mother raised her hand. "All right, Quintilian. I'll put those points to the Council," she said wearily. "Where are you going?"

"I have some unanswered questions."

Hector caught up with me on the stairs. "You've done well, failure. I knew you'd get to the bottom of it."

I shook my head. "All I've done is react to events."

The old man smiled. "Very modest." He continued downwards.

"Where are you going?"

"Back to my books. I've been without them for days."

"More Juvenal?"

"I haven't seen anything here to put me off him."

I got him into a Land-Rover, then walked towards the Transit. Just before I turned out of Moray Place, the lights in the empty gardens went out.

Like the sun in a minor constellation imploding.

I called Hamilton and asked him where Katharine was. She'd stayed in the infirmary with Adam's body. I couldn't think of anything to say to her as I drove to the castle.

The cell where the murderess had been taken was in the depths of the barracks block, at the end of a long, dank passageway. Guard personnel stood at five-yard intervals, carrying rifles with fixed bayonets. I hadn't seen those for a long time.

"I've given instructions to shoot to kill if she makes a break," said Hamilton.

"Brilliant. Don't you realise that she's finished killing? She could have knifed me but she didn't."

The guard commander at the heavy steel door waited for the guardian's order, then unlocked it. The clang as it opened echoed down the corridor and came back at us like a vengeful spirit.

"Christ almighty," I groaned. They had stripped Scott 372 down to her auxiliary-issue khaki singlet and knickers. Her wrists and ankles had been cuffed to a solid wooden chair that was bolted to the stone-flagged floor. "How's she going to make a break?" I asked. "Unless she happens to be related to Houdini, of course."

"You can't be too careful," the guardian said impassively.

"Aren't you freezing?" I said to the prisoner.

Amanda lifted her head. "I'm a cold-blooded creature, citizen," she said, a smile flickering across her lips. "Haven't you noticed?"

I stood looking at her, struck again by how perfectly proportioned her features were. Let alone her body. But she was right. Her eyes were glazed like a reptile's.

"So," she said, giving Hamilton a glance that would have dissolved most men's bowels. "It's interrogation time."

I sat down opposite her and rested my elbows on the table. "I was rather hoping for a confession, Amanda."

My use of that name made her smile again. "You don't have to sweet-talk me, Quintilian." She pursed her lips curiously as she pronounced my name, like she was going to whistle. She repeated it and laughed as innocently as a child learning a new word. "I'll tell you everything, Quintilian. Only you though, no one else. Especially not anyone from the Council." Her tone remained even but I noticed that her fingers – all eleven of them – had tightened on the chair arms.

I turned to the guardian.

He bit his lip then shrugged. "Very well. But the tape recorder is to run continuously."

Amanda laughed, this time harshly. "Don't they trust you?" she asked me.

I waved Hamilton away. A technical auxiliary brought in the tape recorder and set it up. As soon as the door closed behind him, the murderess began to speak.

"You bastard, Quint. I should have been there." Katharine was standing at the window, her back to me. "You owed me that."

I looked at her from the sofa and wondered how much longer I could keep my eyes open. I'd got back from the castle in the early afternoon after listening to the confession for over twelve hours.

"What is this great debt I've suddenly acquired?" I demanded. "It seems to me you owe me an explanation of what you were doing following me out to the middle of the gardens." I closed my eyes when she didn't say anything. "Anyway, I told you. She wouldn't speak to anyone except me."

"Oh, the great Quintilian Dalrymple," she said scathingly. "What makes you so special?"

"She needed someone who could understand what she did." I opened my eyes when I heard Katharine coming over quickly.

"If you're so fucking clever, why can't you understand that I followed you out there because I was worried about you, because I . . . ."

She buried her head in the cushion beside my leg, sobs jerking her shoulders.

I put my hand on her back. "Come on, you'd only have tried to hurt her."

"And what if I did?" she said, looking up at me with wet eyes. "Could you blame me?"

"No." I pulled her towards me. She didn't resist. "But this isn't only about Adam, Katharine."

"Tell me what she told you," she asked quietly. "At least I'm entitled to that."

I nodded, then made the mistake of closing my eyes for a few seconds before I started to speak. Faces flashed in front of me. I made out Caro's and Katharine's, then they were both replaced by the flawless mask of the murderess, her lips moving as she spoke. I opened my eyes with a start and she disappeared. But her voice still rang in my ears, sweeter and more deadly than any siren's song.

"You know, Quintilian, none of it would have happened if Fergus

– Scott 477 – hadn't been on sentry duty at the crematorium the night Gordon . . . the night Gordon's body was taken there."

"Gordon and you were more than just close colleagues."

"Gordon and I . . . Gordon and I knew each other all our lives. Our parents were neighbours."

"In Trinity."

"You have been doing your homework. When Fergus saw from the documents who was in the coffin, he called me."

"Wait a minute. Gordon had a brother. Stewart Duncan Dunbar. Tell me about him."

"That animal? Until Gordon died, I hadn't thought about him for years. Why are you interested?"

"You remembered him after you saw Gordon's body, though, didn't you? That's why I'm interested."

"How . . . how do you know all this?"

"Never mind that just now. What did the older brother do to Gordon?"

"The same thing he did to me."

"When did it happen?"

"Before they packed the pig off to the school for the deaf."

"What age were you?"

"Eight. He . . . why are you making me go over this? I kept it locked away for years."

"You learned things from Stewart Dunbar, didn't you? Like how to use a ligature."

"How do you know that? There's something I don't under-stand here. Do you know the pig?"

"I met him. He had a connection with the directorate."

"Where is he?"

"In a safe place."

"They don't know, do they? Remember the tape."

"What did Gordon's brother do to the two of you?"

"No, I don't want to . . . oh, what does it matter now? It's relevant to your inquiry, I suppose. What you've got to understand is that their house was like Bluebeard's castle. The parents were never there. They were lawyers, fanatical supporters of the Enlightenment."

"Till they were found to have connections with the democrats in Glasgow and exiled."

"That was much later. Who's telling this story?"

"Sorry. So what about Stewart Duncan Dunbar?"

"We never called him by his first name. It didn't seem appropriate. To Gordon and me he was the Beast. His room was like a laboratory. One that belonged to a scientist who'd gone right off the rails. There were animals splayed out on boards, cut open. Rats and rabbits, mainly, but he took the neighbours' cats too. God, the smell."

"And the ligature?"

"When he reached his teens, he began to get even worse. He started doing things to his body – cutting himself, sticking pins into his thighs, putting pencils in his ears. That was how he damaged his hearing. His father found him thrashing around on the floor with the pencil points in his ears and an erection. Oh, and he was laughing."

"The ligature, Amanda."

"I'm coming to that. He got us into his room one day and locked the door before we could resist. Then he went for Gordon. Suddenly he had a leather bootlace round his neck. He passed out almost immediately. I tried to get the animal off him so he concentrated on me. I can still smell his breath. He never brushed his teeth. They were blue with decay. I had to turn away. Then he pulled my pants down and sodomised me. A few minutes later he did the same to Gordon."

"And you were eight years old?"

"That time the parents listened to us. But instead of having him put away, they got him into the deaf school."

"Did you see him again?"

"Only once. After he'd been thrown out. He was proud of it. He ran away not long afterwards. It took me a long time to blot him out. Gordon helped me, we helped each other. But I learned something from the Beast that was reinforced by the auxiliary training programme."

"What was that?"

"The poetry of violence."

I woke with a jerk, sweat all over my face. I was still on the sofa. Katharine's head was against my thigh, her breathing regular. I vaguely remembered sleep overwhelming me while I was telling her what Amanda had said. I lay still, feeling Katharine's warmth and aware of her scent. Outside it was still light though the sun was well down in the west. I would have got up to stretch my cramped legs but I didn't want to disturb Katharine.

So I sat and thought about the poetry of violence. I knew something about that too. I saw the Ear, Nose and Throat Man turning on me, the light falling on his scarred face and rotten teeth. But instead of seeing Caro's body, as I used to when I remembered the butcher, I pictured Amanda. The skin on her arms was smooth, sheathing well-toned muscles. When I'd stood up from the table in the cell, I glimpsed the curve of her breasts beneath the singlet and the lines of her bare, marble thighs.

And her voice went on, running through the catalogue of her crimes in an easy, even tone. Apart from when she was talking about Stewart Duncan Dunbar, she never hesitated. Like the radio announcer reading the inter-barracks rugby results on a Sunday evening.

I couldn't stop myself closing my eyes. I went straight back to Amanda in the cell.

"Fergus called me when he saw Gordon's barracks number on the documents at the crematorium. There was some bureaucratic problem and the delivery squad didn't notice how upset he was. It was the shock. I felt it too. There had been no news of Gordon's death. When he didn't come back to barracks, we assumed he'd been assigned an extra tour on the border. It wouldn't have been the first time."

"You opened the coffin."

"I had to see him one last time. And when I did . . . I knew without even thinking about it that I was going to track the bastards down."

"You thought auxiliaries were being killed for their organs."

"That's the way it looked. They'd taken his brain, eyes, liver, kidneys, pancreas, as well as other parts I couldn't identify. Since the documents were official, I knew auxiliaries must have been involved."

"Fergus committed suicide when he realised what you were doing, didn't he?"

"I'd been using his clothes and boots. He put two and two together when he heard about the murders."

"You used a bootlace like Stewart, didn't you? And you disguised yourself to get us off your trail. That way you gained time to find everyone who was involved."

"And to make them sweat. They deserved that."

"So it was all a question of personal revenge."

"No. I'm a good auxiliary. I wanted to purge the city of the disease that was afflicting it."

"You never thought of going to your superiors?"

"Is that supposed to be funny? Who could I trust? I was already performing at the Bearskin. I'd seen plenty of senior auxiliaries in the audience."

"How did you come to be working there?"

"It was that bitch Knox 96 – Sarah Spence – she recruited me last December. She'd been after me for weeks. I preferred performing to letting her go down on me. Killing her wasn't exactly a hardship."

"You didn't realise she was involved in a sex slavery deal Heriot 07 and the Prostitution Services controller were running?"

"Is that what the medical guardian meant? It makes sense. There were always these young, half-brainwashed citizens wandering around the club. I was too busy chasing the people who killed Gordon."

"It's not clear that he was killed deliberately. I think Yellowlees was telling the truth when he said he only took organs from bodies that were dead before they reached the infirmary."

"It's too late to ask him for confirmation now."

"Your system was to kill every Thursday night. Because . . ."

"Gordon died on a Thursday. I had to keep him alive somehow."

"And you were very careful to leave no prints, no traces to incriminate yourself. When you mutilated Sarah Spence in Stevenson Hall, you took off all your clothes, didn't you?"

"Yes. I dumped the rags I used to clean myself in the barracks furnace later."

"And the damage to her anus?"

"I used my truncheon. With a condom on it."

"To make sure we thought you were male."

"I had it all worked out. I had a good teacher."

"Who?"

"Bell 03. The guy who wrote the *Public Order in Practice* manual."

"You . . . you shouldn't believe everything you read in books. As for the driver, Rory Baillie, you trailed him from the mess?"

"Believe it or not, I didn't intend to kill him. After all, he wasn't an auxiliary. I wanted information from him."

"But it was a Thursday night."

"My only night off."

"What made you change your mind about killing him?"

"I found foreign currency in his wallet. And an infirmary authorisation issued by Simpson 134."

"After you killed Baillie, you planted Fergus's clothes in the Water of Leith to make sure we didn't suspect a woman."

"You found them, did you? It never said in the *Guardian*."

"What about Roussos, the Greek in the Independence?"

"I was after Simpson 134, the nursing auxiliary. She was difficult to get close to. One day I saw her meet the foreigner and hand an envelope over. So I concentrated on him."

"You thought he had something to do with transplants?"

"There are enough tourists in wheelchairs to make you wonder."

"After you sold a double dummy by dressing as a male transvestite, how did you persuade Roussos to go into the linen store?"

"That was his idea. He said he liked doing it in unusual places."

"You know he was alive when you removed his eye?"

"Yes. The fire alarm went off earlier than I thought it would. My incendiary device did a good job."

"You killed innocent people."

"Who's really innocent, Quintilian? I know for certain you aren't. And you're the hero of the city now. I'd rather be dead than a hero in this cesspool."

I sat up with a start, this time waking Katharine.

"Are you all right?" She ran her palm over my forehead. "You're very hot."

"Bad dream," I said, struggling to get the words out. I looked around, suddenly sure that the murderess was in the room with us.

Katharine pulled me to my feet. "If we're going to sleep, we may as well use the bed."

I followed her, glancing back one last time to convince myself Amanda wasn't there. The muscles on my arms and the bruise on my chest were aching. Katharine pulled back the covers and started to take her clothes off. I saw the triangle of hair in her crotch and the dark rings of her nipples but felt no response.

"Can you understand why she killed?" I asked.

She looked across at me and nodded. "Revenge for someone she loved." She shuddered. "I can sympathise with that. From what you said about Caro, so can you."

I sat down slowly. She was right. We were all guilty of murder, in thought if not in deed.

"After the fire I went back to tracking Simpson 134. Eventually I took a chance and went to the infirmary. Someone came down the corridor before I could get her to tell me what had been done with Gordon's organs. I'd already decided that the medical guardian was responsible."

"The nurse almost identified you. She saw your fingers."

"I was lucky then. I thought you might be getting close. That's why I gave up the Thursday routine. Do you think the show I put on for the guardians was a success?"

"Brought the house down. You know, you could probably have got to the border with Yellowlees as a hostage. Some of his colleagues would have done anything to keep him alive."

"Maybe I should have given myself another chance. What will they do with me?"

"Solitary for life."

"Kill me."

"What?"

"Kill me before they come. I'm begging you, Quintilian."

"I can't. I'm not a killer."

"I don't believe you. Besides, this would be a mercy killing."

"What did you do with the organs you removed?"

"They're under a consignment of fish in the Scott Barracks cold store. I was going to send them to the Council when I had a complete collection."

"Jesus."

"Kill me. You can't let me rot on Cramond Island."

"It's too late, they're coming."

"You're no better than the rest of them. You dress up as an ordinary citizen but under the surface you're still an auxiliary. And a coward."

The word shot through me like the volley from a firing squad. I sat up, disentangling myself carefully from the sheets, and went into the living room. Outside it was dark but the curfew hadn't come into effect yet. I looked down at the road in the glow from the streetlights. Suddenly I was certain that I didn't want to sleep again for a long time. In my dreams I couldn't separate myself from Amanda. She'd used the manual I wrote to kill, in the mistaken belief that the city had been selling organs for profit. But even when I was awake, I couldn't condemn her. Gordon, Katharine, Adam, Billy, Amanda and I all had the same background. We were the children of families where love and affection had been replaced by devotion to the cause. The real criminals were in the Council.

The lights flashed three times then were extinguished. Ten o'clock. The realisation crept up on me like a footpad in the night. In the perfect city, the only way to express free will was to commit murder.

Chapter Twenty-one

I finished my report on the investigation as quickly as I could and spent the next week trying to forget the murderess. Without much success. After a couple of sleepless nights and days spent wandering aimlessly around the city, I even considered going back to the Parks Department – after all, I still had the Transit. Katharine talked me out of that. After Adam's cremation, she seemed to accept his death. In the castle they carried out psychological tests on Amanda, followed by what passes for a trial in Edinburgh. I kept away.

The next Thursday Katharine and I were called to the Council chamber. Two chairs had been placed in front of the horseshoe. The medical guardian's place was empty. It looked like a tooth had fallen from an old man's gum.

My mother kept her head lowered over a pile of papers while we were ushered in. Finally she raised it slowly and looked at me. Her face was even more swollen than before and her hair thinner.

"The meeting will come to order," she said, her voice unsteady. "The contents of the various reports on the activities of the self-confessed murderess Scott 372 are noted. Are there any further comments before we close the file on her?"

No one could find anything to say.

"Next business. Public order guardian?"

Hamilton got to his feet. "My interrogation of the Prostitution Services controller is now complete. Steps have been taken to locate the citizens who were sent to Greece. They will be repatriated as soon as possible."

My mother nodded and made a note.

"As regards Heriot 07," Hamilton continued, "he is making progress. The doctors expect him to be able to face questioning soon."

I'd visited Billy earlier in the week. He was just about coherent and had been told he'd be spending the rest of his life in a wheelchair. I couldn't find much to say to him.

"I trust that Heriot 07 will return to the Finance Directorate when he is fully recovered." Billy's chief looked expectantly at the senior guardian as if what he'd said was perfectly natural.

My mother gave me an uneasy glance. "That will need to be discussed at a later date. Heriot 07 is guilty of serious crimes."

"But where would we be without him?" said the finance guardian. "He made all the deals that . . ."

"That will do, Donald," my mother said firmly. "If you'd kept a tighter rein on your deputy, perhaps none of this would have happened."

The old man looked like he'd just stood on a six-inch nail. He waved his hands weakly and slumped down on to his chair. He wouldn't be in a job for long, I reckoned. Running my eyes along the guardians, I was struck by how wan and impotent they appeared – like the survivors of some natural catastrophe who had come so close to annihilation that they would never be able to return to the way they used to live. Even the younger ones sat slackly in their chairs. The only Council member with any life in him was Hamilton. I soon found out why.

"Senior guardian," he said, getting up again and glancing at me meaningfully. "I would draw your attention to the memorandum I drafted concerning citizen Dalrymple. The recordings of the prisoner's confession suggest that he is in possession of information which may relate to the murderer codenamed the Ear, Nose and Throat Man. My directorate's opinion is that there are grounds for his arrest."

I admired his spirit, going into battle with my mother over me. Perhaps he thought she was in a weak enough condition to accept his advice. When I saw her glacial expression, I realised he might well have a point.

Then she drew herself up and turned to him imperiously. "Guardian, without citizen Dalrymple's work this case would not have been brought to a satisfactory conclusion. You of all people must be aware of that." She gave the irony a few seconds to sink in. "I have considered your memorandum and have concluded that further investigation of a five-year-old case is not in the city's interest."

She got that right. Hamilton's face was bloodless. He sat down without looking in my direction.

I suppose I should have been grateful to my mother but I didn't want her to think she'd bought my silence. "What about the medical guardian's activities? Doesn't the city have a right to know what he was doing with the organs he obtained illegally?"

"You never give up, do you?" my mother said with an infinitely weary sigh. "The body competent to judge the rights of citizens is the Council of Guardians and it is perfectly capable of doing so without reminders from you."

"The body?" I said. The joke was lost on them.

"Come on," said Katharine, standing up. "There's nothing for us here."

"On the contrary," my mother said before we got far. "There is a great deal of work for you here."

I slowed down a little, not enough to suggest I was interested in what she was saying.

"I would be gratified if you were both to accept an invitation to join the Public Order Directorate."

I turned to see Hamilton close to cardiac arrest.

"In appropriately senior positions, of course."

I looked at Katharine. Her lips twitched into a bitter smile.

"I think we'll need some time to think about that," I said.

"Don't take too long." The senior guardian's expression slackened. "As my colleagues are aware, the Council will shortly be restructured. That's why we have delayed naming a new medical guardian." She lowered her head. "I shall be retiring."

I wasn't sure whether to congratulate her or ask her why she'd waited so long, so I did neither. "We'll let you know our decisions," I said. "In the meantime, Scott 372 is waiting to be escorted to Cramond Island."

"There's no shortage of guard personnel capable of that task," my mother observed drily.

"She's my prisoner."

"Very well." She was already poring over another file. "Don't lose her," she said without looking up.

I raised my eyes to the ceiling of the chamber and followed Katharine out.

Hamilton came down the stairs behind me. "Look, Dalrymple," he said, his voice unusually tentative. "It was my duty to write that memo, you do realise that, don't you?"

That wasn't worth an answer.

"What about the directorate? Do you think you'll come back?"

I knew the prospect was about as palatable to him as having Patsy Cameron installed as his personal assistant. No way was I going to put him out of his misery yet.

Evidently Katharine's mind was working the same way. "As far as I'm concerned, the invitation deserves serious consideration," she said sharply and walked out into the evening sun.

Hamilton stared after her. "Strange woman," he murmured.

"She thinks the guilty aren't being adequately punished. In some cases I think she's right."

"You mean the murderess?"

"No. Locking someone up in solitary for life is the worst punishment I can imagine."

"Who then?"

"Billy Geddes, for one. That talk about him staying in his job – are you people hypocrites or just cynical bastards?"

"His expertise would benefit the whole city. With the money . . ."

"Spare me the economics lecture. What about Patsy Cameron? I suppose she's back in Prostitution Services."

"No, she is not, citizen. I have my own ideas about what should happen to her."

I wondered if they involved an eighteenth-century costume and a length of rope.

"Guardian, do me a favour," I said, making the words sound more like an order than a request. "Stay away from the esplanade. I want to handle Scott 372's transfer without you getting in the way."

That shut him up.

Twilight had turned to darkness by the time the squad of guards appeared.

"Here she comes," Davie said, pointing to the castle gatehouse.

I looked over from where the Land-Rovers were parked on

the esplanade and watched as Amanda walked slowly towards us, flanked by a heavily armed escort. I felt Katharine stiffen by my side. The prisoner had been given yellow and black striped overalls and labourer's boots, and her hair had been cut short. She still looked like the representative of a superior race. When she caught sight of me, she smiled. She ignored Katharine completely.

"Quintilian," she said. "I was hoping I'd see you again."

We were bathed in light as the vehicles' headlamps came on. The whiteness made Amanda's features even sharper in outline.

"No talking, prisoner!" the guard commander shouted.

"It's all right," I said. "I'm responsible."

Katharine looked at me tensely. "Gag the bitch," she said in a loud whisper. "Are you going to sit in the Land-Rover and have a conversation with her?"

"You don't have to come," I said. "It'd be better if you didn't." I'd tried to get her to go back to the flat but she insisted on seeing the murderess to her cell.

"Don't start that again," she said grimly. "I'm coming."

"Shall we get on then?" asked Amanda politely.

Davie opened the vehicle's rear door and watched as a guardsman secured the prisoner's hands, attaching her handcuffs to the stanchion behind the front seats.

"How many men do you want in there with her?" said the commander.

"One'll do," I replied. "The three of us will be in the front."

"And we'll be right behind you." The grizzled auxiliary strode away to his vehicle.

Doors slammed all around, then engines revved. Katharine and I climbed in. Davie drove off across the esplanade and down on to the Royal Mile.

"So what's next on the agenda, Quintilian?" asked Amanda. She was right behind me but she still needed to raise her voice above the engine noise. "Any more multiple murderers to be caught?"

"Shut her up, for God's sake," Katharine said, turning round to face the prisoner. "If you don't, I will, Quint."

"Calm down, will you?" I looked round as well, first at the guard then at Amanda's handcuffed wrists.

"Bloody right," said Davie. "How do you expect me to drive

with all this racket?" He slowed down to take the left turn on to Bank Street by the gallows.

And suddenly I remembered Yellowlees when the lights went out in Moray Place. Amanda had been cuffed to him but when the lights came on again she was free. I jerked my head back round and saw the intent expression on her face. But before I could do anything, she struck, lashed out with her right foot and caught the guardsman sitting opposite on the chin. His head shot back with a sickening crack and he slid lifeless to the floor. At the same time Amanda slipped her right hand out of the handcuff and looped her arm round my neck. I felt the grip tighten.

"I can kill him in a split second," she shouted to the others. "You know I can!"

I sat motionless, my body taut. She only had to wrench her arm round and my neck would snap like a stalk of dried grass. I knew Katharine and Davie understood that – the hold was one that all auxiliaries are taught. The pressure of Amanda's six fingers at the top of my spine sent tingling shafts all over my body.

"What do you want us to do?" I heard Davie ask calmly.

"Call the escort commander and tell him to get his vehicles off our tail. Be very explicit about what I can do to citizen Dalrymple."

He spoke on the mobile. "Where do you want me to drive?" he asked when he'd finished. We were still on the Royal Mile; he'd aborted the turn into Bank Street.

"Go straight ahead," Amanda said. "We're going to take a trip to the border. Turn right on to the South Bridge and head south out of the city." I felt her lean over. "You. Katharine. Call ahead to each checkpoint and make sure they let us through."

"How did you get free?" Katharine asked hoarsely.

"These handcuffs aren't designed for women. I've got thin wrists." Amanda rested her head on the back of mine. "You were weak, Quintilian," she murmured. "You should have killed me when you had the chance."

I felt her warm breath against my skin. Her body was curiously odourless apart from the faint residue of carbolic soap and the musty prisoner's clothing. Members of the superior race probably don't sweat. Outside it was completely dark. We had passed the last of the suburbs. I closed my eyes and wondered if this was how it would end – a quiet interlude before sudden blinding pain and permanent night. With the murderess's lips against my neck I almost felt comfortable, despite her vice-like grip. I remembered how she looked in the interrogation cell. Firm breasts, the nipples visible under thin fabric, smooth thighs leading to her secret place. How did she feel when she killed? How did she feel with my life in her hands? I lost track of time and drifted away, unafraid, into a limbo. I thought I could hear a guitar playing. John Lee Hooker was crooning "Think Twice".

The next thing I knew was Katharine's voice on the mobile advising the border guards at Soutra not to approach the Land-Rover. I opened my eyes and saw the lights of the fortified post standing out against the dark mass of the hillside that marks the extent of the city's territory. The farmhouse where Caro died was only a few hundred yards away.

"You're going to cross the fence, aren't you?" My voice croaked from parched throat and lips.

"*We're* going to cross the fence, Quintilian." The pressure on my neck relaxed slightly. "You were the one who gave me the idea. I haven't got much else in my diary for the next few years." She leaned closer again. "Besides, I haven't finished purging the body politic."

I felt the blood surge through my veins. The idea of going away with her was strangely attractive, even though I knew she only wanted me to cover her escape.

"Call the post again," Amanda said to Katharine. "Don't worry," she breathed in my ear, "we'll soon be on our way."

It happened in an instant. Before I could speak, before I could tell her that I would go with her willingly, I felt a momentary tightening of her grip, then heard a gurgling noise. There was a viscous wetness on my neck.

"So go, bitch," Katharine said. "What are you waiting for?" She pulled away the arm that was suddenly heavy on my shoulders.

I turned round, the pain from trapped nerves lancing into my shoulders, and saw Amanda fall back slowly to settle on the legs of the guardsman she had killed. The haft of the knife Katharine had taken from Davie's belt protruded from her throat, blood welling up around it like a subterranean spring. By the time I clambered over the seat, the quivering in all her fingers had completely stopped.

*   *   *

"Come with me." Katharine took my arm and led me towards the border fence. "You were going to go with her." She looked at me accusingly for a second then glanced back at the guard vehicles that had pulled up around the Land-Rover. "What's there to keep you in this bastard city?"

"Nowhere else is any better," I said dully. In the dark I was scarcely conscious of Katharine but I could still feel the warmth of Amanda's breath on my neck, as well as her gradually congealing blood. I didn't want to wipe it away.

"Well, I'm not staying. They'll put me in the cell they had ready for her."

"Because you committed murder? I think we'll be able to argue sufficient cause."

She turned away. "I don't want strings pulled on my behalf. Christ, Quint." She shook the wire in frustration. "Why don't you come with me? Don't you want to be with me?"

I couldn't find an answer that would have satisfied her.

"It's torn your heart out, the perfect city." She looked back at me and shook her head. "And still you stay." She tried to pull herself up the high fence.

"Here." I cupped my hands for her foot.

Katharine grabbed my shoulders and kissed me once, hard, on the lips. "Don't turn into one of them."

"Katharine," I asked before I lifted her up, "did you kill her for Adam or for me?"

There was no reply. I helped her over and heard her tumble into the grass on the other side. There was a rustle, then she vanished like the last wind of winter.

As I turned to walk back to the lights I felt something against my foot. I knelt down and found a book. When I picked it up, I caught her scent. I knew without looking that it was the copy of Chinese poetry she always carried, the same one that her brother had in his flat. I don't know whether she dropped it deliberately or not. Maybe she meant it to be my reward for finding Adam.

The next day was warm. I opened all the windows of my flat and let the breeze raise the dust from my bookshelves. Katharine's poems were translated by Arthur Waley, so I slotted them in where they belonged alphabetically. They ended up between Barbara Vine's *No Night is Too Long* and Colin Wilson's

Casebook of Murder. I thought I'd done it quickly, but her perfume came off the spine like a friendly bacillus and made me step back.

There was only one thing for it. I dug around in my tapes for the recordings I was going to send Leadbelly, then found what I was really after: the bootleg of the Millennium Blues concert that packed out the Albert Hall on Hogmanay, AD 1999. B.B. King, Clapton, Thorogood, Moore, Cray, Page, they were all there. This time I wasn't going to listen with the volume turned low and my ear pressed against the speaker. I gave Gilmore Place and the whole neighbourhood "The Lemon Song" and felt a hell of a lot better.

It wasn't long before I saw a guard vehicle pull up. A few moments later, my door burst open.

"Really, citizen, you should be more careful. This music could start a riot."

"Why do you think I'm playing it, Davie?"

"I brought you a couple of things." He threw over a bottle of reasonable malt. "I owed you that from the Waverley, remember?"

"Bit late. But not too late to open it."

It was mid-afternoon by the time we finished it.

"How about it then?" Davie mumbled.

"How about what?"

"The job, asshole. Are you coming back into the directorate or not?" He pulled himself upright with difficulty. "I have a personal interest. You'd need an assistant."

"True."

"Am I going to get an answer?"

"Not yet."

"I didn't let you down, did I?"

"No, Davie. What would I have done without you?"

"Up yours." He slumped down on the sofa again. "Pity about last night."

I nodded, thinking of Katharine and Amanda, still feeling an emptiness that the whisky hadn't done much about. I looked out over the line of rooftops. The sky was the lightest shade of pale blue. Through the window came the roar of the crowd at the Friday afternoon execution. I wondered what had happened to Patsy Cameron. And if my mother had finished reorganising the Council. Was resurrection on the cards for the body politic?

If there was enough new blood, I might be tempted to take the job. On my own terms.

"Oh, I almost forgot," Davie said. "I got you this as well."

He tossed over a small plastic bag. It was an E-string for my guitar.

I had to laugh.